John Sargent looked up to find his enemy falling into step beside him.

"Well, so it's you again," John said calmly. "What's up now? Another spy job?"

"I've come to give you another chance at our offer," the other man said in a low voice. "I know another man who would jump at this chance to make money, but the boss is hit hard by you and wants you to take the job. He feels you'll do a better job than anybody else. But the time has come and you better say yes at once or the other man gets it." Then he added with a sly smile, "Besides there's a little matter of a lady involved."

John gave the man a quick look, then dropped his eyes. "A lady?" he said, feigning indifference. "I don't have anything to do with ladies. I haven't time."

"Oh yeah?" returned the man with a sneer. "How about that little lady you took home the other night? A lady named Kingsley? I'm sure you know her. Well, she's in real trouble now, and as far as I've been informed you're the only man who can help her out."

The man glanced at John, a self-satisfied smile growing on his face as he said, "Now, does that make any difference? How about our offer now?"

Tyndale House books by Grace Livingston Hill.
Check with your area bookstore for these best-sellers.

SOUND OF
THE TRUMPET

LIVING BOOKS®
Tyndale House Publishers, Inc.
Wheaton, Illinois

This Tyndale House book
by Grace Livingston Hill
contains the complete text
of the original hard-cover edition.
NOT ONE WORD
HAS BEEN OMITTED.

Printing History
J. B. Lippincott edition published 1943
Tyndale House edition/1990

Living Books is a registered trademark of Tyndale
House Publishers, Inc.

Library of Congress Catalog Card Number 89-50795
ISBN 0-8423-6107-3
Copyright © 1943 by Grace Livingston Hill
Cover artwork copyright © 1989 by Morgan Weistling
All right reserved
Printed in the United States of America

96   95   94   93   92
 7   6   5   4   3

Whosoever heareth the sound of the trumpet, and taketh not warning; if the sword come, and take him away, his blood shall be upon his own head. Ezekiel 33:4

I

TWO men sat in furtive converse in an inner office of a large warehouse, at this hour almost deserted by the main force of workers who usually swarmed everywhere. Yet though they felt they were alone and safe from all listeners they spoke in low tones, guardedly.

Weaver, the elder man was large and heavy-set, with sharp eyes and firm lips. When he spoke he seemed to dominate the room, as if somehow he had acquired authority over the whole universe.

The other man was smaller, keen-eyed, with caution in his glance. His name was Lacey, and he was good in his line. He was studying the other man as he talked, weighing his words, sifting his expressions.

"We have definite information that the model has been completed and is now in the hands of the manufacturer." Weaver spoke with heavy emphasis.

"Has it been tested?" asked Lacey sharply. "Are they *sure* it will work?"

"Oh, yes," said the boss impatiently, "it's all been worked out. That's why it's important to get this thing going at once. If these things can be manufactured fast enough it will simply revolutionize this war. Anyone with that equipment will be the winner. It depends on who gets there and gets it to working first. And that's why we *have* to find out just what their secret is. We *think* we know, but we're still a little vague over a few points. And that's where you come in. It's up to you to get drawings, measurements, dates when they plan to ship, all the items you think we will need."

"You mean to plant *me* somewhere to find out those things? But man, that's entirely out of my line."

"Of course not, Lacey! I mean you're to contact the man we suggest, or if that doesn't work out, then find the *right* man. One with common sense to keep his mouth shut and work in the most casual way so there will be no hint of suspicion stirred up while he gets all the information we need. It's nothing new to you, Lacey. It's much along the line of your last job, only a thousand times more important. And we think we have the right man, but it will be for you to contact him through your usual workers."

"I see," said Lacey. "Who's the manufacturer? Or isn't that definite yet?"

"Oh yes, that's definite all right. It's not just one manufacturer, it's two. The way they've got it worked out, Vandingham and Company have the main part of the work, and Windlass, Cooper and Crane have the 'accessories.' That's the way they are talking about it among themselves—'Just a few small gadgets,' they say. But it happens that we know these gadgets are the most important parts when they are in the main machine. And then there is a third plant involved, a smaller, insignificant plant that Vandingham and Company are secretly taking over. It's a little dump not well known, and there they mean to assemble the whole, and feel quite sure the world at large will never dream that anything important like that is going on there. The buildings have been somewhat altered so that they are quite inaccessible to the public, or even to other workers in the same operation, and it will not be known that it has anything at all to do with Vandingham's. It's been very cleverly thought out, and it was only by chance that we happened to hear about it through a man who delivers material to them, and he didn't know he was telling us anything. One of our men worked it out of him bit by bit as they were loading up their trucks side by side, and he was canny enough to ask the right questions about where the material was being taken, and didn't Vandingham buy that other plant? So *we* put two and two together. We've got 'em all watched."

"And you mean I've got to get a worker in each one of those plants?"

"No, no, not that, Lacey. We've got it all worked out, I tell you. You see, it is rumored that young Vandingham is taking over the main office in his father's place this fall. It might be part of a plan to keep him out of the draft, perhaps. But anyhow he's to be there this winter, and the idea is—"

"To try and get his father's secrets out of *him?*" interrupted Lacey. "You never can do that! I know those Vandinghams. They're proud as peacocks of their name and position. They would never give each other away, not even if they were having a real civil war in private among themselves."

"No, they would never give away their own secrets. But someone else could do it. Someone who knew them well, who was in their confidence and hadn't any idea how important it was. And I think I've found the very one for you. A young fellow who was in college with young Vandingham, and is rather up against it financially himself. It's up to you to offer him a good sum to get some of those figures and plans and formulas we need. First, that we may be able to produce the same thing, perhaps even better than they are planning, and second that we shall know exactly where and how and when to strike in order that we may destroy their work before it ever gets to the Allies."

"I see," said Lacey. "A fine scheme if it all fits. But I'd be leery about getting the right man into *that* outfit. I've always heard that gang are pretty doggoned smart, and they don't take every Tom, Dick and Harry in with them, even if they do happen to have gone to college with papa's little boy. However, I'll do my best of course. But who's the lad? Do I know him? Is he known in the city?"

The big man looked at him keenly.

"No, he's not very well known. No, you wouldn't know him. He's only a bright kid, just came to the city this summer; came to look after a sick grandmother. His folks are dead and he worked his way through college, but when his grandmother took sick he left a pretty good job he had in the west and came here to look after her. He's been working around at anything he could get since he came, but he'd be open for a good job, because he wants to take care of the old lady. She hasn't anybody else. She's been a librarian for years, living alone, but she had a stroke or two and I guess she's pretty bad off. Anyhow we've found he's looking for something really good so he can take care of her in great shape. It seems she did a lot for him when his folks first died, but about two years ago she lost all her savings in some fool investment, and now he feels it's up to him. So you see it would be easy to get a hold over him. He'll probably snap at the chance. I want you to have him approached by a man that's always been pretty successful getting such jobs across—perhaps Kurt Entry—and I haven't a doubt but he'll be putty in our hands. So now it's up to you to place him, and then keep in touch with him."

"Where's he live?" asked Lacey.

"Just now he's in the quarters where his grandmother has lived for some time, 143 Burton Street. But I wouldn't advise *you* to be seen going there. We've got to work this thing most cautiously, you know."

"Oh, of course. But I'd want to look the lad over before I undertook this. Personally I think a girl would fit into that outfit better than a young man. They'd be more likely to pick *older* men in a place like that, not a kid, especially for a job as particular as you say this is."

"Wait till you see the fellah. He's very dependable— had to knock around a lot. And keen. Besides, I doubt if they'd let a girl get into the place, not on a job as secret as this one!"

"There are always ways for a girl to get places, especially if someone is sweet on her, and I understand that young Vandingham likes pretty girls. I know a girl I believe could get almost any young fellah to show her around the plant where he worked."

"Not a plant like that!" said the older man. "Not a government secret! You try this fellah first. Then if we can't get him, or somebody better, we'll see about the girl."

"Okay," said Lacey. "I'll look him over. What's his name? Where do I meet him? Has he a telephone? How do I contact him?"

"Name is Sargent. John Sargent. Here are the facts," said the big man grimly, handing him a folded paper. "Better let your man contact him, and feel around how he stands before you make an open proposition. If it's necessary to offer a larger salary than I've suggested go ahead of course. The main thing is to get the right man and get him quick. We don't want that invention to slip out of our hands. And Lacey, be sure you get him one of those new concealed cameras. They're as inconspicuous as a coat button. Better instruct him to get pictures of everything, and absolutely on the Q.T. Of course they wouldn't allow a camera to pass the door if they knew it. It's got to be mighty slick work, you know."

"Of course," said Lacey. "What do you think I am, Weaver? A child that needs a nurse?"

"Well, I'm just telling you," warned the boss. "You know who we're answering to, and you don't want to get into any trouble yourself, do you? Now go. I've got another appointment in five minutes, so I guess you'd better fade away before my next man appears. And Lacey, just remember, don't come here unless I send for you. It won't be good that we should be seen together too much."

"But suppose I should need to report to you. Do I phone?"

"Only at the prescribed times and places. You'll find a memorandum on your paper. That's all, Lacey. Meantime, keep that girl you spoke of up your sleeve for any emergency. Good by!"

Lacey stole out by a side entrance and disappeared into another part of the building, and a group of three were announced and took his place.

Lacey went by a back way to a rooming house and locked himself into a gloomy little room where he sat down to study the paper Weaver had given him.

The paper was typewritten, largely in code.

For some time Lacey sat studying it, frowning, tapping his finger nervously on the arm of his chair, staring at the typewritten words on the paper until they were fairly imprinted on his vision. Then suddenly he was startled by the ringing of his telephone and he hurried over to his desk to answer it.

"Are you number 23 of the troop of investigators?" a strange voice asked.

"Yes," said Lacey sharply.

"Then the orders are for you to proceed to Main Street between Twelfth and Fourteenth at once, and observe the workers among the Water Company emergency men. You can see the person under discussion among them, bareheaded, wearing a blue shirt, light curly hair and blue eyes. Walk slowly, pausing now and then casually to watch the workers, then proceed down the street to Filmore's garage, returning five minutes later, walking more briskly, and not seeming to notice one laboring man more than another. You will receive another phone call at one-thirty. That's all."

Lacey took his hat and hastened away.

Lisle Kingsley, walking with her father and mother from Filmore's garage where they had left their car at her father's office, half a block farther on, was halted by an obstruction on the sidewalk. There had evidently been a burst water main that had flooded the street, and the men from the Water Company were working valiantly to open the road and find the broken pipe that had caused the trouble. Some of them were new at the job and not as careful as they should have been to keep the mud and rubble from the sidewalk, flinging dirt and paving blocks and muddy water out of their way and not stopping to see where they landed until a goodly pile had mounted almost across the pavement.

Mr. Kingsley stepped out into the road to investigate and ask a few questions, as the obstruction was almost in front of his office. A number of people were hesitating in dismay, gazing anxiously down at their shoes, and wondering which was the best way to get across. For traffic had been stopped by the spouting water and its consequent flooding of the street, and the road was pretty well congested with trucks, delivery wagons and cars. Also very muddy, as in places the pools were still quite deep though the water had been turned off for several minutes now.

Just ahead of Mrs. Kingsley and Lisle were a group of

irate ladies, one of whom was storming at the men who were working so frantically to put things right.

It was at this moment that the man Lacey arrived among the crowd.

"I think this is perfectly inexcusable!" said Mrs. Gately, a recently rich woman who had married wealth and intended everyone should understand her importance. "Why can't you men keep this rubbish off the sidewalk? It could just as well be left in the road. Just look at my dress! All spattered with mud and filth! And it's an imported frock! Probably the last one I shall ever be able to get from Paris unless this horrid old war stops pretty soon. And they say Paris will be practically destroyed before it is. That is, the old Paris, where all the fashions come from! There! Now you've done it again! Flung a lot of slushy mud over my shoes! I think you men ought to be arrested! I shall ask my husband to have your names taken and see that something is done about this. I shall certainly report you to the officials of the Water Company, and you men will *all* lose your jobs! Then perhaps you will learn that you can't obstruct the regular sidewalk from the garage to the shopping district. I mean what I say! You'll find out! What's *your* name, young man?"

She pointed her beautifully manicured, crimson-tipped forefinger straight at a young man in a light blue shirt, who was shoveling vigorously in the forefront of the workers. He looked up with a quick amused glance.

"Yes, *you! You're* the one I mean! You flung that water right on my foot! I saw you! How long have you been working for the Water Company?"

He gave another quick grin and answered in a clear young voice:

"About twenty minutes, madam. They were short of help and this thing was getting ahead of them. They asked me to take a hand and help. But madam, if you would just step back a little, or go around the other way, you wouldn't be in danger of getting your shoes any wetter."

"You're impertinent!" said the lady, stepping a little nearer instead of backing away. "Don't you *dare* to throw any more water on me, or I'll have you in jail before you know what it's all about."

The young man did not answer. He kept right on working, but suddenly lifted his eyes and swept the crowd with a quick questioning look, and his eyes met Lisle Kingsley's. Their glances held for an instant in mutual amusement, and contempt for the woman who persisted in trying to hold the center of the stage.

It was just for a moment, and then the boy dropped his gaze and went on with his work. The boy had nice eyes, Lisle decided. It seemed that suddenly they were acquaintances in understanding, one in contemptuous amusement.

Then the boy lifted his eyes for another fleeting look, saw a tiny hint of a smile on the girl's lovely lips, and there was an answering grin on his own face. Lisle had time to notice that his blue shirt was just the color of his eyes, and his close-cropped curls caught the bright sunlight like a spot of beaten gold. He certainly was a personable-looking young fellow even if he was doing the work of a day-laborer, and she noticed that he was not slinging mud toward the arrogant expensive shoes of the brawling woman, who continued to address him as though he were the chief offender in her world. Though the same could not be said of two or three other men who were working shoulder to shoulder with him, for they seemed to make a special point of slinging all the slime of the street toward the offending woman. And one, a lowering fellow, with bushy black eyebrows and swarthy countenance, aimed a neat shovelful of dirty water and stones, full on the tiny foot of the lady, soaking her delicate hosiery with a great definite black stain.

"There!" she shrieked, turning a baleful glance at the blue-eyed boy again. "Look what you have done! Now I'll have it back on you. Those were absolutely new stockings and shoes, and you've simply ruined them! And you did it just for spitefulness. You shan't hear the last of this in quite a while! And I was going to a luncheon this noon! How unbearable! Well, you'll have plenty of chance to think this over in jail and be ready to apologize, and then *work* after you get out to *pay* for them, too! It'll cost you plenty!"

Suddenly the big lowering man turned on her.

"You're all wrong, ma'am! You're completely off your base! You're barking up the wrong tree! That kid didn't sling that mud on you. I done it myself, and I'm *glad I did*, do ye *hear*? If you don't know enough to get out of the way when you're hindering our work it's good for you! And if you stick around here any longer I'll do it again! Now, get out of the way, unless you want some more of the same kind, and I don't mean mebbe! You can go talk to the Water Company if you want, but you can't get nothing on us. *We're* not the Water Company! We're just volunteers, passers-by, helping out in an emergency! The head man of the Water Company is standing over there in the road in the middle of all that water. If you want to talk any more, paddle over there and talk to him. Now, *scram!*"

Mrs. Gately blinked and spluttered at the man, her face livid with anger.

"Why—you—you—out-*rag*-eous *creat*ure!" she shrieked. "Who are you anyway? To speak that way to a *lady!*"

"Oh, is that what you are? A *lady*? Pardon my error! I never would have thought it. Okay, boys, sling your mud. The 'lady' *asks* for it!"

He stooped to drop his shovel into the deepest mud,

and turned with the evident purpose of planting an ample quantity straight on the tidy little Gately feet. Suddenly Mrs. Gately started screaming and trying to back out of the crowd, but by this time the crowd had closed up behind her and there seemed no way through. Then the lowering man and a couple of like-minded evil conspirators, seeing their chance, slugged a goodly portion of wet dirt over the imported feet and the furious woman, raising a frantic howl, took a slide on the muddy pavement and sat down with her imported frock in a very wet puddle, till a kindly gentleman, not really knowing what it was all about, reached a helping hand, and drew her, spluttering and resisting, back against the wall.

Somebody took pity on the poor lady and hustled her off to a car, and to her home, and the crowd soon dispersed. But Lisle Kingsley following her mother across the street, gave one more glance back at the blue-eyed boy as she turned away, her own smile still on her lips. She felt somehow that they were friends, she and that young man, and the thought of him lingered with her as she went on her way.

John Sargent as he turned and looked after her furtively, wondered if he would ever see that girl again. He felt a warm friendly comfort from her smile, in a day that had started in anything but a pleasant way.

Then suddenly he heard the words of the two men working next to him. They had paused in their work and were gazing after the girl.

"That's old Kingsley's kid," one of them said, the lowering one who had been so disagreeable to Mrs. Gately.

"Say, is that right?" asked the other one of those who had assisted in the mud slinging. "She's some looker all right! You didn't hear *her* making any outcry about the mud, either, and I bet she has as many 'imported' shoes and 'fwocks' as the old dame."

He twisted his face and his voice into a clever imitation of Mrs. Gately's expressions and tones and the rest of the gang laughed, roughly, and cast appraising glances after the pretty girl who was skirting the wet places and crossing the road.

So, that was who she was, thought John Sargent. Daughter of a very rich man! He had heard of him. He turned a furtive look over his shoulder and took in with a swift glance the sign that glittered goldenly in the morning sunshine over the office door just beyond where he was working. He caught a glimpse of the tall gentleman just entering the doorway. That would be the girl's father. He looked it every inch. Dignity, culture, keenness, distinction. All the attributes that go to make up success in the world today. Then, without seeming to do so, his eyes swept across the street to where he could watch the girl as she walked. She was graceful, slender, with an air of ease and assurance without arrogance. The kind of daughter a father like that man would be expected to have. And *she* had smiled at him, and understood how he was feeling about that silly woman! He would cherish that smile. He probably would never see her again, but she would be pleasant to think about now and then, a sort of ideal.

Lisle crossed the street back to her father's office just above where the water break had been. A slight rise in the ground at that point had left the crossing dry. She came down the street and went into the office door. That seemed to settle it in John Sargent's mind that she was a daughter of the head of that well known and distinguished firm.

And while John Sargent was musing on this matter, the man Lacey stood not far away on the sidewalk studying John.

As it happened there was still quite a crowd standing around and he was in no danger of being observed, for many people were lingering there, watching the work that was going on, and he was not noticeable. As he stood on the sidewalk and looked about him quite casually he noticed his handy-man Kurt Entry standing across from him watching the workers interestedly, but the other man did not look at him, and no recognition passed between them. But that of course was as it should be. And this was not the first time that such a thing had happened, when other operations of the same sort were being planned. Kurt Entry was well trained, and was a good actor. He knew how to erase himself from any given picture. That was why he was hired.

But the man Lacey carried away with him the picture of the young man with the firm line of lip and the gold hair and the blue eyes above the blue shirt. Yes, that was a young man who would have good sense, but wasn't there something lacking in that face for the job they wanted to wish on him? Didn't he lack the dare-devil glint in his eye, or did he? There was something firm and determined about the set of his lips, and once won over to accept the role that he was to be offered, he would stick. He would be a faithful emissary. But would he accept? There was a keen look in his eye. He wouldn't be one to be fooled, to accept a job without understanding what it involved. Still, with a sick grandmother—a funeral perhaps in the offing—money *might* be an inducement. It would take plenty, of course, if there proved to be a congenital fanaticism to be overcome, but money would likely do it. A fanatical twist in the brain would be the only thing that might prevent. Still, he looked withal a merry sort of lad with a good sense of humor, and not every fanatic had a sense of humor. Perhaps it would be as well to send Kurt after him and let him sound him out about a better paying job tomorrow.

Lacey was back in his room a good half hour before the expected phone call came.

"Well, Lacey, size yer man up?" came the boss's sneering voice.

"Yeah. I looked him over. He may be all right, but he looks mighty soft to me."

"You're mistaken. Nothing soft about him. I've been watching him for several months. Got a lot of character, that kid."

"Well, mebbe so, but the girl I'm thinking of is a 'regular.' If you had time I could tell you a lot of jobs that dame pulled off, and she's pretty as all git out. If I know anything at all about that young guy you say is to have charge of his dad's plant, she could work him for almost anything you want. Like to have you see her. She's worth looking at. If you could drop in anywhere you want to suggest I could have her there, and introduce you. You wouldn't need to commit yourself in her presence. She knows her onions."

"You haven't told her anything about this affair, have you?"

"What do you take me for? I should say not. But I've tried her out already on so many other jobs I know just how she'll react, and this would be right down her alley. She'd eat it up. She's plenty proud of her record in the past."

"I see," said the grim heavy voice of the boss. "But I tell you this is no lady's job. It wouldn't be permitted."

"Okay! But I'd like you to meet the lady now she's in the vicinity. You'll need her some time if you don't need her now."

"Well," said Weaver after an instant's pause, "I'll be at the restaurant at the corner of Tenth and Harper at twelve sharp tomorrow. If she's there all right, if not that's the end. This, you understand, is a man's job. Get to work on your man as soon as possible. I'll have the job rounded up for him by morning. That's all!" and the boss hung up.

But about that time Kurt Entry lurched across the pile of rubble at the curb and fell into step behind the young man John Sargent whom he had been watching carefully for the last hour.

A little later a girl in a grubby room of a cheap hotel received a phone call.

"That you, Erda?"

"The same."

"We'll make it twelve sharp tomorrow. Tenth and Harper."

"Very well. Any special line?"

"Nothing new yet."

"Okay!"

2

LISLE went through the outer room where stenographers and clerks were already hard at work. She smiled at one and another of them, and they all smiled back as if they liked her. She had a habit of making even a smile seem an honor.

Lisle had not long to wait: Her mother soon came out of her father's inner office and they started out together on their shopping expedition.

"I think we had better go to the tailor's first, dear, and get that fitting out of the way, don't you?" said her mother. "There may be some changes to make and I don't want him to be held up getting your suit done. You might need it in a hurry. There is liable to be a change in the weather any time now. Also you will have to decide on the fur for your collar, you know. Really, I think dear, that it is smarter to have fur on your collar this year, don't you? It's a little bit more feminine, and I don't want you to look as if you were in uniform, not *all* the time, anyway. You're too young to affect that style."

"Yes, I like the fur, mother. It's certainly more comfortable in the fall before it is time to put on a whole fur coat. But there isn't any special hurry about it, is there, mother? I thought you wanted to see those gloves that were advertised in the paper this morning, and they might all be gone if we don't go to Hayden's first."

"That's true too, but after all there are always gloves of one kind or another. I think we ought to get this fitting out of the way at once. You see Victor telephoned after you went down to the car to say he would meet us at Hayden's for lunch at noon, and we must be sure to get back in time. He said he would get there soon after twelve, and we could go to lunch together."

"Oh!" said Lisle, a kind of blank dismay in her voice. "I thought this was going to be a shopping excursion. Why did he have to barge in? I do hate to have to select things with somebody standing around watching, criticizing, trying to advise. It always upsets my judgment and I take anything, whether I like it or not. Victor always thinks he knows it all, and insists that I shall do as he suggests."

Her mother looked at her in surprise.

"Why, my dear! I didn't know you felt that way. He asked if he might come, and I supposed of course it would be the thing you would want, especially since he may receive his commission as an officer any day now and will probably soon be called away. I couldn't say no, he seemed so eager about it. I didn't think you would want to be rude to him."

"Of course not, mother, I just thought it would be so nice if we could have the whole day to ourselves, and not have to hurry. But it's quite all right. Of course you were right to tell him to come."

Her mother gave her a quick look, noted her troubled face, the slight frown on the girl's soft brows, the disappointed set of the sweet lips, and then her tone changed.

"Lisle, have you and Victor been having a—difference

of opinion? Not a quarrel of course. I am sure you would not descend to anything as unladylike as that, but has something come between you? I noticed you have not been going out with him every time he asked you." She watched her daughter's face while she waited for an answer.

"Why, no, mother, not exactly a difference of opinion," said Lisle, "but he has been sort of disappointing lately. I suppose maybe he's just growing up, but he was a lot nicer the way he used to be."

"Why, my dear!" said her mother, amazed. "I had no idea you felt that way. What has he done? What happened?"

"Oh, nothing, mother! Nothing really *happened*. He just seems so determined that he is going to order my life for me."

"But—my child! In what way?"

"Well, for one thing he doesn't like my college. He says I need to get away from home, that I'm coming up with a very narrow environment, and I didn't like that! I don't think he has any right to criticize the way you and father are bringing me up. He keeps saying I have no mind of my own. And I *do!* I *like* my college, and I don't want to go to any other. I refuse to go to any highbrow college, just to be able to say I've been there. I prefer the way you chose for me to be educated."

"That's very sweet of you, dear, and certainly we do not need any advice in arranging for your education. Your father and I have talked this matter over for several years, and we felt that on the whole we had chosen well and wisely. Also we wanted to keep you near us as long as possible, and I still think it was right. But surely, Lisle, there is some mistake. It does not seem like the old Victor to criticize your family and your life-plans. You must have misunderstood him. He must have been joking. Just doing what you call 'kidding.' He couldn't have meant that. He was well brought up. His mother is very punctilious about behavior. He was taught to be polite almost from his babyhood!"

"Oh, he's polite enough," said Lisle thoughtfully. And then after an instant's pause, "But *very firm!*"

Her mother studied her with a puzzled expression.

"What do you mean by that, dear?"

"He's determined I shall think for myself, even if I do make mistakes, and not always have to consider what *you* would say or think about anything."

"My dear, do you feel the need of more freedom in your actions?" asked the mother with a troubled look.

"No, mother, I don't," said Lisle with a set of her firm little chin. "I've always sort of gloried in the fact that you and father never said 'You shall,' or 'You must,' not since I was a very little child and very naughty. You've always taken me to a quiet place and explained why you felt it would not be a good thing to do, and then put it up to me to decide. And I couldn't help but see that your advice was good. You gave me the feeling that you had had more experience than I, and you had found it wasn't a good thing to do. You gave me confidence in your judgment. It was as if we were going down a strange road together, and you had traveled that way before and found where it led, and where to turn off, and if I saw a side road where a lot of flowers grew and you said it led to a swamp where I might get drowned quickly and no one know where I was, you taught me to think twice about it, and to remember what your experience had been when you took that same path years ago and almost lost your life."

A look of great relief passed over the quiet dignity of the mother's face. Then after a moment she asked:

"And couldn't you explain it that way to Victor?"

The girl's face was swept by a stormy memory.

"I have, mother. I told it to him just like that, and he

simply got that maddening smile on his face, a sort of superior sneer he has, and said: 'Times have changed, darling, and *you* are living in the antique past!' "

The mother looked startled.

"Well," she said, "I'm afraid I shouldn't at all approve of the college *he* attends. It seems to have done something undesirable to him. However, my dear, I suppose it is just a phase of his youth. He will probably get over it when he really grows up and gets beyond that superiority complex. That's what your father feared when he heard Victor had chosen that college. They simply don't believe *anything*. But I'm sure he'll get over that."

"I don't think he will, mother," said Lisle sadly. "He really *is* grown up, you know. He'll be of age in a few days now. You know that party his mother is giving is in honor of his twenty-first birthday. Mother, I wish I didn't have to go to that! I don't like his attitude toward me. It's entirely too possessive."

"Well, dear child, don't worry about that. There may not be any party. Not if he goes to war, and is called soon. But of course you would have to go if there is a party. You are one of his oldest friends, and you are already invited."

"What do you mean, there may not be any party? Of course there'll be a party."

"Why, Victor told me that he wasn't sure but he might have to go away sooner than he had expected. He had a letter this morning hinting that he might be called very soon." Mrs. Kingsley was watching her daughter closely. How would this news affect her child? But Lisle did not wince, did not turn pale, did not even look disturbed.

"Of course, mother, that would be entirely possible. I had thought of that, and almost dared to hope that that might be a way of escape from that party, but it seems so selfish to want it just for my own comfort, when I know Victor is looking forward to it, and I know it means so much to his mother. But you know, mother, there isn't a chance that even that possibility would stop that party. Why, Victor's mother has been looking forward to that party and counting on it for years, and she'll find some way to pull it off in spite of the government. You'll see. I've heard her talk so many times, and she's simply fed it to Victor all through the years. You'd almost think it was some kind of a coronation day. And he's begun to act as if he felt that way about it himself. He *has*, mother. It just made me ashamed for him when he began to talk the other day."

"But Lisle! Child! Don't speak so bitterly! I can't think how you can turn against your old friend this way. Victor is not to blame. That party is a sort of symbol of his young manhood. Perhaps his mother has been foolish about it. She's rather fond of social customs and old family traditions. But you ought not to turn against your old friend for that."

"Oh, I haven't turned against him, mother, only it makes me tired to hear them talk. Why, they are making a lot more of that party than they are of Victor's going off to war."

"Well, dear, perhaps it's something to help ease the pain of their parting. You know Mrs. Vandingham has always been so very close to her son."

"Yes, I know," said Lisle. "But that's no excuse for her making a perfect sissy out of him."

"Oh, my dear! What a state of mind you are in! You never thought that of Victor before, I'm sure."

"No—, perhaps not!" said the girl with a troubled sigh, "though I'm not sure but it was in the back of my mind all the time, and sometimes it would come up and worry me."

"Oh, my dear! Why didn't you tell me? Perhaps we could have done something about it."

"What could we have done? Besides, I wasn't altogether sure about anything."

"Well, at least we could have talked it over and sifted your feeling down to facts. And yes, perhaps we could have done something really practical about it. Victor always used to be amenable to reason. Perhaps he has had no one to talk things over with him. You know his mother is very conservative, and dislikes to bring personal matters out into the open. When Victor was a little child I can remember her saying that it was better not to notice naughty things that he did. He would be more likely to drop them if they were not mentioned."

"Yes, I know. He never talks things over with his mother. He thinks women have the wrong viewpoint on almost everything, and they are not wise advisers of the male sex. That's what he said, mother! Just recently. He never used to talk that way, but now he says he thinks women were made principally to be petted and to make a pleasant home for men. And as for his father, he's too busy to talk anything over with him. Don't you see, mother? That's what is the matter with Victor. He's made his own philosophy of life and he means to live by it. He says they encourage the students at his college to do just that. He told me so the other day, and he said that if girls were brought up that way they wouldn't be so feminine in their ways. But he said he liked them better feminine, that he couldn't bear a woman who was always trying to make him over. And since he said that, mother, I haven't tried to talk anything over with him. It wasn't any use."

"Well," sighed her mother, "I'm just sorry you didn't mention this before. I would like to have had a good talk with him. He always used to listen most respectfully to anything I said. Maybe it's not too late yet."

"I think it is, mother. Victor is very definite in his

'philosophy of life' as he calls it. Just wait till you hear him talk. He simply thinks he knows it all, and I'd hate to have him try to take *you* down, and show *you* where he thinks you belong, the way he did to me. I would just *hate* him if he tried it, mother."

"Well," said the mother with a sigh, "I certainly hope that time will prove you are mistaken. I was always very fond of Victor, and I thought your friendship with him was such a happy healthy companionship. I would be sorry indeed to have it turn out the way you seem to think it has. But don't be too hasty in your judgment. Remember you have been separated for almost a year now, and it would be natural there would be some changes. But those things will probably all be adjusted as time goes on and life falls into its normal lines again. Try not to think too much about it. Just let things work out. Be your old self as far as possible. Avoid discussions, and above all wrangling, even about things that matter. You can state your own belief of course, when necessary, but let it go at that. Don't try to argue. Half his opposition will die out if he has no opposition, I imagine. Now, dear, here we are! Forget all this and put your mind on your suit. I want you to be sure you get the right fur on that coat, because I do dislike to have you uncertain about things you have to wear through a season or two. This is the time to select wisely. Especially now as a war measure, you know. It isn't patriotic to buy carelessly and then fling a thing aside because you are tired of it, and get another. You know we are constantly warned about that. There! See that coat in the window! Do you like that shade of brown fur? I think that would be becoming to you, don't you?"

So they entered the tailor's shop and were at once immersed in thoughts of garments.

But now and again, back in the recesses of her mind,

Lisle caught herself regretting that Victor was to be at lunch with them. Somehow she couldn't seem to get away from annoying memories.

As she put on her coat and adjusted her hat after the fitting she glanced at her watch and noted that it was within a half hour of the time set for them to meet Victor. How annoying! Now there would be no time for her to take her mother to look at the dress she had seen the other day, and was hoping her mother would be as interested in as she was. And there wouldn't be any time after lunch. There never was when Victor was around. He would have some movie, or show, to which he wanted to take her, or he would be planning something, she was sure; and she would have to go of course if he asked before her mother. Her mother was troubled, she could see, because she and Victor were at odds, and she would be morally certain to further any plans Victor had, hoping it might smooth the troubled waters, and bring about a state of peace between the two who had been such close friends through childhood.

She drew a deep sigh as they stepped out into the crisp autumn air, thinking of Victor. Was it riches and position that made him that way? Maybe it wasn't only the college he attended. Maybe he was just lifted up in his own eyes. Well, however it was, she had to meet him in half an hour and be as pleasant as possible through the lunch time. But she would get away from him if possible for the afternoon, so she might as well smooth out the ruffled brow she knew she was carrying and get ready to smile. Certainly she never could get anywhere frowning.

So she went with her mother to select some new shoes to go with her new suit, and had as good a time while she was doing it as possible. It would be good to make mother feel that this matter of a difference between herself and Victor was a trifling thing after all, and nothing to worry about. She didn't want her mother to talk to Victor about it. He would tell her she always ran to mamma with all questions, and wouldn't she ever grow up? She hated to have him talk that way about her mother. No, she would just ignore things. Of course she would likely have to go to that party, much as she hated the idea. It would mean having Victor order her around and tell her who to speak to and what to do, but perhaps after all he might go away to war and escape the party, so she needn't worry.

So she went through the duties of the next half hour, sat with her mother laughing and talking when Victor arrived, and met him with her usual charming casualness. Perhaps after all she had been silly. Victor was very handsome of course, and he had been a delightful friend. Well!

She watched him as he came down the aisle toward the waiting room where they were seated on a leather couch. His distinguished bearing, the almost haughty carriage of fine head and shoulders, the wide dark eyes, the flashing smile. Yes, he was about the handsomest boy she had ever seen, and she used to be so proud to think he was her friend, and had chosen her for the object of his attentions. What had changed him? What had changed her? Or—were they really changed?

His eyes rested upon her as soon as he sighted her, and expressed his admiration. And she knew she was looking well. She had taken pains with her brief opportunity for those few touches she had given to her toilet as she stood before the mirror in the fitting room. She knew that he had always admired the green suit she was wearing, and she knew that her hat was becoming. There was no reason for her to feel that she was not at her best, even though her garments were not new this year. So she met her old friend quite at her ease and held out a pleasant hand of greeting, suddenly aware that her mother was watching with sharp eyes. Perhaps this knowledge gave her tone a sound of formality, though she was struggling to make it as natural as possible.

"Hello, Vic. Nice you could take lunch with us," she said heartily, trying to make her voice sound genuine. "I didn't know you were back from Washington till mother said you had telephoned. Did you have a pleasant time on your trip?"

"Oh, fairly so," said the boy looking her over critically. "You're looking well, Lisle. Seems to me I remember that dress and hat you're wearing. One of your old-time favorites, isn't it?"

Lisle laughed and tilted her chin a bit defiantly. Was he rebuking her for not having been more dressed when he was lunching with her?

"What a memory you have for trivial matters," she replied gaily. "Yes, of course this is an old dress. It isn't patriotic, you know, to get new ones unless you have to."

"Oh, I see. Yes, of course. Well, it's still becoming to you."

Lisle's cheeks were glowing now. Something in her old friend's tone aroused her anger. It was perfectly silly of course, and why should she care? But he acted almost as if it was a personal affront to himself that she was not wearing a new suit. She gave a quick glance at her mother to see if she had noticed it or whether this was just her own imagination, but she saw her mother too had a look of annoyance.

"Yes, we're all doing our best to be patriotic, aren't we, Victor?" responded the mother sweetly, with just a little haughty lift of her chin. "I think that English slogan is so interesting. You know it of course, 'Eat it up, wear it out, make it do!' I often say that over to myself when I'm tempted to buy something I don't really need. I think it is an excellent rule. We want to do all we can of course to help win this war. And indeed it is little enough we can do, we who have to stay at home and cannot go out and fight. We want you boys to feel that you have us all a hundred percent behind you. Did I understand you to say, Victor, that you have your commission?"

"Well, no, Mrs. Kingsley, it hasn't come through yet, but I am sure there is no doubt about it at all. Dad has some very powerful friends in the government, you know, and he can practically get anything he wants."

"Oh," said Mrs. Kingsley, raising her eyebrows slightly. "I must have misunderstood you. But of course, I suppose those things all have a certain amount of red tape to be arranged before things are really finished. However, I understand that plans are being hurried up because of the great need of sending more soldiers over at once, and I suppose it won't be long now before we can expect to be startled by having some of our best friends called. You know it is awfully hard to see those whom we have known and loved for years leave us. Yet we do not grudge the pain of their going because they are of our very best, and only the very best are ready to take on them the responsibilities of this great cause. Just think! You, Victor Vandingham, are really going to war! Aren't you thrilled at the thought?"

Victor regarded her as if she were slightly demented.

"Well, not exactly," he drawled in a new accent he had acquired at college. "One scarcely yearns to go out and get into such a mess of course. And there are a good many reasons why I would much rather stay at home just now. Plans I had made to begin my life in a regular way, business plans and so on. One hates to be halted right at the start this way. But of course if it has to be it has to. However I'll be honest. I'm not just shouting with joy over the prospect. But say, I'm starved, aren't you? Shall we go to the tea room at once?"

In silence Lisle walked beside her old playmate as he led the way to the tea room, while her mother did her best to converse about generalities.

It was Victor who selected the table at which they were to sit, although Mrs. Kingsley suggested that she usually sat in the center of the room where she had a favorite waitress.

"What! You mean that crab-faced woman with the lantern jaw? Forget her, Mother Kingsley. She thinks she owns you. She knows how to put one over on you, Emily, and she works you for all she's worth. The last time I ate with you here she gave me the worst serving of chicken. It was nearly all bones, and I think she personally picked out that serving because I jacked her up on telling you that the cherry pie was all gone when I saw the woman at the next table get a big piece just five minutes before. If I'd had time I'd have reported her. You wait till I show you a waitress that is real. Here! There she is over there! That one with a pink ribbon on her hair that just matches her cheeks. She's easy to look at, isn't she? No lantern jaws on her. She'll give you her prettiest smile and get you what you want in a jiffy. Now, you'll see!"

Lisle giggled softly.

"You mean she'll smile and smile and be a villain still?" she asked pointedly.

The young man flashed a haughty reproof at his old playmate, and walking over to the table drew back a chair for Mrs. Kingsley, and another for Lisle, then turned to a convenient coat tree, divested himself of his handsome overcoat and sat down seemingly well pleased with himself.

The pretty waitress fluttered up and prepared the table for their use with glasses and silver, providing them with menu cards.

The young man accepted his with a grin and a "Hi, Cherry! How are things with you today?"

"All right, thank you, Mr. Vandingham," responded the girl with as perfect poise as if she had been his dinner partner at some social affair.

Mrs. Kingsley lifted her eyes in a quick thorough survey of the girl, and brought them back to the menu. But the girl's flush was permanent and her poise quite perfect, the poise of a well-trained waitress who knew her place, no matter what a daring young man chose to do.

The lady gave her order quietly, with utmost breeding and few words.

"Tomato stuffed with chicken salad, this plate of sandwiches and a cup of tea. Dessert? No, no dessert. I seldom take it at this time of day."

Lisle was ready with her order:

"Vegetable soup and a chicken sandwich!"

"Now Lisle, that's no gala lunch!" put in the young man. "We want this to be a real meal. I'm taking roast beef and mashed potatoes and shrimp salad, avocado pears and hot rolls, unsalted butter, and black coffee. You take the same, Lisle, then we'll come out even. Come on, be a good sport and play up!"

But Lisle sat coolly and looked him down, shaking her head.

"Thanks, no, Vic, I'm taking vegetable soup and a chicken sandwich. You get what you want. It will be all right with me. I'll take an orange sherbet to close with if that will help you out. And now, having settled the momentous question of what we shall eat, suppose you tell us your impression of Washington during this strenuous wartime. Did you like it? Would you be glad if you could stay there?"

Like a child, the young man turned quickly to the new subject offered.

"Washington? Oh yes, it's certainly swell to be down there for a while, only everybody is so terribly busy, and nobody has any time to enjoy life. There's too much traffic, and too many people trying to run things their own way, and even the girls are putting on uniforms and trying to act as if they were the soldiers. It's all right for the women to help in the war problem of course, but when it comes to all the pretty girls dropping their gaiety and attempting to pose as nurses or messengers, or hostesses, or even fliers, I draw the line at that. Girls haven't the mental power to go out for war. They're bound to get silly and make great mistakes. This is a man's work, this war, and women shouldn't try to mess in it just to get notoriety. It isn't desirable for women to get notoriety. They should confine their activities to something more feminine. However they did take time off for a few dances. There are some swell girls down there of course. The finest of the fine. Daughters of senators and officials. I met a girl from Russian nobility who was a stunner. She was clever, too."

"H'm!" commented Lisle pleasantly, "that must have been interesting."

But Lisle's mother was silently eating her luncheon and watching the boy who had been so many years her daughter's playmate, noting the changes that seemed to have come to his state of mind since he had been away, first in college, and then after a brief interval at home, off to Washington, where he was supposed to have been maneuvering some desirable berth for himself during war, with the wise machinations of his father and friends.

Then suddenly the young man turned to her, annoyed perhaps at the silence of the woman who had always seemed to be his old friend and ally.

"Say, Emily," he burst forth nonchalantly, "there's something I've been going to speak to you about, and I guess this is as good a time as any. It's about Lisle. Have you ever considered sending her away to get a little different slant on life? I've been thinking about it a lot lately, Emily, and I felt it was my duty to suggest it to you."

Mrs. Kingsley lifted her eyes calmly and looked into the gay assured eyes of the handsome boy for a moment before she spoke. Then she said coolly:

"Since when have you taken to calling your elders by their first names, Victor?"

"Oh, *that!*" laughed Victor. "Why everybody does that now, haven't you noticed it, Emily? It's quite the thing. All my friends at college do it. In fact I think you'll find that it's getting to be a custom all over the civilized world. Of course my mother practically had a fit the first time I called her Geraldine, but she's getting quite accustomed to it now, and only laughs when I say it. And you'll soon get to like it too, Emily, I'm sure. You see it gives you a personal individuality that you didn't have before."

"No," said Mrs. Kingsley quickly, "I shall not like it. I shall never like to have youths who are practically little more than children, speaking to their elders in what I consider a disrespectful manner, and if you intend to remain a friend to our family I must insist that you do not do it again."

"Oh, now Em—I beg your pardon, Mother Kingsley—I'm sorry you take it that way. I assure you I have the utmost respect for you, but it seems that it would be best for you to recognize the trend of the times, and accept the changes that are coming into circulation. And it is for that reason that I suggested that Lisle might profit by going away to another college for a while and getting a more modern viewpoint, for herself, and for her parents. It has done me a world of good to get away from the elderly and somewhat antique ideas of my parents, and I'm sure it would improve Lisle wonderfully."

"I'm afraid I don't agree with you that it has done you a world of good to go away," said Mrs. Kingsley. "I think it has injured you unbearably, and if I were your mother I should be grieved beyond endurance at the change. Even as merely your old friend I am filled with disappointment in you. I used to count you as a lad of great promise, but now you seem to have been under some stultifying blast that has made you insufferable. I would scarcely recognize you for the same boy we used to know. And I certainly do not recognize any right that you seem to think you have to criticize or advise about the education and development of my daughter."

"Well, right there you are mistaken," said the arrogant youth. "If Lisle is to be my wife some day I think I have a right to suggest how she shall be prepared to fill the position of hostess in my home, and her social position as my wife."

Lisle's eyes began to blaze. She laid down her knife and fork, and prepared to rise from the table, while her mother assumed a haughty manner and answered in a cool voice:

"If," she said. "Yes, *IF!* You certainly have assumed a good deal, young man. There has been no question of marriage with you, and yet you come here as if you were giving an order for a certain style of wife to be prepared for you. You are insolent, Victor, and you do not seem to know it, which makes it all the more insulting."

"Oh, but that is absurd!" said the young man with a grin. "You certainly have known for years that Lisle and I were meant for each other and that neither of us had any thought of anything else but that we should marry some day. In fact I have been debating today whether after all it wouldn't be best for Lisle and me to get married right away, and then I would be in a position to mold her and train her in the things that will fit her for the life we have to live together. It's just as well to be frank about it, don't you think? And then I decided that perhaps it would be as well for her to get a little further training from outside. But really you know, I might be ordered to leave the country very soon as a soldier, and in that case I should insist that we be married at once. I would prefer that myself I think, and then we could have a little enjoyment together before I go, anyway."

Then Lisle, quite white with excitement and anger rose from her seat, and speaking in a low voice that could not be heard at the other tables, said:

"I think this is about all I care to hear of this discussion, and I can settle the matter once and for all. I don't intend to marry you, Victor Vandingham, either now or at any other time, and I do not intend to go away from my college and my home, either, to any place that you can suggest. I do not *want* your suggestions and you certainly do not have any right, nor ever will have any right to make suggestions to me or to my family. Now, mother, I'm going on to have my hair done and I'll meet you at the Red Cross class this evening. Good by, Victor. I think this is probably the last time I shall see you to talk to. I couldn't quite forget what you have said and the way you have changed."

"Now, Lisle, don't be silly!" said the boy. "What's the matter with you? Can't you take kidding any more? You used to be a good sport. I had no idea you were getting so narrow in your viewpoint. Forget it, Lisle. I came here this afternoon intending to take you to the football game. It's going to be a good game and we'll have fun, and you'll begin to understand what I mean. Sit down till I pay this check and then we'll go on to the game and get straightened out. I don't suppose you'd care to go to the game too, Mother Kingsley, would you? I can easily get another ticket."

"Certainly not," said Mrs. Kingsley, rising.

"And I certainly do not care to go either," said Lisle firmly. "I have things to do and engagements to keep. Besides I would not care to go anywhere with you." And Lisle turned and marched across the tea room, stepping into the elevator that was just closing its door. It was the most thorough turning down that Victor Vandingham had ever had, though he was not greatly depressed by it. He had faith in himself and his own charm and felt he could soon win Lisle back to himself again. He would punish her for a few days and then win her back.

So he lingered till Mrs. Kingsley had gone, had a few low-spoken words with the girl Cherry, made a tentative date with her for the evening, then went gaily away.

3

LISLE Kingsley as she walked out of the tea room and went down in the elevator was so angry she could hardly see where she was going. She couldn't remember ever to have felt so indignant before! To think that Victor Vandingham had *dared* to talk that way to her mother, and about her! Actually taking it for granted that he and she were to be married, when he hadn't ever said a word about it to her! Just coming out in the open and announcing that it was going to happen, as if his word was law!

Lisle's ideas of marriage were very sacred and beautiful. When she was quite a little girl her mother had told her bits of stories from her own romance. She had told how she was walking along one day and saw a young stranger, very tall and handsome with a pleasant look in his eyes, and then how she had met him at a friend's house at dinner one evening, and how he had called to see her, and taken her places, and what nice times they had had together. Picnics and parties and lectures and concerts. Those brief pictures had lingered in the mind of the child, always culminating in the final love story.

How daddy had told mummy he loved her and how they had planned to be married and spend their life together. The little romantic touches were very tender and quite sacred in the memory of the young girl as she was growing up. A fitting pattern for the story of the lover who would perhaps come into her own life some day. But strange to say she had never quite visualized Victor as that lover. Victor was a friend, yes, a good playmate, but the lover she had vaguely looked forward to would be very different from Victor. And so it had come to her as a sort of a shock to find that Victor had been considering that she *belonged* to him. And she didn't want to belong to Victor *always*. Oh *no!* Not in any way but as a friend. It had angered her, almost terrified her, to have Victor speak of marriage as a sort of business arrangement to be entered into as if he were taking her over to support and mold, instead of as a beautiful sacred state of joy as she had always felt it was. It wasn't just for fun, like going to a football game or a party to dance together. Why didn't Victor feel as she did? He had a good father and mother. He must have seen a few ideal marriages in his life. At least he knew *her* father and mother and their beautiful life. He had spent many hours in her home playing and had had ample opportunity to see how they cared for one another. Could it really be true that since he had been away to college he had accepted such different standards? She couldn't believe it. He must just have been joking, surely, as her mother had suggested when she first told her of the change in Victor. Of course he could not have been really proposing marriage. He wouldn't do it in that way. He was only trying to be exceedingly daring, probably rather enjoyed the idea of shocking her and her mother. Perhaps he felt that such an experience would make them understand what he had been trying to suggest, that she should go away to another college for her closing year.

Well, if that was it he would be disappointed, for she certainly did not wish to go away. She *would not* graduate at any other college than her own, where she had been working now for three happy years. She did not want new associates, new ways and standards. And perhaps it wasn't such a bad thing that they had been angry with him and she had left the restaurant. It might bring him to his senses and make him understand that he could not talk to them in this casual new way he had learned.

But the uppermost feeling in her mind was one of shame for him. To think that he had so changed! She wasn't in love with him. By no means. She hadn't ever thought of love in connection with him. He had just been her nice boy friend, and now he wasn't even nice, not the way he acted today. But perhaps after he had thought it over he would realize what he had done.

Well, he ought to be ashamed. He ought to realize that everybody was not like his new-fashioned friends. And if he liked that sort of thing she didn't want anything more to do with him. But surely now, after this, she wouldn't be expected to go to that party!

Of course there would be mortifying explanations if she didn't! She would have to write a note to Mrs. Vandingham. Oh, she *couldn't*! How could she explain without telling her what Victor had done? And that would involve such an endless situation. Victor would be brought into it and be required to make an apology. She could see him now, in his new role, laughing it all off, calling it a joke. And *making his mother believe it!* That would be the worst. And she *couldn't* go to his party now. Even if he did apologize he would somehow make it apparent to the assembled town that there was some special arrangement between them. He would claim they were going to be married or something, and do it so publicly that she couldn't deny it without making a fool of herself.

Tears stung into her eyes as she walked along the street. Oh, she couldn't go to the hairdresser's now and sit through a long session, being asked questions! Because the hairdresser felt herself to be a privileged character, having been serving the family of Kingsleys through long years. No, she would go home, straight home, and telephone the hairdresser calling off the appointment. Then she could lock herself in her room and cry if she wanted to, without fear of questions. She was relieved that even her mother would not be at home. Then she would have time to think this thing through and find out just what it was all about, this whole matter that hurt her so. If it was any secret feeling in her own heart she must ferret it out and do something about it.

So she stepped into a drugstore, telephoned the hairdresser, and then took a taxi home. She didn't want to run the risk of even meeting some friend on the street and having to stop and talk. She wanted to get this trouble out of her system once and for all and not just spend time being angry. That wasn't a healthy thing to do. She wanted to be at peace with the world, and until she had thought this thing through she couldn't be. Her own natural world into which she had been born had been tipping and tilting ever since Victor got home in the spring, and now today it had turned completely over. What was she going to do about it? Something had to be done at once. Perhaps she had better arrange to go out west to see those cousins she hadn't seen in years, and get herself through the time of that awful party. She certainly wasn't going to it anyway, now, not after today!

So she entered her home, and calling to one of the servants that she had returned she ran up to her room. Locking her door she flung off her hat and coat and threw herself down on her bed in a sudden paroxysm of weeping.

She was not a girl given to tears and they soon spent themselves. She sat up and wiped her eyes, went and washed her face, and then began to look herself over. What was she crying about? Why did she feel so broken up about what had occurred? So humiliated? She wasn't in love with Victor, no, of course not. But he had been a good friend and it was a shock to find him so different from what she had always thought him. But why waste tears on him? She must snap out of this.

Then the telephone rang, and she slipped out in the hall and across to her mother's room to answer it, struggling to take a deep breath and get the huskiness out of her voice.

"Yes?" she called cheerfully in a voice that would do for any stranger. There were no tears in the sound.

And then it was her mother, calling most anxiously.

"Oh! Oh, Lisle! Is that you? Are you really at home? Oh, I'm so glad!"

"Yes, mother. I didn't see going to the hairdresser's just now and I called it off. She didn't mind. She had somebody waiting, and was glad to be able to take them. But how did you happen to call here?"

"Why I called up Miss Harris and she told me you had just called and asked to be released. Lisle, child! I'm sorry you are so upset. But I don't wonder of course. Now, dear, what do you want to do? You need to get your mind off this foolish matter. Would you rather meet me at Hathaway's and get through our shopping, or shall I come right home?"

"Oh, mother, I don't believe I want to shop any more today. We'd be sure to meet somebody and somehow I don't feel like talking with outsiders. I've just got to get things straight in my mind before I will feel like talking."

"Yes, I understand, dear. And I'll be right home. You and I need a good old-fashioned talk together before we go any farther."

"Oh, mother, you haven't got the shopping done you had planned. Those gloves, and all those other things on our list. You go on and get them. I'll be all right."

"No, dear, I'm sort of upset myself. I have no further interest in shopping, and especially not without you."

"Oh, then, mother, I'll come right down and meet you. I don't mind, *really!*"

"No, dear! I'm tired. I really am! That conversation we had in the tea room sort of took my strength away. I'm coming. Good by!"

So Lisle hurried around and got herself ready to be cheerful by the time her mother came. They were that way, the Kingsley family, always playing up for each other. Never allowing depression to cloud the family sky.

So Lisle changed into a little blue dress with daisies embroidered in a circle about the neck line, a dress that had been a favorite of the family for three years. It wasn't quite in its pristine freshness, but it was one of the dresses that Lisle had hunted out from the store closet when she and her mother had decided to be patriotic and not buy any more new clothes, nor *any*thing that they did not absolutely need. Her mother always said that the blue of the fabric in this dress exactly matched Lisle's eyes.

As she stood in front of the mirror tucking a cute little blue bow among her curls, there came a memory of that boy working in the street this morning whose blue eyes matched his blue shirt, and she smiled at the thought of how he and she had smiled at one another. Strange! Just a working sort of fellow, but he had a really sunny smile! Strange that that little incident should have left such a pleasant impression on her memory!

When she had made herself tidy-looking for her mother she got out a bit of needlework she was working on, with Christmas in mind, and made ready to be as cheerful as possible and have one of the real talks with her mother that had always been such a delight to her. Mother had a way of searching her soul without seeming to do so, and planning ways to set anything right that proved to be out of kilter, a way of soothing hurts and giving courage to go forward in forgiveness and kindliness.

So by the time her mother arrived half the work of healing was done, because the daughter was ready to accept any suggestions that her mother would have.

Lisle saw that her mother was more disturbed than she had owned over the telephone, and she immediately set to work to soothe her, so that when they sat down before a delightful fire in the library, Lisle with her bit of petit point in her lap and her gold thimble on her slender finger, there was a real smile on her face, and no trace of tears left.

The mother was sitting in her own comfortable chair, with her head back, a look of rest beginning to come over her weary features. And so they began to talk.

"Now, Lisle, my dear, I think if I were you I would just put this whole matter out of mind entirely and forget it," began her mother.

"Why, yes, mother, of course," said Lisle briskly. "But mother, you did see what I meant when I said Victor was changed, didn't you?"

"I certainly did!" said Mrs. Kingsley. "I couldn't have believed it possible. It seems incredible. But then, I suppose that is the trend of the times. A ruthlessness of thought and speech, that of course sometimes covers the deeper lovely feelings that used to be counted the better emotions. Of course it may be caused by a lingering adolescence. A dislike to speak in gentler terms. I don't know. I've been trying to figure it out on my way home, but I really can't fully understand it. I have always been so sure that Victor was courteous, and that he was deeply attached to you. I couldn't have believed that he would be so blunt and rude as he was today."

"Well, mother, surely you see after what happened today that I simply *can't* go to that party! You understand how I feel about it, don't you?"

"Why, of course, dear! I've been thinking of that, too. I have been hoping that something will occur in time to stop that party entirely. In fact I can't see how his mother can bear to go on with a party when her son is liable to have to go away to war very soon. Parties are occasions for gaiety and joy, and not for sorrowful times. One doesn't want great hordes of people around when the heart is aching with imminent partings in the offing."

"Yes, I know," said Lisle. "I don't see how she can. But mother, somehow it never seemed to me that she cared for her son that way. She cares more for how he will look to the world, than for what he is. She—wants him to—show off, mother! She really does. I think she is a great deal to blame for the way Victor thinks and acts, now that he is grown up. She has taught him to look out for such things, to get everything for *himself*, get all the breaks, and evade all the hard work and hard things."

"Yes, I'm afraid she is to blame a great deal. But still, Victor has a good mind. He might think these things out for himself."

"Mother, I don't think he has been taught to think, not reasonably. I think in all the teaching he has had, *himself* has always been made the center, and now that he has reached the age when he considers himself grown up, he feels that he can assert himself and take what he wants out of life, and nobody dares to prevent him. I don't think I ever really allowed myself to think that clear through to the conclusion before. But for several years, whenever I've been seeing him for a few hours, at a party or some game, I have noticed that more and more in him, although for the sake of old times I hated to admit it. But I couldn't help seeing it, and it troubled me a lot. It somehow interfered with all my early standards and spoiled a lot of my childhood memories."

"My dear! Why did you never say anything about it before?"

"Well, I don't know. I think I did come near telling you several times during vacation, but I always hesitated because it seemed to me that if I admitted such a thing enough to tell you about it, that would make it true. And I just couldn't bear to spoil things. But this time, well, I was really upset when I heard he was taking lunch with us, or I wouldn't have let you see it. You see he said a lot of things yesterday, when he took me to dinner and for the evening, that disturbed me, and I hadn't had a chance to think what I could say in reply that would make him see what I meant. I never like to quarrel you know. But there were some things he took for granted that I couldn't let go, and I wanted a chance to think them over before I saw him again. But oh, mother, the way he talked this afternoon, that was *awful!* Taking it for granted he was going to *marry* me, just like that, without ever having asked me what I thought about it! It was so as if he was making a bargain, or buying a horse or dog. I just hated it! Even if I'd cared anything about him I would have hated it. Do you think I was wrong, mother? Was I just a silly child?"

"I certainly do not think so, my dear. You were perfectly right. I was deeply offended for you myself. I was outraged at him! I felt he was fairly insulting. But, my dear, I blame myself for not having seen this coming and saved you from the experience this afternoon."

"No, mother, you mustn't blame yourself. I should have told you before. Though those things that made me so indignant before were nothing to what he said this afternoon. Is marriage like that, mother, just a sort of a commercial arrangement? Mother, daddy wasn't like that with you, was he? *I'm* sure he wasn't. He didn't just tell you you had to marry him at a certain time, not even asking you if you wanted to. Men can't do that, can they? Because if they can I will never *never* get married. Not even if I thought I loved a man would I just walk after him when he said I had to. Would you, mother?"

There were tears in her eyes and voice now, and she was almost on the verge of breaking down again.

"Why of course not, dear. That is not true marriage. There is no real marriage where there is not love, and true love does not order the beloved one. A joyful marriage can only be where there is real love, and tender courtship, and a real lover would never force his attentions on one. I cannot think that Victor understands, or that he is really grown up. His whole performance this afternoon was like a selfish wilful child."

"But mother, I think he believes that is the modern way and that you and I are old-fashioned. That is what makes it all so hopeless. Not hopeless either, mother, for I do not feel it matters very much if he is like that. Oh, he is an old friend, I know, and one hates to lose the companion of one's childhood. But he isn't important to me, really, any more."

"Are you sure, my dear? Oh, I would be so glad if I could be certain that that is true! For nothing that I can think of would seem more terrible to me than to have you married to a young man with such standards. Or broken-hearted because he had turned out to be what he evidently has become. I used to be so glad that you had a boy friend like Victor Vandingham, but now I am greatly thankful that we have discovered what he is before it is forever too late! Oh, my dear!"

"Well, now Emi—I beg your pardon, Mother Kingsley—just what fault do you have to find with me? What's the matter with me that you're making such a scene about? You certainly put on a dramatic act in the tea room. I didn't know either of you were capable of that. I thought you were too well bred."

It was Victor Vandingham's voice that drawled into the conversation lazily. They had not heard him coming. He had just walked into the house much as he used to do in the old days when he was a mere child, listened a moment to locate the low voices he could hear and then walked straight to the library door. The door had opened stealthily and he stood just behind Mrs. Kingsley's chair before he spoke. Then he calmly stalked over to an unoccupied chair near the fire and slumped down into it, gracefully, his hat in his hand, swung carelessly, very nonchalantly, he looked from the mother to the daughter and back again.

"Well, really!" said Mrs. Kingsley springing to her feet, her pleasant eyes fairly snapping with indignation, her whole body expressing dignity and utter outrage. "Since when did you start walking into people's rooms and interrupting private conversations? Haven't you humiliated us enough today without this? Of course in your childhood days when you were a friend of the family you had the privilege of walking in unannounced, but I consider that by your conversation this afternoon you forfeited that right. I certainly am disappointed in you, Victor, and—ashamed of you!"

"Now, what did I do, I ask you? Didn't I ask your daughter to marry me? What is humiliating about that?"

"You announced to my daughter that you were *going* to marry her," said Mrs. Kingsley. "That is not the way an offer of marriage is usually made. Especially between young people who have seen very little of each other for nearly four years, and who are both rather young to be even considering marriage at present. But even if you were not so young you certainly know that there are ways of conducting such a suit for a girl's hand that you have entirely ignored. Why would you think any girl would *want* to marry you with such an invitation? The veriest savage would know better than that."

A wide devilish grin overspread the handsome face of the boy.

"Oh, you mean all that antique junk about love? Why, where have you been that you don't know that that kind of mush is entirely out of date? You've known me for years. You know what my family is, and that I am financially able to support your daughter in a style even better than she has been accustomed to all her life. What's the idea of your giving me the high hat that way? Haven't I a right to demand certain things of the girl I've decided to marry? You've kept her down to your own notions so long that she really doesn't have a mind of her own, and you've made her old-fashioned to the extent that she can scarcely hold her own with young people of her age. I say it's a shame, and I was only trying to be frank and make you understand. But if you can't see it that way just call it a joke, and let it go at that. I was only joking, and I certainly think you both ought to be able to take a joke. You used to be able to see a joke, what's become of your sense of humor?"

"I see no humor in making a joke of sacred things," said Mrs. Kingsley.

"The bunk! What's sacred about what we were talking about, I'd like to know? We weren't talking about religion."

"You were talking about marriage!" said the lady coldly. "It is the most sacred relation on earth. It is the foundation of the family, and of all right human relations."

"Not any more," said the boy importantly. "Not since divorce has become so common, so almost universal. You can't put over that old stuff about marriage being sacred. I tell you it's been clearly demonstrated today that marriage is what you want to make of it, and if the man is the head of the house, it's his business to order what the marriage shall turn out, see? So it's up to the man! And I was just showing you that I understand my part in this arrangement." He grinned affably at them as they sat there speechless, unable to believe their senses that their erstwhile friend could so have changed.

"And just what have you come here for?" asked the mother haughtily. "I thought when you first came in that you had come to apologize for all your rudeness, but you seem only to be adding more insult to what you have already said."

Then that impish grin broke out on the boy's face once more, an echo of the look he used to wear when he came over to tell some joke after school when he was a child.

"Say, I was just kidding! Can't you understand? I just came over to say so, and to tell you I really want to take Lisle to that football game. Come on, Lisle, forget it all and let's have a swell time the way we used to do!"

"I don't think that would be possible," said Lisle with a haughty lift of her pretty chin. "I'm afraid I couldn't forget some of the awful things you have been saying."

"But haven't I just told you I was only kidding?"

"Yes," said the girl with an understanding look in her young eyes that seemed suddenly to be looking deep into life and knowing many things that had hitherto been hidden, "I know you *say* you were only kidding, but you see I don't believe that! I have known you a good many years, Victor, and I know pretty well *when* you are telling the truth and when you are only kidding, and I *don't believe* that you are entirely amusing yourself by taking us for a ride. I am quite sure that you were trying out a new standard of life which you have recently acquired, and I don't like it. I don't want to have anything to do with it, and I won't hear any more about it. And now if you will excuse me I have a lesson to prepare for my Red Cross work this evening."

Lisle arose and started toward the door, but suddenly Victor sprang to his feet and burst forth in his old impulsive way, walking over to her and grasping her wrists familiarly:

"Aw, don't be that way, Lisle! Be a good sport and go with me to that game. I really want you, and I really came after you, and I swear I'll make you have a good time. Come on and let me show you I mean it."

Lisle drew away from him.

"No, Victor, I can't go. I don't want to go. I'm fed up with this whole subject, and I would much rather stay at home and work."

"Aw now, Lisle. You aren't going to be a flat tire when I went to all the trouble to get these special tickets just for you. You might try me out just for one hour and let me prove to you that I'm not so black as you have tried to paint me. Come on, Lisle, for the sake of old times, and the days when you and I were pals! I can't bear to have you get this way. It isn't like you. It isn't according to your old code. You always were fair with everybody and you're not being fair with me now when I've apologized for my thoughtlessness. I'm only asking another chance to prove to you that I'm the same old guy you used to like. Come on, Lisle! Don't be a quitter!"

Lisle looked troubled and drew her hands away.

"I'm not a quitter, Victor, but it seems to me that you

are. You had good standards and principles when we were children, and now you have cast them all aside. I do not like the way you talk."

"Say, Lisle, be yourself, and give me another chance to show you. Just one more chance, Lisle! Be a little fair to an old friend!"

Victor knew how to make his handsome eyes plead, how to use his expressive voice in wordless arguments, how to throw utter sorrow and despair into his mobile face, till one glance his way would make strong argument for him, bring doubt in the mind whether one was quite fair to him.

Lisle turned perplexed eyes toward her mother.

"Should I, mother?" she asked.

Her mother gave a troubled glance toward the boy, and then looked at her young daughter with worried eyes.

"I—am sure—whatever you decide to do will be right," she said hesitantly, but there was question in her own voice.

The boy grew even eager:

"Aw, now Lisle, be your old self. Stick to your old code! Be fair to me just once more!" he pleaded.

So Lisle's face, though it did not soften, grew decisive:

"Very well," she said almost coldly, "I'll go, this once!"

"But you can't go in that dress," said her mother rousing. "You'll have to dress, and it's getting late." She glanced at the clock. "Besides it's growing colder."

"Take your time," said Victor settling back in his chair again with a look of almost defiant triumph in his eyes.

"I'll put on my fur coat," said Lisle, "it's right here in the hall closet. I won't be a minute."

"That old shabby coat," complained her mother

distressfully, as Lisle made a dash across the hall and came back sliding into her old beaver coat, and a little brown felt hat.

"It's all right," said the girl with a wry smile. "It really doesn't matter what I wear. Come on, Victor! Let's get this thing over!"

"Oh!" said the young man with an offended grin. "Is that the way you're taking it? Well, come on! I'll see it through no matter what odds you give me!"

And so with unsmiling faces they went away to their test, and the mother went to the window and watched them with troubled eyes. Had she done right to assent to her daughter's going? Would harm come from it, or would there come a possible reconciliation? And would that be good for her child, or ill? She turned away from the window with a sigh after they were out of sight, and in her dignified conservative way did what she understood to be right in the way of making a troubled prayer to offset what harm might be done.

4

JOHN Sargent walked a full block before he realized that there was someone walking in step with him, long loose steps, as if they were old friends. Then, as they crossed the next corner and a good many other pedestrians turned away down the side street, the man was still there. John turned and gave him a quick look, taking in the keen eyes, the slouching gait, the assured set of head and shoulders.

The stranger met his gaze with a steady look, and then spoke.

"Well, you've had a busy day, haven't you? I been watching you quite a spell off and on. You're a good worker. Seems like you ought to be able to hold down a better paid job than the one you were at."

"Thanks!" said John, giving him another quick searching glance, but saying no more.

"You been working for this company long?" asked the stranger, after waiting in vain for a more comprehensive answer to his first remark.

John gave the man another sharp look.

"Awhile," he answered shortly.

The other man studied him a moment.

"They pay you pretty well?" he asked insinuatingly.

"What's that to you?" John barked out quickly.

"Oh, nothing. Nothing at all," said Kurt Entry apologetically. "I just was thinking a man like you in these times would be worth a good deal of money to the company he worked for, that is, if you always worked as hard as you did today. It's that reason I asked about wages. Some don't appreciate how hard a man works, and pay as little as possible, and I happen to know about a job that pays real money. I wouldn't wonder you might fit in there if you cared to apply."

"Yes?" said John in a tone of unbelief. "I've heard people talk that way before. Then you come to enquire, and it doesn't turn out to be so much. You hunting for a job?" John looked the man up and down with the air of being a contractor searching for laborers.

"Me? Oh no. I got a job. Pays me good. I just happen to know about this other job. It's just velvet!" and he mentioned an incredibly large sum somewhat under his breath.

"Oh yeah?" said John and gave him another sharp look. "What's wrong with it?"

"Eh?" said Kurt Entry giving John a surprised look. "What's wrong with what? The job or the pay?"

"Both," said John crisply. "People don't pay that much to anyone unless there's something crooked about the work or the place where the money comes from."

"Oh!" said Kurt, lapsing into a non-committal attitude. "Well you see it's this way. There's need, in a certain place I know, for a man who can be trusted. A man who knows how to keep his mouth shut and obey instructions; and being a pretty good judge of human nature, I took you for that kind of man, see?"

John's brows drew together in a puzzled expression. He was thinking fast.

"Is this a government job?" he asked sharply.

"Well, yes, in a *way* it is. It's very important, and that's the reason they can't trust every Tom, Dick and Harry."

"I see," said John, "but the government doesn't send men out to contact strangers on the street with a proposition like yours. What kind of a sucker do you think I am?"

"You don't understand me, kid! I just took a notion to you and I thought you would fall for such a lot of money."

"What made you think I would?" said John Sargent with his eyes narrowing.

"Well, I heard you had a grandmother you were taking good care of and I thought you would enjoy having a little real velvet to help with your job."

"But you haven't answered my question yet," said the boy. "What's the catch? I know there's a catch somewhere, for I'm not great enough for some big man in the government to have gone lulu over me. Answer me the question, and I'll answer you. What is it they want done that anybody couldn't do?"

"Well, it isn't anything great, kid," said Kurt. "Just a little matter of observation, and of being able to report on certain things as soon as they're planned so that other people can keep up with the times. Nothing out of the way at all."

"Like what?" asked John, watching the other man now keenly.

"Oh, just keeping ears and eyes open. Finding dates of shipments, formulas, getting descriptions and measurements. Know anything about photography?"

John lifted his head alertly.

"What if I do?" he asked.

"Well, there's plenty of dough in knowing how to get a good picture of important things. I know that fer a fact."

"Meaning what?"

"Well, I'm not just saying what I mean. Not till you say you're ready to deal with me. And you don't need to worry about my commission. All I'll ask will be a measly little ten percent on what you make."

"Oh, so that's the catch, is it?" said John with a grin.

"What do you mean? There ain't any catch. This is straight business."

John continued to grin.

"Ten per!" he sneered. "Paid in advance, I suppose?"

"No sir. You don't pay till you get yours, and that'll be plenty soon after you deliver the goods, see?"

"Yes, I see," said John. "I see your trick, but I'm from Missouri and I don't snap at the first drop of the hook. Besides, it was you that brought this up, not I. It sounds fishy to me."

"Nothing fishy about it, son. It's genuine business, if you're interested."

"Well, I'm not interested," said the lad. "I'm not interested in rackets of any kind, and this sounds to me about the worst racket I've heard yet."

"No racket about it, young fellah! Just an honest-to-goodness way to make a little easy dough. I thought you looked like a man that could put a thing across in great shape if you just once got it into your head to do it. I sort of took a liking to you when I heard how respectful you spoke to that sour lady that was trying to take a rise out of you, and you wouldn't rise. I liked that in you, and I says to myself, That's just the man for that job I heard of, and I'd like to be the one to connect him up with it. I sure would. It's an all-right proposition, and I'd like to see it well done. It's a job I would have taken on myself if I hadn't been so well suited with the job I've already got."

Kurt Entry gave a sidewise glance toward his victim and smiled his oily smile.

John Sargent turned and faced the man by his side.

"What is all this about anyway, stranger? Are you an agent for some group, or something? And what would this work be I'd be supposed to do? Answer me straight! I won't listen to any more of this hedging business."

"Sure, I'll answer you straight. You wouldn't have so much to do beyond the ordinary mechanical work in the plant. Just keep your eyes and ears open for what is needed, and know how to report it. Just mebbe a picture now and then of something important. Plenty of pay, and very little extra work."

John suddenly turned on the man and glared at him.

"You mean that you want me to be a miserable spy against my own country and what they are doing to defend our freedom? Is that it? Well you can get out, you louse! And take the answer back, *NO! Never* will I lend myself to such treason, not for all the money in the world! That's flat and final! Good by!" John Sargent swung himself aboard the bus which had just stopped to let a passenger off, and was now about to start. But Kurt Entry's voice pursued him as the door was closing: "Well, kid, think it over. I'll be seeing you." But when John looked back at the corner the man had vanished.

Two blocks farther on, John Sargent swung off the bus again, and made his way to a police station where he reported what had been said to him, and then hurried to his grandmother's comfortable little apartment. She welcomed him with her eyes and she flashed for him her poor twisted smile. Then John Sargent prepared a delicate meal for her and fed it to her, made her comfortable for the night in a gentle way he had, and as she slept he sat and brooded over the state of things that had been opened up to him that afternoon, and his very blood boiled with indignation. Was it possible that such traffic as this was really going on in his own beloved land? Hiring spies and treachery? He had read of such doings of course, but had never half believed them until now. And couldn't that guy tell from just looking at him that he wasn't that kind of a fellow? Well, he'd show them. If that stinking sneak came around again he wouldn't even look at him, but he'd see that the police got the high sign before it was too late to catch him. A long time he sat beside that simple bed and watched the sleeper, his thought growing more and more tempestuous. How his very soul ached to be in the great war struggle to set his world free from such horror. He had heard the men talk where he used to work, even if he hadn't had time to read the papers or listen to the radio. The war news traveled fast around the gang as they worked, sometimes even anticipating the things that were happening, so that the men almost talked about things before they had really occurred. He knew that every able-bodied man ought to be out defending righteousness. And yet he knew that for the present his duty lay here with this dear invalid. She had spent years working for him, helping him through till he would have his education. And now she was laid low, and didn't even know what dire distress had come upon the world.

Or did she? How much had she seen from her small world in her library before the blow had fallen upon her? She was a reader, quick to know the signs of the times. Once when he had been home for a few days in vacation time she had spoken of the possibility that the war-torn world across the sea might even send the struggle to America.

"Oh, I hope you won't have to go away and be a soldier, John," she had said with a sigh.

There had been a prolonged silence, and then the boy had replied:

"But Grandmother, if war should come to defend a righteous cause, you wouldn't want me to keep out of it, would you? You wouldn't want me to be a slacker?"

And she had given him one yearning distressful look and said with another deep sigh:

"No, of course not, John."

And so he knew in his heart that if even now he could tell her all that was going on in the world, and how America, their own dear land had been called to do its duty and go out to fight for victory and freedom, Grandmother's tired eyes would flash with their old fire, and her locked lips would try to form words which would bid him go and fight with the rest, and not to let her necessity be a hindrance to his doing his duty.

But he could not leave her now. She was all he had left, and she had worn her own life out trying to help him. It wasn't as if she were unconscious now, and wouldn't know the difference if he was gone. He knew that his presence was a great joy to her. Her eyes told him that. But he had a strong belief that real duties never conflicted. There would be a way out somehow if circumstances changed.

But whatever came, while he was here at home at least, there would be things he could do for the cause of defense. He had a fairly good promise of a job he would be likely to get in a few days. It would not only enable him to make his grandmother more comfortable, but he would be definitely doing work that was needed in the war.

At present he was hiring a pleasant elderly woman to care for his grandmother during the day. She wasn't a regular nurse, and he wanted very much to be able to afford a professional nurse. Perhaps that would come pretty soon. But at present Mrs. Burke was doing her best, between looking after two little grandchildren when their mother was out working. It wasn't an ideal arrangement, but it was the best he could afford now. Perhaps something better would come pretty soon. It was for these reasons that Kurt Entry's suggestion of more money had at first caught his ear and made him listen briefly in spite of his better judgment. But now as he thought it over his lip curled at himself to think he had even *seemed* interested in the stranger.

And then came the thought that perhaps here was something he could do for the war interest. He might be able to trace down some of these treacheries that were going on in the country. He would keep that in mind and be on the watch for suspicious characters. He wasn't a trained detective of course, but in these days everyone must be on the alért, ready to help in every way.

Then he began to think about the man that had accosted him. Perhaps he ought by good rights to have questioned him more. Perhaps he should have found out where this work was going on that they wanted him to spy on, and then let the owner himself be warned. But, on the other hand, would that mean there was danger of getting himself involved and suspected of something unlawful? He should be careful of that of course, not for his own sake but because of his grandmother. He must not do anything that would involve his staying away from her while she was in this critical condition, liable to have another stroke at any time, the doctor said. She depended upon him. He could not bear to think of her anguished eyes searching the room in vain to find him. No, he must be cautious about whatever he did.

To that end perhaps he should avoid all contacts with such men as that stranger, at least for the present. But then it wasn't likely he would be approached again, not by that man anyway. The way he vanished so quickly showed that.

Or did it? Would he come again some day when he was least looking for him? What approach would he use the second time? And what should be his own reaction? Apparently interested, or not? And how much could he count on those police? They had asked a good many questions, but would they be on hand when needed?

These and other questions relating to fifth columnists kept thrashing themselves over in his mind until his brain grew weary and his eyes heavy with sleep, and after listening to his grandmother's steady breathing and making sure she was as comfortable as could be expected, he slipped into the small adjoining room. It was little more than a big closet, only large enough to hold a cot and a small pine table, the only place he could call his own. Yet it was just right, for lying here he could hear if his grandmother needed him, could watch over her in the night.

He was soon ready for the night, and as he dropped down on his hard little cot and drew the covers up, strangely there came to him the face of that beautiful girl he had seen on the street that day, that girl whose glance had met his own. Why did that girl so continually haunt him with her pleasant beauty? She was no one he would ever be likely to know, nor even speak to. And yet since he saw her early in the day there had not passed a minute when the memory of her had not come to haunt him, to taunt him as with something unattainable. He was half angry at her for having made such a strong impression upon him, wholly angry with himself for allowing the vision of her to come and go in his memory this way. He thought he had downed it, swept it out of his mind. But just tonight he had happened to glimpse an item in the society column of the newspaper, a department in which he had no interest whatever, and never consciously looked at, linking her name with Victor Vandingham's. Vandingham, the man who had been his particular aversion in college. The man who had been the cause of more than one humiliation during their scholastic years in the same institution. The one who had assumed the right to ignore him, to discount him on every possible occasion, to sneer at him because he did not have the money to finance the various enterprises in which Vandingham had been interested. The one who had prevented his being elected to membership in the finest fraternity, and whose deciding vote had kept him from a number of honors his fellow students were ready to give him. And this young man was a close friend of the girl whose face and glance kept coming back to him! This must not go on! The paper even hinted very plainly that she was engaged to Victor Vandingham! And he was haunted by her vision as if in some subtle way her spirit belonged to him.

Fiercely he frowned and turned away from the thought of her. No woman should tempt him to let his thoughts dwell on her, no matter how brave or beautiful a vision she might be. She was not born into his world. And he doubted if he would ever find one who would fit into his life. He was fashioned of harder clay, meant to fight and die for freedom perhaps, that others might enjoy. Not meant to live at ease for happiness.

So again and again he disciplined his thoughts, until he felt he had almost forgotten how she looked, and the thought of her was far away. A moment of weakness, he told himself, the result of a longing that sometimes came over him for his mother, whom he could just remember. A beautiful mother, sweet and tender with him, and gentle to everyone. Beautiful, too. For even a child knows beauty, and to the little one who first judges womanhood by the face of his smiling mother, his ideal grows great, so that he is not easily satisfied by one who does not measure up.

The man Kurt Entry did not appear for some days, and John Sargent began to feel that he must have dreamed the whole occurrence. Several times he had seen his policeman friend hovering on the outskirts of the group where he was working, giving a wink and a lifting of the hand toward him as had been agreed upon between them, and John could only lift his brows and shrug his shoulders as if to rest himself, showing to the officer that the man had not appeared. So the policeman blended into the distance and disappeared.

Then one day, quite two weeks from his first appearance, Kurt Entry returned to the roadside. Of course it was not in the same location where John had first seen him, but again he stood most casually as an onlooker for a few seconds, and John glanced up to see him looking straight at himself, a half-amused smile on his lips as if there were a secret understanding between them. John was ready for that. He ignored the glance, swept his own eyes across the crowd and dropped them down to his work again. He did not look that way again. Later when the day was done and Sargent started for home he could not see the man anywhere, and when he passed his policeman friend who had suddenly appeared, he nodded his head as agreed upon to show that he had seen his man again.

To an observer the policeman showed no sign that any communication had passed between them, and John passed on his way home. Three blocks farther on Kurt Entry fell into step beside him.

"Well, how about it, young fellah? You thought that matter over yet?"

John looked up with apparent surprise and no recognition in his glance.

"Thought what matter over?" he asked indifferently.

"That little matter of getting yourself a larger salary."

"Oh! *That!*" said John. "I'd almost forgotten that. You see I never place much significance on a proposition unless I know who's behind it. And of course the way you made it out I wouldn't touch it with a ten foot pole, not even if the angel Gabriel was financing it. I'm an American. I'm not a traitor!"

"Now see here, young fellah," said Entry, "you got me all wrong the other night. I wasn't proposing any illegal thing at all. You didn't stay to hear me explain. You just went off half-cocked on that bus, and my news is too private to shout to the universe. It's government secrets, you know. And my proposition was an all right proposition with reliable people behind it. People who'd never go against the government, not for worlds. As loyal people as you'd care to meet anywhere. Reliable and respected people as there is in the city."

"Yeah? Who, for instance?"

Kurt Entry's eyes narrowed. He cast a furtive glance behind him and then sidled nearer to his companion and lowered his tone:

"Know anybody by the name of Vandingham?" he said in a sepulchral whisper.

John Sargent looked up with a quick wonder in his eyes, instantly concealed.

"Seems to me I've heard the name," he said, thoughtfully, almost disinterestedly. "So you mean *they* are the people that are offering this big salary. Is that right?"

"Not on yer life it ain't," said Entry. "They are the folks that are *making* the stuff on the government job. They'd be the folks you'd be working for, see? But the big dough would come from an entirely different party, and *they'd* be the ones you'd have to satisfy. The folks that want the dope."

"Yeah? Well, who are they?"

"Oh, that's a military secret," said Kurt Entry. "You wouldn't likely come in contact with them at all. You'd get your check through the mail perhaps, or money order, or whatever, I don't know which, or else sometimes in cash through a go-between."

"*You*, do you mean?" asked John with a quick glance at the man.

"Oh, no, not me," said Kurt. "I never handle the

money on such deals. I just get my ten per. You see I'm pretty busy myself, sometimes traveling for my firm. But when I hear of a good thing like this I like to help my fellow men by passing it on, and also make a little money myself on the side. I figure it's only fair if I put you on to a lotta dough, that I should have my share for making it known to you. Ain't that so?"

"I suppose it's all in the way you look at it," said John, and continued on his steady gait, breaking into a merry whistle now and again.

Kurt Entry stalked by his side, giving him a sidewise curious glance, amid a growing impatience.

"Well, what say? Shall I put you down for my man? It doesn't do to be too slow accepting a good thing, you know. Vandinghams are hiring men right and left, and they *may* get all their places filled if I don't give them your name tonight. You've got to get the job, you know, before you'd be in a position to give out facts."

"Yeah, I see," said John grinning. "There's always a hitch somewhere."

"What do you mean, young fellah? There ain't any hitch. It's just common sense. You can't do my folks any good unless you're in a position to get their information. Now, once for all, are you interested in getting that job with Vandinghams?"

"No," said John soberly, "I'm not interested."

Kurt Entry gave him a sharp look, and then suddenly became aware of two men approaching. They were not in uniform, but Kurt Entry was well versed in the art of escape and allaying suspicion. His eyes narrowed. He lowered his head. Let his feet drag a little as if he were about to turn back. Looked up at John and said in a low tone:

"Then I'm afraid I can't promise to hold this any longer for you. I shall probably not return unless I find there are still openings. Good by!" and he scuttled diagonally across the street to an alley and disappeared. But John, with an eye toward the approaching pedestrians, and a grin on his lips, shouted: "Definitely, not interested."

The two men approaching turned their eyes toward the place where Kurt Entry had disappeared, and plunged across the street themselves, giving John a hurried salute as they went.

5

AFTER the football game there was a formal truce between Lisle and Victor. That is, it was formal on Lisle's part, and warmly friendly on Victor's. For Victor had been on his good behavior the rest of that afternoon and took great pains to be attentive and interesting. He told at length about games he had been seeing elsewhere, bought candy and peanuts and pennants and flowers for his girl, just as he used to do when they were very young. He acted out the old-time comradeship. Sometimes she wondered at him greatly. For though she was pleasant the old comradely friendliness was missing from her manner and he must have noticed, even though he was not of a fervent nature. It suited his purposes at the time to keep Lisle in the old intimacy, for he had been surprised beyond measure at her reaction to his behavior at the store, and at present it wasn't in his plan to have any disaffection arise.

For in truth his future was rather a muddle at present. The party, the war possibilities, and any chance that he might find a place in the scheme of things that would enable him to remain honorably at home made it desirable that there should be no disaffection, no gossip, no outward break between the families. Therefore Victor put aside his newly acquired insolence and was just a boy friend as he used to be. This attitude on Victor's part made it very much easier for Lisle to continue her friendliness. Although Lisle was just a shade more distant than she used to be, quieter, more silent, not quite so joyous and smiling, more dignified, a bit cool.

But it didn't seem to bother Victor in the least. With his nonchalant self-assurance he went calmly on his usual way, taking it for granted that whenever he got ready he could easily change his old friend's attitude, and bend her to his will.

But Lisle on the other hand was not quite as ready, as in former days, to accept all his invitations, or to take it for granted that of course he was always to be her escort. She was often now seen in company with other young men, and acted as if it were a matter of course that she had other friends besides himself.

If Victor did not like this he never let it be known, just took it for granted that of course if he asked her first and wanted her badly enough, she would be his companion, no matter who else had chosen to ask her.

But Lisle was quietly working it so that she would have a number of other escorts, and was not always available when Victor came to claim her. Sometimes this state of things distressed her mother, who had always been fond of Victor, and felt that his family were beyond reproach. She had excused his conduct at the store as being only the freak of a boy who was playing a prank, and she was often dismayed at the definite hostility toward the young man that she continually saw in her daughter. She was always hoping that there would soon be a better understanding between the two young people. She was a woman who found it very hard to give up an ideal that she had cherished for years. So, whenever Lisle went out with Victor, and seemed fairly happy about it, she drew a deep breath of relief and kept hoping that the lad would forget his new found standards and return to the ways of his childhood.

But Lisle was by no means happy in the company of her old friend. She seemed to have had her eyes opened to a great many things in him that did not satisfy her, ways that she had never noticed before he went away to college. She went through her engagements with him in a continual state of protest and anxiety, in fact a state of defense.

Not that she ever spent time in argument. She was not of that nature, but now that she was beginning to see more clearly, Victor was no longer her ideal friend, and she sometimes had hard work to keep up the semblance of enjoying a pleasant occasion. Continually she was hoping that Victor would presently be called away to wherever he was going in the scheme of war work.

But the days went on, and Victor was still hanging around, apparently doing nothing but having a good time. Playing tennis and golf, playing polo sometimes, out in his motor boat or his handsome high-powered car, as long as gasoline was to be had. Not making much show of sacrifice in any way because his land was at war. Only going on as always having the best time he could and denying himself nothing.

"The war will cure him of that," said Mrs. Kingsley. "He doesn't really know what it's all about yet. But he will. Wait till he gets out among the other soldiers!"

"Sometimes I wonder whether he's really expecting to go at all," said Lisle one day. "He keeps talking of that party of his as if it was an assured fact, as if it was the end and aim of all existence. And of course the time is going on and the date is almost here."

"Yes," said her mother, "and dear, if that party is

really to come off of *course* you'll have to attend it, and we ought to be thinking about a dress. It is to be very formal, you know."

"Well, I don't feel like spending a lot of time and money on an evening dress when we are at war and ought to be thinking about other things. Little children starving and needing clothing. I don't think it is at all right. And of course an evening dress isn't really essential. You know we are being urged not to buy anything that isn't absolutely necessary."

"Yes, I know, of course, but I'm afraid this is really necessary, my dear. You know Mrs. Vandingham has always been a very close friend of ours, and I'm afraid she will be hurt if you do not take as much pains about a dress for her son's party as you have done for other parties in the past. And you know Victor has always recognized your old dresses, even if you have worn them only once. He'll be sure to tell his mother."

"Yes, I suppose so," said Lisle with a sigh, "but I don't like it! Mother, it almost seems wicked to be dolling up this way when a lot of the boys we know are actually dying to save our country from awful peril! Mother, do you know, they think Richard Gerrick was killed in action? Or at least, maybe it's missing in action. I don't see why Mrs. Vandingham is willing to have a great party now when everybody is anxious and worried, and we don't know what dreadful thing may happen next."

"Are you sure they are going to have it, dear? Have you asked Victor about it lately? I think that would simplify things greatly if you would just speak of it, and ask if it is really coming off, or will he be called to serve before it is time?"

"Perhaps," said Lisle with a troubled glance. "I'll see, if there is a good chance without seeming to drag it in, but I'm almost afraid to mention it lest he will go off into one of those fits of modernism, the way he did in the store. It just makes me sick every time I remember that."

Well, I scarcely think he will," said her mother. "I think he realizes we didn't like that at all. You'd better find out if possible. And then, perhaps we can think of a way to fix up one of your evening dresses that you have worn before. There's the wine-colored tulle you haven't worn much. I don't believe Victor ever saw that on you, and you could liven it up with a white sash edged with pale blue that would give a patriotic touch to it."

"Perhaps," said Lisle without enthusiasm. "All right, I'll try to find out." But she went away listlessly, as if she did not relish the task before her.

But as it happened, Lisle didn't have to do what she dreaded at all. Victor took it all in his own hands.

He arrived at the house the next evening, his eyes shining with the look Lisle had learned to interpret as the glow that came when he had got his own way. Her heart sank, for somehow she knew that something must have happened. Victor was not going to be steadied and strengthened into the man he ought to be, but was likely going to be allowed to go on and do as he pleased. How this could possibly be when one considered that he was going to have to deal with the government, she could not explain. Although she knew that some people had what they called "pull" and found ways to carry out their own wishes, even in opposition to the laws and regulations that had been laid down for the guidance of the country. Victor had always been one of those who found ways for priority above others. She wondered what he had done now that gave him that look of having won over against great odds. And suddenly she realized that it was a look such as his mother wore at times when she had succeeded in getting her own way.

So, soberly, with searching eyes, she sat herself down to listen to his eager tale.

"Well, Lisle, it's all settled at last, and now you can plan to go down to the store in the morning and select your dress for the party. You haven't said anything about it so I judge you haven't bought it yet. But there's no time to lose now, for everything's all fixed up, and it's only ten days off, you know."

"What do you mean, Victor? Only ten days off? Do you mean you have to leave for the army as soon as that?" Lisle asked it calmly, not at all as if she were in the least excited.

"Leave!" shouted Victor with a laugh of triumph. "But I don't have to leave! Not at all! I'm to stay right here for the duration! Isn't that great?"

"Oh!" gasped Lisle. "Do you mean you have been *rejected?* But on what grounds? You're perfectly healthy, aren't you?"

"Rejected, nothing! Not on your life I haven't been rejected! I've been asked to stay at home and take over the management of my dad's business. You see it's quite important. He's been selected to make some important things for defense. I'm not at liberty to tell what of course, and I'm to have charge of the office! Of course you know—or maybe you hadn't heard,—that Dad hasn't been well for almost a year now, and the specialist he's been to has said positively that dad can't run the business alone. He needs my help, as of course I'm the only one close enough to him to know all about his affairs. So the government has arranged to have me take over. Of course if dad gets better he'll be back here now and then and keep in touch with things, but I'll be the chief executive, and I'll be no end busy. I'll have to be going back and forth to Washington constantly, and working night and day. And there'll be no chance of my having to go to camp and be put through all that drilling and training dope and that fighting business. I'll be right here in one of the most important—if not *the* most important plant in the whole United States. Of course there'll be other people associated with us in the work, but I'll be practically the head of the whole shooting match. Isn't that great, Lisle? Can't you congratulate me? Haven't I just landed on my feet again, like I always do?"

"Why, yes, it does seem that way, doesn't it? That is, if that was what you wanted. Personally I'd rather go and fight, for I'd feel more as if I were really doing something worth while. But I suppose your plant must be very important, too."

"Oh, it is, Lisle! It's about the most important plant in the whole country. We have a new invention that is practically going to make over the whole operation of war, and bring victory, so I feel I'm far more important here than if I stuck on a uniform, and swelled around shooting people. I never did have much of a yen for that sort of thing anyway. Of course when I was a kid I used to fight and all that, but I wasn't brought up to be a fighter. Our family always felt there were better ways of settling differences than going out and seeing which side could kill the most people, anyway, so I'm just as well satisfied. Although of course if I'd gone I was practically promised a major's commission, and all that. But seeing dad and the government need me here, I'm entirely satisfied."

"Yes?" said Lisle, trying to be appreciative. "Well, it's fine that you're pleased, and of course your mother will be glad to have you at home after you've been away so long at college and other places. What is it you're going to be, Victor? An executive in your father's office?"

"Well, practically that, but it's quite an important executive of course. And now, Lisle, can you arrange to go down and get your outfit tomorrow morning? I'd like to go with you and help you select it. It's all kinds of important to me how you look at the party, you know, and I shall have plenty of time to trot around with you and look things over before you decide. I'm not to take over the plant till the week after the party, so I'll have plenty of time."

Lisle was still for a moment, looking thoughtfully at her old playmate. Then she spoke, slowly, gently:

"That's very kind of you," she said, "but it won't be necessary. Mother and I have arranged to take care of that."

There was a quiet dignity in her manner that was not like anything he had ever seen before in the usually docile girl, and he looked at her in amazement. What did this mean? She had always seemed glad to have him go shopping with her. He frowned.

"What's the idea?" he said. "I certainly have a right to have a say about what you shall wear at my party, haven't I? It's a great time for me. You don't seem to realize that I shall be coming into my majority, and I certainly want my best girl to appear just right."

"You speak as if it were to be a sort of coronation affair," she said smiling. "But now about your suggestion. I am sorry if I don't usually dress to please your taste. You often used to admire my clothes, I remember."

"Oh, yes, they've been well enough when you were nothing but a high school girl, but you must admit that this occasion calls for a little more sophistication, and your mother's taste isn't always that. You see she hasn't got it into her head yet that you are grown up, and I think it's time that you did some choosing for yourself. It's just what I was telling you the other day. You let your mother think for you, and it's time you were on your own. So you and I will go down tomorrow early and pick out something rare. Don't tell your mother about it until afterward, and see if after all she isn't pleased with our taste. She certainly wouldn't want you to wear something that I disapproved, would she?"

"I'm sorry," said Lisle calmly, "I really don't think that it would occur to her, or to me either, that you had anything to say about what I shall wear to your party. If you can't trust me to dress fittingly I think it would be better for me not to come at all."

"For Pete's sake, Lisle, what's got into you? You never acted this way before. Is your mother still angry over that misunderstanding we had at the store the other day? Because if she is, after all the humble pie I had to eat, I think it's time that we had a little more plain speaking. I think it's time she kept her hands off our affairs once and for all. And I demand that you and I shall go down and select this dress ourselves. That can be a sort of test proposition between you and me."

A flame of anger burned in Lisle's eyes, but she kept them veiled for a moment, her lashes down. Then she lifted them calmly, her voice quite cool and steady:

"Well, I'm sorry to disappoint you, old friend, but that will not be possible, because, you see, I am not buying a new dress."

"You're not buying a new dress? You don't mean to tell me you are coming to my party in some old rag that everybody's been seeing you in for dear knows how long? The kind of thing you've been bringing out of the past ever since I got home!"

Lisle smiled.

"Sorry," she said, "haven't you heard that our country is at war and we are asked not to buy unnecessary things? But I don't believe even you will call my dress an old rag. However, if you don't like what I'm wearing when I get to your party you can just give me a high sign, and I'll slip home the back way and nobody will be the wiser. But as for letting you select my dress, even if I were getting a new one, nothing doing. And I don't quite understand why you think you have a right to even suggest it. Now, if you would like to see that book we were talking about the other day, I happened to find it this morning when I was going through the bookcase. I'll get it for you."

"Hang the book!" said the indignant youth. "I don't care if I never see it. I want to know what you're proposing to wear at my party. If it isn't right, believe me I'll make the biggest row you ever heard of. Now, I demand to know. If it's already bought I want to see it. What is it?"

"I don't care to discuss the matter any further, Victor, and I fail to understand why you should have any more jurisdiction over my garments than you do over those of any of your other guests."

"Why certainly, I have more interest in what you wear. You're my best girl you know, and I've got to be pleased by the way you appear!"

"Or else?" said Lisle lifting her eyebrows quietly.

"Or else I'm off you for life," said the young man wrathfully. "Do you think I want everybody criticizing your dowdiness when you appear for the first time in public as regularly belonging to me?"

"Oh, but I shall not be appearing that way," said Lisle sweetly. "I'll just be one of your childhood friends, that's all. And there will be so many people present that nobody is going to take particular notice of what I'm wearing. Besides, most of my friends are being very careful to dress quietly on all occasions. It's a matter of patriotism, you know, so I don't think you need to worry. But you'll have to rid yourself of that idea that I belong to you in any special way, for I do *not*, and I wouldn't care to have people think I did. In fact I should stay away entirely if I thought you would put me in any such position as that before people. I am not your best girl, or any kind of a possession of yours, and I want that very plainly understood before the time comes."

"Say, now, look here, Lisle! You're acting awfully strange. Of course I want people to understand that you and I are engaged, and that we are to be married very soon. I thought my party would be a good time to announce our approaching marriage, at least quietly, if not formally."

"But we're *not* engaged, Victor! And we're *not* going to be married, so that's entirely out," said Lisle almost wearily. "And I refuse entirely to be made a party to any such appearance. If you are going to keep on with any such nonsense I'm not coming to the party at all! And I mean that!"

"Now, Lisle, you're not being kind," said the boy stormily. "You didn't use to be like that. You always were co-operative. I don't like the way you act at all. I come over here to make arrangements to take you shopping and you get high-hat and decline to go. And besides, I had some shopping of my own that I want you to help me with. We're going down and select you an engagement ring tomorrow morning the first thing. Now, will you be good and do what I say?"

"No," said Lisle gently. "That's quite out of the question. I'm not engaged and I don't intend to be engaged to anyone at present, and I certainly don't want an engagement ring. You'll just have to put such ideas entirely out of your calculation, if you want co-operation from me."

Then the telephone sounded a clear note in the hall and Lisle said: "Excuse me please," and hurried to answer it, while Victor pranced angrily back and forth in the living room, and met her with the blackest of frowns when she returned.

Lisle came back to the room with a pleasant smile on her face.

"Sorry to interrupt our conversation," she said, "but Mrs. Carlisle is bringing her niece and nephew over to introduce them. They are visiting her for a few days from Boston, and she wants them to meet some young people. Of course I had to tell her to come."

"I don't see that you did," said Victor haughtily. "You could have said you were going out, or had guests or something. You knew perfectly well that I had important things to talk to you about, and that I wouldn't want an audience."

"Why, no, I didn't," said Lisle calmly, "I didn't know you had anything more to discuss. I thought we had said all there was to say on that subject, and it would be a good thing to have a little change of scenery. I thought you'd stick around and get acquainted too. I've heard this niece is a very pretty girl. Her name is Bernice Brandon, and her brother is Arthur. Have you met them yet? We might have some music. I hear they both sing."

"Oh, my word! *Sing!* I suppose they have voices like a lot of cats on the back fence."

"Oh, perhaps not so bad as that!" laughed Lisle.

And then the doorbell sounded through the house.

"Great Scott, Lisle, you don't suppose they're here already? Let me get out. I don't want to see those dopes!"

"Oh, you can't do that, Victor. I told them you were here."

"I should worry what you told them. I'm not going to be bored with a lot of dopes all the evening. Not on your life. I'll see you in the morning, Lisle. I'll be here at ten on the dot, and I don't want you to keep me waiting!"

But already the front door had opened and the three visitors had reached the entrance door of the living room.

And then they were inside the room, and Mrs. Carlisle was facing the irate Victor with a smile on her face.

"Oh, good evening, Mrs. Carlisle," said Lisle stepping forward graciously, with perfect poise. "So nice you could come over," and Mrs. Carlisle introduced her young people. Victor meantime had backed away from the doorway and was standing sullenly over by the mantel while these formalities were going on. Lisle thought to herself that it was a lucky thing that there was no other exit from that room or Victor would certainly have sought it and vanished. In fact she wasn't at all sure what he would do next, for lately he seemed to have discarded all his courtesy, in spite of his mother's care in training him. Lisle wasn't at all sure he would be even decently polite to her guests in his present state of mind. And it was all she could do to keep her gracious smile on her face and coolly turn and say, "You know Victor Vandingham, of course, Mrs. Carlisle." And then she dared to lift her eyes impersonally to Victor's face, and saw to her astonishment that he had come forward pleasantly, with eyes of admiration toward the niece and was ready to acknowledge the introductions with his best manner. So! That was that! Victor was conquered for the moment, and she drew a deep breath of relief and gave herself to seating her guests pleasantly.

"Excuse me a moment," she said, "I'll call mother," and slipped out of the room, leaving no choice for Victor but to sit down and talk with the guests.

When she returned she found Victor seated on the couch with Bernice Brandon eagerly engaged in a lively conversation, proving beyond a doubt that he could be entertaining if he chose. That was the meanness of him that he could be agreeable and didn't often choose to be.

Mrs. Kingsley came down in a moment and as they engaged in general conversation, Lisle watched her erstwhile lover being agreeable to the other pretty girl. So Victor was still easily influenced by beauty. She smiled to herself as she watched him furtively, saw his handsome eyes light, saw his alluring smile. And suddenly it came to her how unpleasant it might be to have a man like Victor for a husband. In more ways than one he would be hard to live with.

As she thought back now in quick retrospect over the past she recalled how Victor had always wanted his own way about everything, and if he didn't get it he just wouldn't play, and always managed to break up the whole game for everybody and make an unpleasant state of things all around.

No, decidedly she wouldn't ever marry him. Not even if she loved him, which she was suddenly sure she did not. It would be horrible to marry a man who thought he was always right in everything, and who would brook no difference of opinion, nor allow his wife to do as she pleased in anything.

So it was a great relief to her to sit smiling and talking with Arthur Brandon, really enjoying his conversation. He was little more than a shy boy yet, but he had read a great deal, and he knew what he was talking about. He was really interesting. He was not only well read but he was well versed in music and a number of scientific subjects, and before long they were launched into some truly deep discussions, which made Lisle entirely forget that Victor was present.

He however appeared entirely satisfied with Bernice Brandon, and did not seem to notice that the girl whom he had just been saying was engaged to him was deep in talk with another fairly personable young man. And somehow it gave Lisle a great relief to realize that when the time came to make him definitely understand her own decision, she need not feel that he would suffer in any way. Unless perhaps it might be through his pride, that any girl whom he had honored would reject his hand. Well, that was a relief to know, for now she felt beyond the shadow of a doubt that he did not love her, and never had. She doubted if he knew what love meant. And it was no wonder that he called it "Oh, that *mush!*"

In the midst of these thoughts she managed to keep fairly well in touch with the conversation that was going on about her. Then her mother spoke:

"Lisle, dear, did you know that these people are fine musicians? Don't you think it would be nice if we were to have a little music?"

"Oh, lovely!" said Lisle. "Do you play or sing or both?" she asked Bernice.

"Oh, a little of both, although we mainly sing," laughed the other girl. "My older sister usually plays our accompaniments when she's around, and our little sister plays the violin. But they are neither of them here of course. I'm not much on accompaniments, and so Arthur and I seldom sing much when we are away from home, it is so hard to find a good accompanist. But my aunt says you are a fine pianist."

"I play," said Lisle modestly, "but I never was much on singing. I haven't a great voice. And not caring for my own voice makes me shy of singing. But come on, let's have some music!"

She went over to the piano and sat down, pointing to a pile of music. "What shall we begin on?"

The other girl hesitated.

"The other gentleman? He's musical, isn't he? We've been talking about the symphony orchestra."

Lisle looked at Victor.

"Yes, Victor sings, sometimes, when he wants to," she said with a smile.

And so presently the four young people were singing. Victor lifting a lazy tenor and joining in with the other voices, and Lisle coming in with a soft true alto.

Mrs. Kingsley sat and watched them all, studying Victor, and thinking with relief that he was acting quite like his better self. Perhaps after all Victor would mature and come into his own, come back to the promise of his younger days. It had been such a happy thought to feel that Lisle's future was to be laid in pleasant pastures, with a good young man for her companion. Such a terrible shock to hear him talk as he had talked that day in the store restaurant. Could Lisle ever forget that? Could *she?* And yet as she looked at the young man now it seemed incredible that he could ever honestly have meant those sentiments he had expressed then.

Suddenly the evening was over and Mrs. Carlisle arose with hasty apologies for staying so long. Victor with grace and dignity accompanied Bernice to her aunt's, all of them expressing the joy they had had in the companionship, and especially in the music. For their voices had proved to blend well together, and even Victor had swelled around and said how good they all were, and how well their voices "went with his."

So that night when Lisle at last went to her rest she was well content at the way the evening had worked out. Nevertheless, she was firmly resolved that she and Victor would *not* go shopping together in the morning.

6

WHEN Victor came to the house the next morning to get Lisle she was gone. She had arranged to go out with two other members of a committee who were making arrangements for a nursery school to care for the young children of the women who were going into the factories and defense plants to work. It was a wonderful plan and Lisle was deeply interested in it. So she was very glad that the rest of the committee chose this special morning to get started with the work.

Lisle did not have much opportunity to talk with her mother before she left, and it had been quite late when the guests left the evening before, so Mrs. Kingsley had not heard any report of what had passed between her daughter and Victor. She did not even know that the whole wartime situation had been entirely changed for the young man. So when Victor came in and asked for Lisle he was told that she was out on committee work and no one knew exactly where that work was located.

Naturally Victor was much annoyed. Not only had his girl ignored his suggestions, and turned down his plans, but she had gone away and made it practically an impossibility for him to get in touch with her. This, regardless of the fact that it was important for him to be at the jeweler's at a certain arranged time, to look over diamonds under expert advice. He was so upset at this change of his plans that he finally demanded to see Lisle's mother, and complained in no uncertain language about her daughter's conduct.

Mrs. Kingsley's reaction was quiet dignity.

"Suppose you sit down, Victor, and talk quietly. Let me understand this whole matter. You see I have not heard anything about it at all. Do you say that Lisle promised to go out with you this morning?"

"Well, not exactly promised," said the young man haughtily. "But she knew I wanted her to go for we had been talking about it, and she knew why, and then those people came in and we had no further opportunity to talk. But she knew perfectly well what I wanted, and now she has done this! Gone off without leaving any word for me. I didn't think Lisle would treat me that way."

"I'm very sorry if you think she has been unfair to you," said Lisle's mother, "but I am sure there is some reasonable explanation. I know that she has been appointed on this committee, and of course it is important that it get its work started immediately. She perhaps started to explain this to you and thought she had done so, not realizing that you would not understand why she could not go with you this morning."

"No, she didn't say a word about her old committee," said Victor crossly. "She just didn't want to go. In fact she said she wouldn't. But I, of course, thought she was kidding. You see I had an appointment with a very important man and I wanted her to go with me. Well, I may as well tell you, we were to select the diamond for her engagement ring. I naturally wanted her to choose the one she liked the best, and to take the advice of this expert. And if a thing like that isn't more important than any old war committee, I'd like to know the reason why."

Mrs. Kingsley looked at the young man with startled worry in her eyes.

"Wait, Victor. I'm afraid I don't understand. You say you asked her to go with you to choose her engagement ring? Did she understand that? Are you *sure?*"

"Why of course," said the boy with his old cross tone. "I told her."

"Well, but I don't understand, Victor. Had you asked her if she would marry you? When were you engaged?"

"You heard me tell her we were going to be married the other day at the store."

"But *telling* her you are going to marry her is not asking her if she is willing. What makes you think she is willing? What did she say when you asked her?"

"Oh, she just laughed and gave me a lot of back talk that she didn't want to marry anybody, and all that, but I knew she didn't mean it. Girls never mean things like that. We've always expected to get married, ever since we were kids. And I don't like the way she is acting. Now I'm in a heck of a fix. Got a diamond expert coming all the way from New York to meet us and she won't be there! If that isn't standing me up, then I don't know what is."

"Victor, have you ever told my daughter that you love her?" Mrs. Kingsley's voice was very clear. Her eyes searched the boy's face as she spoke, and the young man lifted his chin in offended haughtiness.

"Mrs. Kingsley, you and I have always been good friends, but I think you are going a little too far this time. I think that matter is strictly between Lisle and myself."

Mrs. Kingsley looked at him in perfect amazement for an instant, and then she arose and said quietly:

"Oh, very well, then I suppose the matter of how Lisle decides to treat you will be another thing strictly between Lisle and yourself, therefore I shall not need to trouble any more about it. I'll ask you to excuse me now. I have important matters to attend to at once. Good morning!" and she turned to go out of the room. But Victor quickly intercepted her.

"But that isn't all," he said, still in his complaining voice. "I offered to go along with Lisle and help her select her dress for the party at our house. There isn't so much time, you know, and I want to be sure she looks just right."

"Oh, *indeed!*" said Lisle's mother. "Well, I don't wonder that Lisle went away without explanation if you said that to her. Certainly we won't need to trouble you to pass censorship on Lisle's clothes. I think you had better go home and think over the things you have been saying and doing, and you may possibly find out why Lisle did not care to wait for you."

"But don't you think we ought to decide such things together, Mrs. Kingsley?"

"Why no, I don't see that it is a matter that you have anything to do with. A woman selects her own garments."

"Well, what is she going to wear? I want to know. I think I have the right. What is the color and style? I thought I'd like to suggest some ideas to her. She hasn't bought her dress yet, has she? Or *has* she?"

"Why Victor, I'm not sure, but I think whatever she decides upon, it is already bought. You see we felt very uncertain as to whether that party would ever come off—at least at this time. I understood that you were to be called to war any day now."

"That's all off," said Victor coldly. "I'm not going to war at all. I'm needed at home for defense purposes. I'm to take over the management of my father's business.

He hasn't been well, and the government has awarded some very important work to our plant. I'm to take over in the office as soon as my majority party is over. So you can see why I'm anxious to get everything settled up and my life started the way it ought to be, and I don't think Lisle had any right to stand me up this way."

"Oh!" said Mrs. Kingsley, with a sound in her voice as if it were a lovely balloon that had suddenly been pricked. "Oh! Well in that case I'm afraid I can't help you any. And about the matter of Lisle's dress, I think that is entirely her own affair, to wear whatever seems suitable to her. Good by!" and Mrs. Kingsley went out of the house, walking swiftly down the street in the direction of her morning errands. But by the time she had gone the first block she began to feel that Lisle had better sense than she had thought she had. This young man was not a person to whom she wanted to trust her only daughter's life. Not the way he was now, anyway. She had thought, she had hoped that Victor had not really changed, that he had just experienced a small season of aberration at the store that day, and that he was later reverting to type. But the way he talked today Mrs. Kingsley could see that Victor really had changed, taken on new ideas, new views of life, that were quite impossible. She could not blame Lisle for turning against him, for running away from a shopping expedition with him, running away even from a gorgeous diamond ring, for anything that a Vandingham would purchase would of course be gorgeous. But decidedly with his present developments he was anything but desirable.

Victor stood watching her go down the street with amazement and utter incredulity in his face. He had not dreamed that again he would encounter such unbelievable victorianism in the people he had been sure were his devoted slaves. Always Mrs. Kingsley had been so kind to him, always suggesting pleasant things that Lisle might do to make a happy time for him. He could not understand it that they did not want his advice about Lisle's dress on such an important occasion, that they actually seemed to resent his suggestions as if he were interfering. And as for the ring and the marriage, they were actually ignoring the idea as if he were a child and had no right to ask her to marry him. And making so much of that antique idea of *love*, as if that were important. Well, of course if they insisted on living on traditional ideas he might have to give in and give them a line of talk, what he had come to look upon as "mush" talk. But it would go sadly against the grain to back down on the ways he had been learning the last four years, and he would hate to think afterward that he had to get his wife by such an ancient method. Where had Mrs. Kingsley been that she didn't know that romance and all that was the bunk? Couldn't she look around her and see how many divorces there were and remarriages? Why, people didn't think anything of it today. They married because they enjoyed each other's company for a while, and when they got tired of each other and saw someone they had a better time with, they got a divorce and annexed somebody else. Well, it wasn't easy to teach elderly people new ideas, and he supposed he would have to give in for a while until he and Lisle were married, for he could see that Lisle was in no state to give up her early beliefs and standards, and she would need to live in a modern world for a while, away from her people, before she found out what a little fanatic she was becoming.

Well, probably the best way to bring her to her senses would be to ignore her for a few days. Even bring another girl around and let her see him going *hard* with her. That Bernice would do as well as anyone perhaps. She was pretty and quite interesting. Of course she was due to go back to Boston in a few days, but perhaps if his mother invited her to the party she would stay for it. He would see about that at once. Go right home and tell his mother to send that girl an invitation. And perhaps there were other girls he could think up that would put Lisle on her toes to bring him back to her. But he wouldn't be too quick to do that either. He must get her good and anxious before he gave in and returned to her side.

So Victor hurried home to get an invitation sent off to Bernice, and her brother. Of course the brother was a bit young for his coming-of-age party, but as he and his sister were visiting here it was probably the proper thing to do to invite him.

It was on his way home that he caught his first glimpse of another girl, a girl he had never seen before. She must be a stranger in town. She certainly was a glamour girl all right if there ever was one. Exquisite complexion, lovely eyes, silver-blonde hair low on her shoulders in the very latest roll, daring make-up. Ah! That was sophistication! He wished he had Lisle there to point it out to her, his ideal of the way *she* ought to dress and make-up. Would there be any way to get Lisle to see her? That was the kind of girl who could bring Lisle to her senses if any other girl could, and let her see how she would lose him if she kept on in her present staid old-fashioned style.

He looked so hard at the new girl, really staring at her, that she stared back at him, and finally gave a slow understanding smile, with a lifting of her long gold lashes that the boys at college used to call a "come-hither sweep."

As he came nearer to her his eyes said things, and he half hesitated, then came forward quickly with his wholly engaging smile, and lifting his hat gaily said:

"Say, I've met you somewhere before, haven't I? Tell me where, glamour girl. It certainly seems that we are old friends?"

The girl turned on a warmer light in her eyes and a subtler smile.

"It does seem that way, doesn't it?" she said easily, pausing as if they were old acquaintances.

"Well, say, this is great!" said Victor. "You're just the one I was longing to meet. How about a date with me? Going anywhere to lunch?"

"No, not definitely."

"Good! Then we'll make it definite. Ever try the Dark Star restaurant? Then come, I'll show you something new."

The girl looked him straight in the eye with a quizzical expression, and hesitated.

"Who *are* you?" she asked coolly. "I'm a little particular who I choose for my friends."

"Oh, *are* you?" said Victor. "I hadn't thought so, but that's all right with me. I'm Victor Vandingham. Ever hear of me?"

"Why, yes," said the girl, "I think I have. Are you related to the V. C. Vandingham of the steel plant?"

"I sure am!" swelled Victor with a grin. "The very same. He's my father."

"Well, that's interesting," said the girl. "Sure, I'll take lunch with you. What do I call you? *Mr.* Vandingham?"

"No, that's too formal for the way we met. You'd better call me Van. That's what I was called at college. And what do they call you, little one?" He smiled down into her face, and sincerely hoped that someone in the Kingsley house was looking out the window to report this drama to Lisle. For Victor seldom put on an act without an eye to a possible audience.

The girl looked up nonchalantly and answered:

"Oh, my name is Erda. That's enough for the present,

isn't it? The rest wouldn't mean a thing to you yet, anyway," and she turned with a smile, slipped her hand within Victor's arm, and modulating her step to his, walked on up the street with him.

"We'll take a taxi downtown," said the young man, "and later if we decide to go somewhere else I can phone to have the man bring my car down. Okay with you?"

"Perfectly okay with me," said Erda smiling, and stepped gaily on, entirely at her ease.

So that was what Victor Vandingham was doing, instead of choosing a diamond for Lisle Kingsley's engagement ring.

7

WHEN Lisle returned to the house about the middle of the afternoon her mother had just come in and they sat down together to have a cup of tea and some sandwiches, for neither had had time for lunch.

"Did Victor come over for me this morning, mother?" asked Lisle.

"Yes, he did, and he was certainly angry that you were not here, and more rude than I would ever have believed he could be. He said you promised to go shopping with him to buy a new dress for his party, and to select your engagement ring, and you stood him up! Is that true, Lisle?"

"No! He asked me to go, but I told him I was not buying a new dress, and that I didn't want an engagement ring for I wasn't engaged and didn't intend to be. He got very angry about the dress. Asked if I was going to wear some dowdy old rag. He said you were old-fashioned and wouldn't know how to select the right kind of a sophisticated dress, and a lot of stuff like that, just as he talked that day in the store. He said he and I were to be married right away, and he wanted the wedding date announced at the party, and everybody invited. Oh, mother, he was simply impossible! And then before I could do anything except to say I wouldn't go and I didn't want to be married, or have an engagement ring, Mrs. Carlisle and her young people came in. You know how late they stayed and how he went home with them. There simply wasn't anything I could do about it. I hadn't had a chance to explain to him that I had to go to a committee meeting, and I didn't think it mattered anyway since I had told him I didn't want him to go shopping with me. Oh, mother, do you think I should have stayed at home for him after he had been so outrageous?"

"No, my dear, you were perfectly right to go, and besides I explained to him that you had a committee."

"And mother, do I have to go to that awful party? I know just how he will act. Just as if I was his property."

"Well, we'll see my dear. I really think you could manage to keep somewhat in the background if you tried. Just be sweet and dignified and don't give him a chance to say unwelcome things. You must remember there will be a great many people there, and you wouldn't need to be too early, you know. I had hoped there wouldn't be any party, but it seems it is to go through."

"Yes, mother, and did he tell you he is not going to war at all? He's going into his father's plant."

"Yes, he told me," sighed the mother. "It's rather disappointing of course. I think he needs the discipline of the army. But perhaps the responsibility of business will do the same for him."

"I doubt it," said Lisle sharply, and her mother gave her a quick look. Was Lisle deeply cut by all this? Oh, she hoped that her child would be saved from having a broken heart.

But Lisle, after her talk with her mother, seemed

quite gay, as if her heart had been unburdened and she felt relieved. Her mother watched her carefully the next few days, and drew a relieved breath whenever Lisle came in with a smile. Perhaps her daughter would escape sorrow, but it had seemed so beautiful to have those two children grow up together and care for one another. But Lisle was by no means pining away, and her mother wondered. Had she some other interest that she had not told about? Some young man perhaps in her classes at her university. Perhaps that was it. She must keep a close watch, for sometimes when a natural friendship was broken a girl would take to anyone who was good-looking and admired her. She must be careful that Lisle made no unwise contacts. That mustn't happen twice to Lisle.

And what would she have said if she could have known that the only young man whose smile and merry eyes had lingered in her child's memory she had seen first working on the street with common workmen. Mrs. Kingsley wasn't a snob, or at least would have been dismayed to find that she was, but she had been brought up with a firm belief in class distinction.

Lisle was happy and fully occupied with her war work now, and especially with the little day nursery in which she and some of her friends were interested. She grudged the hours when she must leave it all and hurry down to the city to her university classes. But this her parents insisted was the right thing for her to do, to finish her college course and be ready to graduate with her class.

Lisle was a good student, never neglected her studies, and arranged her hours so that she was able to carry out all the plans she had made for war work. So when Victor, after philandering a few evenings with Cherry and her ilk, and with Erda more than a few, concluded it was time to get back to Lisle and bring her to time, he found she was out.

She had gone that evening to take the place of one of her older friends who was ill, and who was a teacher of a Red Cross class in the lower end of the city. She was not familiar with that part of the city, but was at once interested in these new people, and lingered afterward to answer eager questions put by some women who were both poor and ignorant. It was late before she started home. And because they as a family were being most careful about conserving gas and tires, she had gone on the bus that night. But when she arrived at the corner where she should take the return bus, no bus came along. She had probably missed the one she intended taking. Or had she made a mistake about which corner she should wait? Then suddenly as she stood there uncertainly, looking at her watch, casting anxious glances in the direction from which she thought the bus should arrive, the sirens began to shriek for a blackout, and one by one the lights in the buildings and houses around her went out. Then all at once the street lights were gone, and there was utter darkness. It seemed to Lisle she had never seen such dense black darkness in her life. She turned this way and that in her bewilderment, and realized that she was completely turned around. She did not know which way to go. She wanted to hurry, but how could she hurry in utter darkness, and in a region with which she was not familiar?

Then she saw a blue light flash from a doorway. A man was standing in the door with a flashlight in his hand, covered with blue cellophane! Perhaps it was an air warden! She stepped over to him and asked where she could go to telephone for a taxi. But he shook his head. There was no telephone near by and no taxis could be had during a blackout.

"Come inside," he said pleasantly. "You will be perfectly safe in here until it is over. This is a rather tough neighborhood for a lady to be alone, you know, but this is a Bible class. You are Miss Kingsley, aren't you? I'm John Sargent. You don't know me, but I've seen you before. Come this way and I'll put a chair for you just inside the class room where you can listen. Sorry we're all in the dark, but we haven't got our blackout curtains up yet."

He flashed his blue light, she got a glimpse of his face, and suddenly she knew him. He was the man with the blue eyes she had seen in the street working that day. She had never forgotten him. She looked at him in a daze of wonder. She felt as if she were among friends. A Bible class! Surely that would be all right. How wonderful that she had found a place like this, for now she realized that she had been frightened. She sat down and relaxed, conscious of the presence of other people in the room, a goodly number of them. How strange that she should meet that man again and in a place like this!

Then suddenly her attention was caught by the speaker, the teacher of the class of course.

"People are asking," he said, " 'Why doesn't God stop this war? Why does He allow such awful things to go on?' And we turn to the Bible for an answer. Has God ever done this before to the world? Allowed terrible things to sweep over a calm and prosperous people? Allowed whole cities to be destroyed, beautiful memorials laid waste, treasures of art and artifices utterly disfigured, human lives by the thousand, yes, by the million, cast off at a stroke? Has He ever allowed that before? The answer is yes. And why has He done it? Turn in your mind back to the first chapter of Isaiah and see how God sent word through the prophet Isaiah to the kings of Judah of the calamities that were to befall them as a consequence of their sinfulness, their forgetting of the

Lord, 'Ah sinful nation, a people laden with iniquity' he calls them. He brings to their remembrance their great sin of forsaking the Lord, of provoking the Holy One of Israel. So the reason of those wars and that destruction that God sent to His people is not far to seek. And we, in this day, are we wondering why God is letting us see so much trouble? 'We haven't done anything wrong,' we say. 'Why *we* are called a *Christian* nation, yet we have to give up our sugar, and our coffee, and most of our meat and butter too, besides our gasoline and our tires. No more holiday rides. And some of us have to give up our sons, and our own lives. Why should God let all this come upon us? Why should He be so cruel when we are a Christian nation? We are not sinful like Hitler or the Japanese!' Oh but we are forgetting all the time that sin, the main sin, the real root of all sin is unbelief. 'But we do believe in God,' we cry out. 'We join the church, we give to missions, we help the needy. Why, certainly we believe there is a God. We even believe in Jesus Christ, and that He is God's Son. Certainly we are believers and why should all this happen to us? We cannot believe that God would let such people as ourselves suffer this way. Some of our sons and brothers and sweethearts are even being killed.' But you know that is not belief, just accepting with your intellect all those doctrines. To really believe we must individually accept what Christ did for us in taking all our sin upon Himself. He paid the penalty of death by shedding His own blood on the cross in our stead. A true believer accepts Christ as his own personal Saviour. And it is not atheism, but unbelief, mere neglect of God, that is the great national sin. And it is to show the nations what their sin of unbelief has been, that he has to bring them through tribulations, that he has to let war come and kill their sons, destroy their homes, make desolate their goodly works which their hands have wrought and of which they have been so proud. And God through all this horror of war is yearning over His people, whom He has loved and who have forsaken Him and gone after strange gods, gods of silver and gold, the work of their own hands. Oh, those sins of the nations of the Old Testament, how they mock us with their similarity to our own times, our own world, and these sad days in which we are living now, with perils in the offing, and not so very far off either. God is calling His people today by the war which He is allowing.

"But some are thinking that wickedness is perhaps stronger than God, and the devil is getting away with it. No, *never!* Our God knows what He is doing. And these experiences we are living through are not things that Satan has sprung upon an unprepared God. 'Known unto God are all His works from the beginning of the world!' Acts 15:18, and nothing can take Him unaware. 'For ever, O Lord, thy word is settled in heaven.' Psalms 119:89. So God, before the foundation of the world, knew that you and I and our world today were going to have to go through all this turmoil and awfulness. He knew about just your life, and my life, and how the war was going to make us suffer. But He knew also what it was going to do to us, how it would purify some of us. The important thing to Him is whether you and I shall come through it to know Him, our Saviour, and to be like Him, be 'conformed to the image of His Son.' His object in all this is that you and I shall be like Christ, and ready for an eternity with him."

There was more of this. The speaker went on to tell of other wars in the Old Testament times, and of God's sanction for wars, that through them evil should be punished. He showed how God often used one wicked nation to punish another and then punished the nation he used because they were puffed up, thinking they had won the war by their own strength.

And Lisle sat there in the dark listening, filled with wonder, startled into thinking, brought suddenly face to face with a living God whom she had never realized before, amazed that the Bible had truths like these for bewildered souls in every perplexity of their human lives. She had never taken in the Bible before as anything more than a beautiful inspirational book, filled with traditional stories and vaguely related to life as a whole, supposed to be in some way connected with God and salvation for the time that comes after this life. She believed it of course because she had been brought up to believe it, but more as a family precaution against lawlessness and ill-breeding, than as something that involved any obligation to her personally. And now suddenly it seemed that it did, though she just couldn't have told why. This teaching seemed somehow to destroy all the former steady foundations of her life and made her feel that she had been walking in a dangerous way, and she didn't just understand why, nor what she ought to do now.

Vaguely she felt that someone had taken the chair beside her and there was suddenly a sympathy in her heart for all the unknown people in that dark room who were listening with her to this most startling message. Then suddenly the blue light flashed just a wink and she realized that the person beside her must be John Sargent. The knowledge was strangely pleasant, but did not distract her thoughts from the teacher's words which suddenly there in the darkness made a figure shine out, a figure with divine light in His face, looking toward them all, with nail-pierced hands and face that bore glory and love. She saw for the first time in her life what Jesus Christ was, and what He wanted to be to her. Did the speaker just *tell* all that? Could mere human words paint a picture like that in the dark, that brought a light to her soul she had never known before, a light of whose existence she had never before dreamed? Afterwards, thinking back, she could not remember words, only truths, great new truths that she had not known before. Did other people besides this little group among whom she found herself tonight, know these things? Did her mother and father know them, and live their placid lives without ever speaking of them, not even now and then?

Then all too quickly that siren blared forth, proclaiming the blackout was over, and the lights in the room sprang up and gradually she could see the people around her, and could watch the face of the teacher. He brought his lesson to a close with the great proclamation that this Jesus who was now in Heaven, the Jesus who had died for them all, and had risen from the dead, and been caught up to Heaven, was coming back to claim His own! Was coming soon! He had said so Himself. And all these people evidently believed it. Lisle looked from one to another of those about her, looked up to John Sargent who had stepped away to see that the lights went on when the sirens blew, but had returned to the chair beside her.

So she looked up and met that same smile, those same blue eyes tender with reverence now, as he smiled. And her look of wonder filled him with a great ecstasy.

Then the little company burst into soft singing, started by a sweet voice:

I have seen the face of Jesus,
 Tell me not of aught beside,
I have heard the voice of Jesus
 And my soul is satisfied;
For He shed His blood on Calvary,

And He saves me by His grace,
And I find my all in Jesus,
My eternal resting place.

They sang it so tenderly with such clear voicing of the words that they seemed to be wrought into her soul, and she tried to remember them for when she would be away.

Then there followed a tender prayer, and when Lisle lifted her head and looked again at the young man beside her it was as if his eyes told her that it was all true that she had been hearing. That he had tried it and he knew.

But he only said when they stood up and the group were beginning to go quietly away:

"If you can wait five minutes I'll be glad to take you to wherever you want to go. You see I'm janitor here tonight and I'll have to see that the fire is right for the night and the door is locked."

"Oh, thank you," said Lisle looking a little startled at the thought of going back into her world again. "I don't know whether I would be able to find my way home or not. I got rather turned around in the blackout."

"All right, I'll be with you as soon as I can," he said.

And then all unexpectedly a plainly dressed girl with shy eyes came up to her and said "Good evening," and Lisle, taking a lesson from those she saw about her, put out her own hand and grasped the girl's which was held out awkwardly. Somehow she felt as if these people were almost kin to her in some strange subtle way. How it would have amused Victor to know that she felt that way.

"You are a stranger here," said the other girl. "We hope you'll come again."

"I would like to," said Lisle, giving her a warm smile. Then the teacher came by and stopped to speak to her cordially, and others nodded good evening. How warm the world was growing since these war times had come. Or was it these people who studied the Bible that seemed so different from others? Lisle wondered if her mother had ever been to a Bible class like this one.

She could hear the furnace being shaken down beneath the thin flooring. That was John Sargent down there. He said he was janitor tonight. Did that mean only tonight, or was it his regular job? Could it be possible that being in this Bible study atmosphere had given his smile that rare quality?

The people went out with seeming reluctance. They seemed to love the place and each other. But they were soon gone, and then John Sargent turned out the lights, locked the door, and they started.

"If you'll just put me on a trolley or bus somewhere and tell me where to get off, I shall be all right," said Lisle. "I hate to trouble you, and I'm really not afraid."

He smiled pleasantly.

"Well, the trolleys and buses in this region are rather uncertain quantities. Perhaps we had better walk a little way till we find a taxi. I'll be glad to go with you to your door if you don't mind walking with a stranger."

"Why," said Lisle with a little ripple of a laugh, "you're not a stranger, are you? I think we were introduced by Mrs. Gately one morning on the street when she was protesting about getting her imported dress spoiled. Wasn't she too funny? But—" and her voice grew sweetly grave, "we have been seeing the face of Jesus together tonight and that makes us friends, doesn't it?"

"It does," he answered solemnly with a deep ring to his voice. "I'm glad you're like that!"

"But I'm not," said Lisle thoughtfully. "At least I never was before tonight. I think I've you to thank for the vision I got tonight. I didn't know there was teaching like that in the Bible."

"Well, I only discovered it myself a few weeks ago," said the young man. "A fellow workman asked me to take his place here for a while as janitor, because his wife was sick, and so I found the Lord."

"Why!" said Lisle. "That's like my case. I had no idea when I came over to this part of the city to take the place of a Red Cross teacher who wasn't feeling well that I was going to get caught in the dark and walk right into a place like this. It's wonderful. And—I wonder if I haven't found the Lord, too. I never heard anybody talk the way you do. I'm a member of a church of course, and my people have always been church people, but I really never heard anyone say that you could 'know' the Lord the way that teacher said. The way you have said. There can't be many people who know these things, or surely I would have heard of them."

"Well, I've found out that there are a good many, but of course there are a lot of the other kind. The ones who are so interested in the world and doing as everyone else is doing that even the war hasn't waked them up yet."

Her heart warmed to that.

"Are you doing something in the war?" she asked suddenly.

"Well, not much yet," said John with regret in his voice. "I came home in my last year of college to take care of a dear old grandmother, who has practically worked herself out to help me, and now her life is hanging in the balance. I can't go while she needs me, but it may be a matter of only a few days, or at most months, the doctor says. Of course she doesn't know there is a war on and we are in it, though she sensed it was coming some time ago. If she knew she would want me to go at once, no matter how much she would miss me. But she is paralyzed, and cannot talk. She can only press my hand, but I can see by her eyes that it means a great deal to her to have me there sometimes.

I couldn't go while she is that way, and so I am waiting."

"Of course," said Lisle warmly, and she began to wonder if Victor would have done as much for even his mother. Not if there were no glory in it, she was immediately sure. Oh, it was dreadful to have her one-time friend fall so far short of fineness and loyalty. And here she was comparing him unfavorably again with an utter stranger. And yet he wasn't an utter stranger. He was a child of God, a saved person who had been seeing the same vision that she had seen tonight.

"I think you are doing so right," she said slowly, almost thinking aloud. "I wish I could do something for your grandmother. Who is caring for her while you are working?"

"I have hired a practical nurse. She is a kindly elderly woman, very sincere. Grand is well cared for. Of course her wants are few."

"Could I send her a few flowers now and then?" asked Lisle shyly. "She wouldn't need to know who sent them. She wouldn't know me. She might enjoy a flower. Flowers are such sort of heavenly things. It might just reach her and please her. But if she thought about them at all you could let her think you sent them. Or if she ever got well enough to ask you you could say a friend of yours gave them to you for her."

"Thank you," he said, his voice husky with feeling. "I appreciate that a lot. We are strangers to you."

"No, not strangers any more," said Lisle. "God's children. Will you give me her address so I can send the flowers?"

He paused under a street light and wrote on a card from his pocket.

"It seems I have no right to let you do this," he said hesitantly. "I can never likely do anything for you."

"Oh, but you are. You have. You are doing something now. And you saved me from the street when I was alone and frightened. Besides if it had not been for you I would never have heard that wonderful Bible lesson, and I feel that it is going to make a great difference in my life."

"I am humbly glad if it will do that," he said.

And suddenly they reached her home. Without stopping to talk about it they had walked on all the way. He looked up at the brilliantly lighted house, wide and stately and luxurious, and she said eagerly:

"Come in a little while. I'd like you to meet my mother. She will be so grateful to you for looking out for me during the blackout."

He flashed her a pleasant look from his blue eyes.

"Thank you," he said, "but I couldn't. I have things to do yet tonight, and I must go to work early in the morning."

"You—are—with the Water Company?" she asked hesitantly.

"Oh, no! That was only to help out in an emergency. I'm working at the shipyard."

"But that's defense work. That's the next thing to fighting."

"Yes, but I'd rather be out fighting. I'm able-bodied and so that is really my place, you know, if it weren't for my other duty."

"Yes, I understand," said Lisle briefly. "You would feel that way. But now I thank you so much for what you have done for me, and I hope I shall see you again before long. I want to get back to that Bible class some day when I can make it possible. So then good night." She put out her hand to his with the same graciousness she would have shown to any of her society friends. John Sargent took the touch of that small hand in his with him to cherish, as she had been cherishing his first smile, and they went on their ways out into the troublous world, with the vision of their Christ between them.

Mrs. Kingsley wasn't home yet from an evening dinner engagement and therefore Lisle had no questions to answer about the blackout. Perhaps her mother did not even know there had been a blackout, since most of her friends were provided with blackout curtains and lived in their usual blaze of light behind them while their world was in darkness.

Lisle went straight to her room, prepared herself for rest, and then took out her Bible that had been a gift when she was very young. A beautiful Bible, and beautifully kept, with scarcely a mark of use, though she had idled through a supposed course in instruction in it in college.

She turned the pages almost awesomely, as one might approach a familiar friend whom one is for the first time just discovering as being of royal blood. She had to look in the index to discover where Isaiah was located, but when she had found it, she pored over those first chapters that had been touched upon in the class that night, and was fascinated as she read the verses, finding that the new truths she had heard that night fairly leaped at her from the pages, and became alive and real with a clear sense that they would never have meant to her before, and she found herself thinking, "Oh, is that what that expression meant? Why I never dreamed before that it was anything but a lovely essay or poem with no relation whatever to anything in existence today!"

Finally when she was ready to lie down and sleep she knelt beside her bed. All her life she had been in the habit of what she had always called "saying her prayers," but tonight was different. Her heart was coming to a Presence she had never sensed before, and as she knelt once more that vision of the Christ stood before her closed eyes, in the semi-darkness of her room, and so she knelt with her heart laid bare before her new Christ. Not asking for anything, just waiting before Him, acknowledging her new knowledge of what He had done for her.

When she lay down in her bed her heart was singing softly:

> I have seen the face of Jesus,
>   Tell me not of aught beside,
> I have heard the voice of Jesus,
>   And my soul is satisfied.

Somehow as she drifted off to sleep, mingled with the music in her heart, she found a silver thread of consciousness was twisted, consciousness that another soul understood and was a sort of partner in this knowledge of salvation that had come to her tonight. And there was just a bit of wistfulness that war horrors and restrictions might be over and she might somehow come to have this stranger young man for one of her friends. Definitely Victor could not compare with him.

8

THE next morning she awoke with a kind of wonder in her mind. Had all that really happened the night before, the blue light, the meeting with John Sargent, the dark room and the message? More especially the vision she had had of the Christ? Could that all have been a dream, or just a figment of her imagination?

She sprang up and looked in her handbag where she remembered she had placed the address John had given her. Yes, it was there. Mrs. John Hartley Sargent. A pretty name. Poor dear lady! She must send some flowers that morning. Roses? Deep crimson and pure white together. That would be bright and sweet, and those fall crimson roses had such a spicy heartening perfume. Surely even sick senses could see and smell such roses.

She must not send too many, as if she were showing off her wealth. She wanted the roses to speak of kindly loving friendship to the dear lady whose grandson loved her so.

She decided she would not speak of this. It was just a little private thing she wanted to do. Her mother might not understand her sudden acquaintance with this stranger. She might be on the alarm. Mothers were that way sometimes. Strange that they so readily surrendered to the correct people, of good standing, large fortunes! Well, what did it matter? She likely would see very little, if any more, of this man, and it was foolish to worry her mother over something that would never need to trouble her at all. Something that she would scarcely understand. She sensed that her mother had been sheltered all her life, and was afraid of anything that was not exactly conventional. So when she went down to breakfast, and after her father had gone to his office, while she and her mother sat talking, her mother asked:

"Where were you last night during the blackout, dear? They tell me there was a blackout, though of course I didn't hear of it till afterwards. I hope you were not out in it. I really don't like this new fashion you have of running around evenings without an escort. I do wish Victor would come to his senses and come back and take care of you."

"Oh, mother! Don't wish that! I don't want him back. But I was quite all right, mother dear! I went into a place where they were having a Bible class and stayed until it was over, and then one of the class members brought me home."

"Well, that was kind, I'm sure. But it certainly would have been more congenial to you to have had an escort of your own kind."

"I'm afraid, mother, that I shall never again feel that Victor Vandingham is one of my own kind. I've been feeling more and more of late that he just isn't. He tries me almost beyond endurance, and I shall be so very glad when that terrible party is over. I somehow feel all out of harmony with a party of that sort."

"Well, now my dear, you mustn't let your feelings run away with you. You don't want to get narrow just because Victor has displeased you."

"You don't understand, mother. I think I'm growing up and beginning to understand what things are worth while in this life. Do you know, mother, I enjoyed that Bible class so much, what I heard of it! I'd like you to go down there with me some time and see if you don't like it. I'm sure you would. The teacher was very interesting, and brought out truths I've never heard before."

"Oh, indeed! Well, that was nice, since you were stranded there and couldn't get away. But my dear, you must be careful not to let yourself get morbid, and fanatical. That isn't a healthy way to grow. You don't want to let one disappointment blast your whole life."

"What do you mean, disappointment, mother? I'm not letting anything blast my life. Victor doesn't mean that much to me, and I guess never did. But I certainly am definitely disappointed in him. He is acting like a young king about this silly party, and I hate the thought of going to it."

"Well, that's a foolish way to take it. Don't make that much of it. Just take it in your week's program, no more, no less. And you know you simply must get that matter of your dress settled. Perhaps the easiest way will be to just run downtown this morning and buy a new one."

"No, mother! I wouldn't toady that much to Victor, and I don't think it's right to spend a lot of money on a foolish dress I won't likely wear again till this war is over, and then it will be all out of fashion."

"Well, then get out your dresses and decide. I telephoned Miss Rilley to see if she could give us a couple of days to make any alterations your dress may need, but she is engaged in a factory helping to do something in the work of making airplanes I think. Then I tried Miss Howe, but she is taking nurse's training. There doesn't really seem to be anybody we know and trust by whom we could hope to have alterations made with any satisfaction. I think perhaps you better take it down to the department store, or Madame Sibilla's. Perhaps that will be the simplest."

"No, mother," said Lisle firmly, "I'm not going to have any alterations made. I'm wearing the dark blue tulle, with a white silk girdle, and I'm sewing a lovely deep red silk cord on the edge of the sash myself. Then it won't cost a thing. I have the red cord. Your idea about our country's colors was just the thing, and I'll wear my string of pearls and my pearl star in my hair. I don't believe Victor has ever seen that dress, but if he has I don't care. It's what I'm going to wear. Now let's forget it, and I'll try and get through that party somehow. I only wish I didn't have to go. 'Tomorrow night. tomorrow night,' I keep saying over to myself. I only wish it was over."

"Why, my dear! I am distressed at your attitude. If you go with that thought in your mind I am sure it will come out and be seen. You mustn't let it appear that you and Victor are not as good friends as ever. When you get through this party you know you can drop him if you still want to, but really, for his mother's sake, and because there will be a great many gossipy tongues set wagging if there is any change noticed from your usual attitude, you must go through with this and carry it off in your usual brave sweet way."

Thus her mother counseled her, and with a sigh Lisle went up to her room, laid out the things she was to wear, got everything in good shape, and then sat down to put the scarlet cord on her girdle. She wanted to be sure that her costume was beyond criticism early in the day and then she could rest easy.

But after the sewing was done, and she had tried on the girdle to make sure it was all right, she locked her door and threw herself down on her knees beside her bed. Somehow she felt the need of being in touch with her new Counselor, and though she was new at real prayer and scarcely knew how to voice her needs, she cried out for help.

"Dear Christ," she whispered, "it seems that I am going to a place where You will not be. Or, *will* You be there too? For I know that You are everywhere. Please help me to remember all the time that You *are* there too. Please show me how to act, and help me not to do anything that will be displeasing to You. Help me if Victor or his mother ask me to do what I do not feel is right, to find a way out without making a scene, or being discourteous. You'll have to show me how, for I always get angry when Victor is so disappointing, and I know getting angry does no good. Help me to be strong and sweet, and not to forget You are there too!"

She was still for a long time after she ceased voicing her petition, seeing dimly once more the vision that had come to her the night before, and its memory soothed her troubled spirit.

Then she rose and went down in response to the summons to lunch, and her face, though not exactly bright, was full of peace.

"You'll be all right, Lisle," said her mother with a smile. "Just remember that your family is every bit as good as the Vandingham family, and hold your head up."

Somehow her mother's encouraging words struck a harsh note on the spirit that had been bending low in prayer, but the words she said in answer startled her worried mother.

"Mother, it wasn't meant to be this way, was it, when the world was made?"

"What way? What do you mean?" asked the mother anxiously.

"Why, people caring about families. Why should one family be any better than another? Why should we care? God made us all. Didn't he mean us to be alike?"

"Why, my child! How strangely you talk! Of course, but not everybody chose to be 'alike' as you say. Some went one way, some another, and it's what we have become that counts. Some have worked hard and gained wealth, and prestige of course which follows wealth, and some have been lazy and haven't tried. So there is a very great difference now in the families of the earth. Fortunately for you your family has been one of the best and greatest. Your ancestors on both sides have had notable people, writers and thinkers and statesmen, many wealthy business men, some great inventors. I doubt if even the Vandinghams can number as many outstanding names."

Lisle looked troubled.

"But mother, after all, does that need to count so much? Isn't it pleasing God that counts most?"

"Why, yes of course, Lisle," embarrassedly, "but why are you talking so much about God? You aren't going to turn fanatical, are you?" She gave a little laugh apologetically. "You know, dear, that would be most unfortunate. You would be likely to make people think you had a broken heart, and if you should give up Victor you don't want people to think you are broken-hearted."

Lisle laughed a sweet ripple of amused laughter.

"Mother! If you can't find something real to worry over, you make up something. I declare I never heard anything so funny. The idea of my having a broken heart over Victor! Why mother, I've lived without him for four years and more, and I'm not going to collapse now without him. In fact I think I'd be relieved if he would just fall in love with somebody else and let me alone. He is getting to be a regular pest and I don't know what to do about it. If only he'll behave at the party I'll be too thankful. Now, mother, if you'll please come upstairs and see how I look in my dress. I've got the girdle all fixed, and I do hope it passes your critical eye, for *I* think it's lovely."

"I'm sure I shall think so too, dear, for you have excellent taste."

And so it proved, for both mother and daughter were well satisfied with the effect when Lisle arrayed herself and posed before her mother.

Then the girl went off to her day nursery work for it was time for her "shift" to begin.

She went happily, humming the line or two of the chorus she had heard at the Bible class the evening before.

"Come back as early as you can, dear, and get a good rest. That will make tomorrow evening better if you are rested when you start," called the mother, and Lisle answered sweetly, "I'll try, but I doubt if it will be possible."

The next night Lisle had a good rest after dinner before she dressed. It was not her intention to go to the next house early. She had declined the invitation to take dinner at the Vandingham home, much to the vexation of her hostess, who had at the last minute to accept a substitute of Victor's, a girl named Erda. She looked dubiously at the stunning ash-blonde who appeared in the most daring dress she had ever seen in town, but there was nothing to do but make the best of it, for Victor had brought her in just when she was so annoyed with Lisle for not coming. She had expected Lisle to help her with last minute plans and decisions, but Lisle had sent word that she couldn't possibly get there until after dinner as something had come up that made it impossible.

Victor's mother was not completely obtuse. She had not lived with her son all his years without knowing that he sometimes did things that offended even his best friends, and she wondered what Victor had been doing now. And then when Victor produced this arrogantly beautiful ash-blonde she wondered the more, and put on her most worried expression, letting the dinner conversation lag again and again, until it was mainly confined to talk between Victor and the girl. And even that was anything but satisfactory. Victor was sullen and disagreeble, acting like an arrogant young king who was about to be crowned as Lisle had suggested. Victor's mother rightly judged that Lisle was at the bottom of this also. Had Lisle seen him going around with a girl like this and stayed away on purpose? Or had they had a quarrel? If so the promise of the evening was not at all bright. And she had worked so hard to have everything right!

In the interval between dinner and the time when the guests began to arrive for the evening she vanished, striving vainly by the aid of powder and brick red rouge to erase the traces of the few tears she could not help shedding after that awful dinner. She had left Victor and Erda down in the library having what Erda laughingly called a heart-to-heart talk to get acquainted.

Erda's job she had set herself was to find out as much as possible about the Vandingham plant, and throw out feelers, for even if the young man Kurt Entry said they were trying to get should undertake that job, she felt that she could be of valuable assistance in more ways than one if she could just get an entrance to the place. So she wanted to test out Victor and see if there was any chance of a job in his office for her. Of course she had posed as being well off, but she was making a great deal of wanting a real defense job so that she could feel that she was honestly doing something in this great war in the country of her adoption.

But she didn't make much headway getting information on the plant from Victor. The truth was he didn't really know much about it yet. He had never taken an interest in business, and had declined, hitherto, all his father's offers of a partnership, and a chance to get ready for it during vacations. He just didn't know any more about that plant than the outside of the buildings. It was to him simply a dirty place where workmen had to labor to make an income for his dad. That was all. And he couldn't imagine why this girl should be interested to ask so many questions. But at last he vouchsafed to tell her that he was taking over himself in a few days now, at least for the duration, as they were making some parts of a very important invention that was to be used in war. And when she eagerly caught at the idea and said:

"Why, that's great! Aren't you just thrilled? Say, why can't you take me into your office as your private secretary? I couldn't think of any job I'd like better, and I'd do good work for you. I'm thoroughly competent. I can give you references. I'm a super-typist, and stenographer."

"Say! That's great!" said the young man. "I'll see if I can't arrange it when I get things going. Of course it will be somewhat up to dad right at the start, and I'd have to go slow. They haven't had any but men in the office heretofore. That's dad's idea, but of course when I get going it'll be up to me, and I'll be in a position to say what I want, and *get* it. Say! It would be great having such a dream of loveliness around in a grimy old office of a steel plant. But maybe you wouldn't be willing to work in such a place. You see the office has to be right down by the works, and especially now when the government has stepped in and given us some secret contracts that it won't do to have known by people generally. That's one reason dad will be hard to persuade. He doesn't believe in having women messing in men's work. But me, I'm a different proposition. I can do a great deal better work if I have a few women around me, jollying me along. And it would be just great if I could have a dream of loveliness around like you. Life would be worth living and all that you know. I'll see what I can do, baby, and you stick around and don't take over anything else yet awhile."

So Erda sat happily with a glint in her narrowed green eyes, and a triumphant curve on her pretty sensuous lips.

Then the maid appeared and asked Erda if she would like to go to a room and freshen up for the evening and led her away, and Victor lazed out to the dining room where the sideboards were beginning to display wines of different kinds, and took a copious drink. Then his eyes sought the window where in the gathering darkness he could see the Kingsley house, and notice that there was no light in Lisle's window. So, that was what she was going to do, was it? She was going to pretend she was called away, or sick or something, and she wasn't coming to his party at all! Well, if that was what she was going to do he was off her for life and he would see that she understood it thoroughly.

The truth of the matter was that Lisle was lying down then, taking her rest, and trying to gather strength for the ordeal of the evening.

Victor got himself ready for the evening, and went down to take another drink. This was a habit he had acquired in college, and had learned well how it would bolster him up when he was ill at ease, so when he finally stood in line to receive his guests where his mother had arranged for him to be, he was gay and hilarious, talking loud, and greeting everybody in the latest accepted style. And his troubled mother stood worriedly in her place and tried to rally her forces. She knew that when his father came to stand with them he would notice Victor, and see that he had been drinking. He didn't approve of young men drinking too much, and so early in the evening! It was shocking! She would have liked to burst into tears and run away to hide. How could her boy do a thing like this, bringing that awful girl to dinner? It must be all Lisle's fault. Lisle who had always been his friend, to desert him on this his great night! This night that she had dreamed of and planned for for years! And Lisle to spoil it all! Where was she anyway? Wasn't she coming at all? What would people think?

She turned sharply, intending to ask Victor if he knew where Lisle was, and why she was so late. Had she said anything to him about it? But Victor was talking to that lynx-eyed girl Erda, and of course she couldn't say anything before her.

Then suddenly there was Lisle. Mrs. Vandingham gave a startled look at her loveliness and fairly fell on her neck with joy.

"Oh, my dear Lisle!" she said. "I have been so worried. It would have simply spoiled the whole affair if you hadn't come. And we were terribly disappointed that you couldn't be with us at dinner!"

"Oh, I'm sorry, Mrs. Vandingham! I'm not that important you know. But I didn't mean to upset your plans," said Lisle sweetly. "Am I very late? I thought I would arrive about the time the rest of the guests did."

"Well, no, not so late, it is only that you are usually with us from the start at anything, you know, my dear. But now you are here I shall relax and enjoy myself. And now let me introduce you. Victor, here's Lisle, don't you see her?"

"I certainly do," blared Victor. "When did I ever fail to see Lisle? But I'm not sure I shall speak to her, coming late this way, and on my coronation night as she called it. How do I look, darling? Like the king you said I would be?"

Lisle gave Victor one of her steady looks, and perceived with a chilly little feeling around her heart that things were going to be pretty bad, for Victor was drunk. She had never seen him out and out drunk before and it shocked her. She had never been used to associating Victor with drinking. That is if he drank he probably did it quietly, and she had never seen him like this. But now he was boisterously drunk. She did not answer, but turned away to move on down the line, till he put out a detaining hand.

"Hi, darling, you don't get out of it that easy. Let me make you acquainted with my other best girl, Erda Brannon. You two ought to be the best of friends, my two best girls! How about it, Lisle? Take her under your wing, will you?"

But Lisle gave one glance at Erda, flashed her a quick cold bright smile and turned away sharply, slipping on down the line and mingling with her friends, presently lost in a group of those she knew well.

Poor Mrs. Vandingham flushed deeply beneath her brick red rouge and giggled nervously. "Oh, Vickie," she gurgled, "you always will have your little joke," and she turned to renew her giggle for Lisle's benefit, but found that Lisle was gone. But when she turned back to Victor there was only a stupid look on his face as if he had been slapped, and the girl beside him was staring off haughtily, astonished. If Lisle had seen them both she might have felt that she had won the first bout of the battle, or she might have felt condemned that she had found no way to meet the onslaught of the enemy but by the world's methods. Just now, though she was laughing and talking brilliantly with a number of young men in uniform and girls in brilliant evening garb, she was suddenly remembering that she had not come alone to this party. There was One who had promised to be with her. Was she honoring Him? But of course she gave no sign of these thoughts as she went on, looking gay and bright and happy.

Mrs. Vandingham bustled up and claimed her attention later.

"Oh, my dear! How darling you look! That dress. I know that must have come from New York. It has the New York look. Somehow nothing around here can quite come up to New York, can it? And it looks so new and fresh and quite in keeping with the times with that charming girdle. It *did* come from New York, didn't it, Lisle?"

"Why yes, Mrs. Vandingham, it did originally, about two years ago, but I've never worn it around here I guess. Though the girdle is new. I made most of it myself!"

"My dear!" said the lady with a quick look around to be sure no one had heard. "How clever you are! But don't tell anybody. They think it is absolutely new. I heard some of the girls talking about it."

"Did you?" said Lisle amusedly. "Well, I'm glad you like it. And what a lot of uniforms you have present. Isn't it grand so many of the boys are enlisting? And how enthusiastic they are."

"Yes," said Mrs. Vandingham with a quick droop of sadness in her face and voice, "I suppose it is, but I think of the mothers. How terrible it must be for them. I can't be thankful enough that my boy had had such an important post given to him. And that he will not have to go away. Of course he is broken-hearted that he cannot go out with the other fellows his age, but he was needed here. His father has not been at all well for the past year, and it was only with the help of Victor that he dared accept the assignment the government had given his company. Of course it was very hard on Vickie, but there are no losses without compensations, and of course it means a great deal to me that he is to remain at home. I know you too will rejoice in that fact."

This was one of the trying situations that Lisle had known she would have, but fortunately just then a group of old friends came up to introduce two soldier boys and she did not have to reply.

The evening dragged itself along, hour after hour, and Lisle avoided the neighborhood of Victor who seemed thoroughly engrossed with the girl Erda, though occasionally he came around where she saw his face furrowed with grouch. You never would have taken him for a king being crowned that night. His handsome face was all of a frown, surly was his expression, and only now and then a grim smile appeared and that was directed at Erda.

There was good music, and of course there was dancing, and once Victor stalked over to Lisle and asked her to dance with him but she shook her head and told him that she had promised one of the soldiers to take him up to the library and show him a couple of choice engravings, portraying some ancient notable battles of the past. She decidedly did not want to dance with Victor. There was no knowing what he might not take it into his head to do if she did. He was evidently out for revenge, and he would have it somehow. But she reflected that her mother and his mother would both consider it a great breach of etiquette for her not to dance at least once with her host, and so when she came back from the library and found him waiting in the hall for her, claiming her as a partner without even asking again, she submitted, moving gracefully, impersonally to the music, her eyes across the room, her lips silent and grave.

All her life Lisle had been accustomed to dance, a little, though she was not especially fond of it. Her mother's code had been moderation in all such things, and an extreme and ladylike demeanor that made her dancing more of a picture of grace, like one of the muses, than a modern form of amusement. There was none of the modern yielding of self to the partner. She kept him at a discreet distance, in spite of his fierce effort to draw her closer.

"You are making a fool of yourself," he muttered. "Nobody dances that way now! I ought to have shown you how they do things today since you seem to have been out of the world."

She gave him a brief bright smile and then said gravely:

"Is the world, then, such a pleasant place to be that one should try to follow all its ways?"

"Oh, you're simply impossible!" snarled the young gallant.

"Yes?" said Lisle. "Suppose we stop then," and dropping her hand from his arm she turned and quietly stepped out of the whirl, vanishing across the room and out a door. Swiftly by a way that the years had made familiar to her as a child, she went to the room where she had left her cloak and her little white fur-edged shoes, hurriedly donned them, slipped down the back stairs, and out through the servants' entrance, unobserved, for the servants were all busy serving now. So she went across the snowy lawn to her home and happily up to her room. Her mother was out that evening, so there was no need to report on her experiences, and she could get quiet and think everything over.

She undressed in the dark, because she did not wish to afford any idle speculators over at the Vandinghams' the satisfaction of knowing that she had gone home and gone to bed. Her room was on the side of the house toward the Vandingham house, and while it was not likely that the gay guests would think to look out across the lawns, notice her light and call attention to it, it was altogether likely that Victor might take occasion to do so, and she did not care to give him the opportunity.

Victor had been drinking more or less all the evening, and while he had not been quite so hilarious as when she arrived, he was still pretty well under the influence of liquor. To have had his hot breath fan her face, heavy with the odor of liquor had been unpleasant to her in the extreme. It wasn't that she hadn't been where these things went on, occasionally, but she had been a girl happy in her studies, fond of simple pleasures, and just hadn't cared for this sort of gaiety. And now to find Victor like others whom she had known and avoided stirred her to deep disappointment. She might not wish to marry him, but it *hurt* her to be ashamed of him. She hadn't thought Victor had taken to drinking. She was almost shocked. Yes, it must be true that she was old-fashioned. Dowdy in her ideas. Well, she was, and a conviction grew in her heart that she was right in being that way. And her Companion, her escort for the evening, was He pleased at the way she had conducted herself? Did He like all this dancing and drinking? Were places like these parties good for His children? She must look into that some day, that is if she ever had occasion to feel the necessity of going to another one. Should her new Christ's child put herself in such a place?

Well, there had been soldiers in uniform there this evening, the uniform of their beloved country. Suppose that the party had been given by the enemy, and that many present were in enemy uniform. Should a loyal American deliberately stay among them, except for state reasons under orders? Well, here again was something she must look into. But not tonight. She was tired and disappointed and had reached a place of parting where her old life and a new one separated. It made her sad and yet there was a deep gladness beneath it all.

As she laid her head upon the pillow she could hear the strains of the music from the other house, far enough away now to lose some of its wild blare. But presently as she remembered last evening, and her vision, a soft sweet memory brought other strains:

> I have seen the face of Jesus,
> Tell me not of aught beside

and she dropped off to sleep with a smile on her lips.

9

THAT very afternoon as John Sargent left the shipyard and began his short walk to the trolley that would carry him to his grandmother's apartment, an elderly man walked up to him and asked direction how to get to the center of the city. John told him clearly.

"If you get on this car I'm taking it will take you within a block of where you say you want to go."

John swung himself onto the car, found a seat and settled down. He was annoyed when the other man followed him and took the other half of his seat. It was the more annoying because there were plenty of other seats the man could have taken, but he followed John closely and indicated that he wanted to take the outside of the seat next the aisle.

"I'll just sit here with you," he said cheerfully, "then you can tell me where to get off."

John drew a faint sigh and accepted the company of the stranger. This new patience was one of the things he was learning at that Bible class, and not always did he remember it. But after an instant's thought he moved over and gave the man a little more room. Then he pulled out the morning paper from his overcoat pocket and absorbed himself in its pages, though he had already read as much as he cared to that morning on his way to work. But his companion was not abashed by the paper. He opened up a conversation, and was not in the least troubled by John's inattention.

"It feels good to sit down," he said. "I've been all day long hunting for a job. Queer, isn't it, just because I have a few gray hairs, and no bunch of references? You see my references were burned in a little rooming house where I was staying. It got on fire, and I barely got out alive with the few clothes I could manage to scramble on as I climbed out the window to the ladder the firemen had brought. And while I wouldn't of course have any trouble in getting more, it happened that all the places I had worked that would have mattered were in the far west, and it would have taken time to get them. Of course if I hadn't lost my money too I could have called people on the phone, long distance, but you can easily see what a time I've been having."

"Yes?" said John, giving the man a quick glance.

It was a fantastic story. Was the man a superior kind of crook, or what? He certainly wouldn't be expecting to get anything out of a working man on his way home from work, would he? Or would he? Sometimes workmen had soft hearts and were gullible. He knew he was himself occasionally.

"Well, how did it come out?" he asked as he turned over another leaf of his paper.

"Well, it hasn't come out yet," said the man with a sigh and a good-natured grin, "but I guess it will in the end. I heard of a job this morning, and I went without lunch and spent the nickel to phone. I took a chance. The man I had to call was the same name as an old fellow workman of mine, and it turned out to be the same man. He's at the head of the personnel in this big Vandingham plant. Do you know it? I hear they're making some new kind of a secret weapon that is going to do big things in this war and hustle it up in great shape, and they're crazy to get workmen at once. But of course they have to have reliable men, that they can trust, to keep their mouths shut, and that's where I had the advantage. This head man knew me, and I tell you he was glad to hear my voice. They want to begin work right away, and they need more men badly, only so many are gone to war, and so many haven't had the training, and so many are strangers, that it is hard to get the right men. The only thing was he wanted me to hunt up another man to spell me, half time. He said they always got along better if they knew each other, or were sort of buddies. He said it would be to my advantage if I could find some old friend in the city, or somebody I knew and thought I could sort of go partners with. But I can't find any old friends. I called up several names I knew, one had a son who used to be a buddy of my son, and I knew if I could get hold of him I'd be in the velvet, because my son used to say he was bright as they make 'em, and the work was right along his line, welding. If I could just get him for my assistant I'd be sitting pretty. But when I called I found he had joined the army same as my son did, and was already overseas. So that was that! And then I unearthed another name, but the whole family had moved west, and I found I'd have to go on my own. But the more I thought about it the more I felt maybe I could find somebody, just anybody, who was looking for a job, and take him along with me. And when I saw you I took a notion to you. I liked the way you walked, and the way you held your head, and I knew I'd never be ashamed of you if I buddied up to you, so here, I'm telling you. Would you like a chance to rake in a whole lot of money? Of course I know the shipyard pays well, but nothing like this job. You could be a rich man if you kept at this long. How about it, buddy, would you be willing to go along with me and take on this job? You know the Vandinghams are a good people to be with. You can't find much better. And now the government's behind it there isn't a question. How about it, man? Will you come with me and get the chance of a life-time making your pile? It's a job you can't match anywhere else that I know of. Want to go with me and try for it?"

"Thanks," said John indifferently, "I have a job that I'm very well satisfied with and I don't care to make a change at present."

"But wait, young man, till I tell you what these people pay," said the stranger, putting out a detaining hand as John rose and signaled that he wanted to get out.

"That wouldn't be a consideration with me at present," said John determinedly. "I'm perfectly satisfied with my job, but thanks for thinking of me. I hope you succeed in getting what you want. Good by," and John swung off, made for the nearest drugstore which wasn't far away, and called up his officer friend.

The man on the bus rode on a few blocks and was lost in the dusk of the evening. His name was Lacey.

Later that evening he called on one named Weaver.

"Nothing doing!" he said with a half-triumphant note in his voice. "He says he's not interested."

"Well, keep at him," said Weaver. "He may come around yet. It sounds as if he is just the man we want, in spite of his reluctance. They say he has a lot of character. What's that? The girl? Oh, yes, I liked her all right, but I still think the young man is our best bet for the Vandingham outfit. The old boss has some very decided notions, and one of them is that he doesn't like women around business. You can't go against that."

"But I think there may be a way for the girl to work

too. She's got ways of her own. She's been scraping acquaintance with young Vandingham and got a bid to his party. She might work it through him."

"You don't say! Well, that shows enterprise, and if she can work it it's okay with me. But I'd still try for the young man. A man's invaluable where machinery is concerned. A girl doesn't always understand some important point that a man would know intuitively. So keep on trying for the young fellow. See if you can't get in with him. Profess to have failed in your own attempt to get into the plant, and ask him to help you. Maybe that will work."

"Okay!" said Lacey. "But I still say I don't believe it will work. The boy's got something in his mind that makes him allergic to the idea."

"That so? Well, perhaps there's something in that. They might not have been good friends in college. Look up records. Find some other student who knows them. See what he says. If there was rivalry between them you might work it on the line of revenge. Sometimes a strong-minded guy like Sargent would yield if you told him there was a chance to get it back on Vandingham. But you'd have to buddy up to him and get pretty close to make him own that, before you could do anything about it. There's another thing, too. This man Sargent has a pretty good reputation around town wherever he's been. He's known to be honest. Goes to some queer kind of a Sunday School, is thoroughly trustworthy. And that's a good reputation to have in a business like this. Nobody would suspect a fellow like that if it ever came to a showdown."

"Yes, that's all right," said Lacey, "once you get him going and into the job too deep to get out and tell. But the trouble with this conscientious kind is they're too honest to start in something that seems a bit shady. I doubt if you can ever win this guy over. He's too genuine to fall for it, no matter how much money he could make."

"Is anybody really that honest and conscientious if he once gets a chance to get away with a big thing like that, and no strings to it?"

"Could be," said Lacey. "I've seen 'em occasionally."

"Well, keep at it. You can't do more than fail! And remember, we don't fail in our business. We've got too much to lose. Of course if worst comes to worst there are ways to *make* anybody do as we say. You understand."

"Yes, I understand. But this is not the old country. These people will not fall for everything. They have courage. They are proud. They have a sense of right and wrong, which we over there have forsworn. We have a different standard of life."

"Lacey, you need to go back and take another course if you don't know how to win over a needed fellow. This one has all the qualifications we need, and there are not so many any more who have since the men are going into the army. Of course in the old country we have ways to train the stubbornest of them to do what they are told, but not here, *yet*. Say, how about turning your girl loose on the lad? She looked to me as if she were better fitted for that sort of work than the actual spying in a plant where they are all men and where she would not have the mechanical knowledge to understand what she was doing. But she might persuade your young man to undertake the job. She's pretty enough. Get her to work on young Sargent."

Lacey shook his head.

"Not his type. He doesn't have much to do with girls. I've never seen him with a girl but once and that was to protect her from a bunch of drunken bums during a blackout and then take her home afterward."

"Who is she? Did you find that out?"

"Yes, naturally. She is the daughter of the millionaire Kingsley. He steps high when he does fall for a girl."

"H'mmm! Is she a good looker?"

"Yes, but in a different way. More refined. More old-fashioned. You wouldn't get her stooping to win a young man. Besides, I've heard she is engaged to young Vandingham."

"The very thing, Lacey! You can get around her. Get her to make Vandingham take her into the plant, and then approach her wisely about the great job there is for the right young man. Perhaps she will induce him to go into this, talk to him about how much good he could do with the money."

Lacey shook his head decidedly.

"You don't get me," he said contemptuously. "They are neither of them that type. The girl would never stoop to coax a young man to do anything, not even to get him to give money to some cause for which she was working, war work, or defense or something of that sort. She is reserved, and dignified and lovely. And he is reserved also."

"Very well, then, I'll tell you what we'll do. Kidnap the girl and let the boy know she is in trouble. Then employ a bum to tell him he knows where she is, and will tell him if he will get certain information from that plant for us. Try the chivalrous line and see how that works."

Lacey still shook his head.

"I'll try it if you say so of course, but I don't feel either of those people would yield. They are wholly American, even to death. They have the same qualities you are trying to inculcate into your army."

"Nonsense! They haven't been trained as our young men are trained. They are a fun-loving giddy set. Why our men have been bred and born to fight and to count self as nothing, for the glory of the whole earth. These

Americans are soft. They are thoughtless and careless. They'll do something that looks good to them and seems to be for their own good, and when they find out what it has done to them they'll collapse, and do what they are told if the promise of release is sufficient."

"No, you're wrong there! These two young people have been born and bred to honor. They drank it with their mother's milk. They have not succumbed to the worldliness and modernism that so many are full of today. That young Vandingham has, and that is why he can be influenced by Erda, but the other girl, Lisle Kingsley, has an exalted view of life, also is devoted to manners and customs. You would find it hard to kidnap a girl like that and get her into a dangerous situation."

"Oh, no, you wouldn't. Not if you picked your kidnapper, and you and I know plenty could do it."

"Yes. It could be done. But there would be plenty danger in trying it. The so-called righteous indignation of the wealthy and fashionable, of the respectable church-going community would be roused and the dogs of the law would be turned loose upon us."

"Those are things we have to expect and avoid," said the big bully whose name was Weaver. "Those are the things we are trained to overcome and beat. You know how! Now go and accomplish. I don't care how you do it, but I want that lad, and that other girl if possible and I don't care how much it costs. When is the next blackout? Watch for that. It's an excellent time to carry out any schemes. Does that Kingsley girl go every night to that Red Cross class in the southern part of the city?"

"No, but she goes to a dinky little religious gathering of some sort. At least that's where she took refuge when the young man was with her."

"Oh! So that's the game is it? The religious angle. Well, that oughtn't to be hard to beat. The element of fear would likely help a lot. Work it out, Lacey, and let me know tomorrow what you plan. Time is going fast, and the quicker we get this thing under espionage the better. It's about the most important thing we have to do just now. This plant has got to be watched in the right way. The man that makes this possible is due for advancement. You know what that means. Now go, and see how quick you can get some action."

The two men parted and Lacey went on his way back to his desolate room to get on the telephone, call up his satellites and work out a plan.

Lisle Kingsley, all unaware that her name had been set down among the victims that the saboteurs were arranging to use to attain their ends, went happily on about her war work, Red Cross classes, and her university course. But none of these at present led her into a neighborhood where plans such as had been discussed could be easily carried out without detection. And approaching examinations kept her busy with her studies, too busy to go to the Bible classes which she longed to attend. Thus God protected her.

John Sargent wrote her a brief and deeply grateful note after the lovely flowers reached his grandmother.

I can never tell you what those flowers did for my grandmother. To understand it you would have had to see her eyes when she looked at them, and to have known her expressive eyes through the years as I have done, to read the almost glorified look of wonder that she wore when I brought them near to her face and she caught the Heavenly fragrance. I know she smelled them for she drew deep breaths, as if she was fairly reveling in them. Then her eyes looked at me with a question in them. You see she knows I would not feel I could *buy* flowers just now, and she wanted to know who sent them, so I told her it was a friend of mine whom I had told about her, and I gave her your name. I think she knew the name. Your family of course is well known, and there was surprise in her eyes that I should know you. So I told her of the blackout and how we came to know one another. I told her about the Bible class, and there was great joy in her face, a kind of glory, if it is right to use that term about a human being. So I thank you from my heart for your kind thought of my dear grandmother and for the flowers.

I do not know if you have been to the class again, because my work has been changed to the night shift and I work from four until midnight, so have missed the class myself much against my wish. But I trust that the Lord will guide you into His truth.

I am enclosing a little booklet that you may like to see, about the soon-coming of the Lord.

Thanking you again for your kindness,

John Sargent

Lisle kept that letter among her treasures, quietly, not even telling her mother about it. She felt her mother might not understand, and of course since she would not be likely to see this young man again, at least not often, if at all, it didn't matter. It somehow seemed to her that this was something all her own, something she didn't want to talk over, or have reasoned about, or torn asunder by worldly traditions. She was not going to make anything of it in her life, and why should it be necessary to discuss it? It wasn't as if there were danger in it for herself or anybody else. It was just a little happening that was a pleasant thing to herself, and would be spoiled by having objections raised. Only, what objections could there possibly be? She had sent some flowers to a dear old lady who was a hopeless invalid, with perhaps not long to live. And her grandson, who had helped her when she was frightened, had written a polite note thanking her. That's all there was to it. If her mother ever came upon it she would let her read the note. She would know at once by its whole tenor that it was all right. Perfectly courteous. And of course there wasn't anything wrong in her sending flowers to an old lady. It couldn't possibly be misunderstood. There!

But she put the letter away carefully, and now and again took it out and read it, just to reassure herself that there was nothing about it she need regret.

The little book John had sent her she read and re-read, and in time wrote a brief pleasant appreciative note thanking him.

One evening not long after she received the little book she was walking to her day nursery work, and noticed some rough looking men watching her. Drunk, were they? She wasn't sure. But she didn't like their looks. They seemed to be discussing her. A taxi was passing just then and she hailed it and got in, glad to have it turn a corner and whirl her quickly from their sight. The occurrence lingered in her mind and worried her, so that she hesitated to go walking in the lower part of the city alone, and was always casting an anxious look around for those same men, yet she was never sure that some she saw in the distance were not the same ones. She tried to laugh herself out of it, but finally fell into the habit of taking a taxi whenever she went into the lower part of the city.

Victor by this time had "taken over," as he called it, in his father's business. That is, he had a large and beautifully equipped office, though those who were watching saw no sign that his father, because of Victor's activities, did any the less than he always had done. The only difference seemed to be that expensively furnished office of Victor's, through which the most important people entered passing through to see his father in a plain inner office. There were no frills on the elder Vandingham's private office.

And it was not long before Erda Brannon was established as Victor's personal secretary. Thus she was in a position not only to see everything that was done at the plant, but also to read all the private confidential correspondence, and to understand just how and what and when everything happened that was of special interest to the enemy. But of all this of course Victor was unaware. He was much intrigued with Erda for the present, and whenever he turned his eyes toward the Kingsley house, or felt a stab of compunction for the way he was neglecting his erstwhile "best girl," he drew an ugly look down across his handsome face and told himself it was "good for her." She would learn she couldn't treat him like the dirt under her feet and expect him to continue to dance attendance on her. He would keep this up till she learned her lesson thoroughly, and then he would go and condescend to her again. She would come around soon enough, he assured himself, when she saw that he meant business. This spurt of war work and day nursery, and hard study couldn't deceive him. So he continued to laze around his luxurious office, idly reading a mystery story, or flirting with Erda, while she plied her trade of finding out all she could about the secrets of the war plant. He made no attempt whatever to curb her eager interest in the machinery, and the mysterious parts their plant was making for a supposedly secret weapon that was to revolutionize war and win the victory for the Allies. But Victor, for the time being, had little thought for anything of this sort. It didn't appeal to him to take much pains to guard the secrets that his father considered sacred. It seemed to him a lot of mere tommyrot, just making a great fuss about nothing, to create an impression on the enemy, nothing to it at all, he said.

But it never occurred to him to question the necessity which was keeping him there in a fine office while his contemporaries were fighting and dying for a real cause. He had heard his mother's "sales" talk so much that he actually began to believe that his own part in the war was very necessary.

Sometimes behind her hand, behind his back, Erda smiled a contemptuous smile, marveling at how blind he was.

Then one day Victor caught a glimpse of Lisle Kingsley as she came down the steps of her father's house, watched her graceful tripping feet, the swing of her lithe body, the tilt of her lovely head, and the old attraction returned to him in full force. Lisle seemed to be as happy as when she was a child. His punishing had not reduced her to humility and pining. She carried a brief case and had the mark of being on her way to classes. Silly, that she could interest herself in learning, mere learning, when she might even now be his wife and have a home of her own, an enviable position in society. She was too well satisfied with things as they were. It was high time he went back to her.

So that evening he went to call with the same old nonchalance as always. He gave no explanation or apology for his absence of weeks, just walked in and began to carry on from his last contact. That was the way to treat such breaks. Just ignore them.

However it was not Lisle but her mother who was sitting in the living room knitting when he walked in. He paused an instant and looked quickly around the room.

"Where's Lisle?" he said, as if he had a right to demand her presence.

Lisle's mother looked up and lifted her eyebrows coolly:

"Oh, good evening, Victor," she said politely. "Lisle is out this evening. Won't you sit down?"

"Where has she gone?" he asked, ignoring her question.

"Why, I really don't remember. She has so many engagements these days that I don't always keep track of them. Did she expect you this evening?"

He eyed her curiously.

"Do I have to telephone every time when I want to see her?"

"Well, perhaps, if you really want to see her. You certainly didn't expect her to sit at home awaiting your pleasure to arrive."

"Getting smart, aren't you Em-ly?"

Mrs. Kingsley made no reply to that, just kept on knitting, counting stitches. After another one or two insolent remarks Victor said:

"When will she be home?"

"Well, I'm not quite sure," said Lisle's mother. "Would you care to sit down and wait? There are some magazines over on the table if you'd like to read."

So Victor settled down to read, turning the pages idly, snapping them half angrily as time went on and Lisle did not appear, and Mrs. Kingsley continued to knit silently.

And when at last they heard Lisle's key in the lock, heard her enter and come lightly across the hall and toward the door, humming a soft tune, they both looked up. She dawned on the living room like a bright lovely star, her eyes shining, her cheeks glowing.

"Oh, mother, it was nice you sat up for me! It always looks lonesome in this room when you're not in it."

"I always like to sit up until I know you are back. Where have you been this evening, dear? I forgot to ask you."

"Why, we had to sing for some of the soldier boys down at the Red Cross rooms. It was fun, mother, and the boys enjoyed it so much!"

"That's nice. But see, you have a caller. He's been waiting some time!"

Then Victor unfolded his languid self from the big chair where he had slumped, and turned a frowning face toward the recalcitrant maiden, as if she were somehow to blame. She had been having a nice time, had she? Well, it was high time he came back and took possession of his property.

10

LISLE turned a pleasantly bright look toward her old playmate and lifted her eyebrows a trifle.

"Oh, I'm sorry you had to wait," she said quite formally. "Did you want to see me for something important, Victor? If you had told me you were coming I would have tried to be home earlier."

Victor eyed her with a scowl.

"Oh, yes? You certainly would not! You've avoided me on every occasion for weeks! And you walked out on me on the great night of my party!"

He fixed her with a gaze as severe as if he had accused her of the unpardonable sin.

A series of expressions like fleeting clouds in the sunshine passed over the girl's expressive face. One could almost read the history of that evening party from her eyes. And then like a veil suddenly dropped over the scene a gentle haughtiness enveloped her, and she looked steadily, almost sternly into his bold spoiled eyes until they began to take on a shamed look.

"Well,—*didn't* you?" he burst forth again, his anger flaring up resentfully. "*Didn't* you, I say?"

Mrs. Kingsley cast a quick look at her daughter's cool face and wondered where she got her poise. This was all a new story to the mother. Lisle had not told much about that party, and her mother had thought it best to let well enough alone and not question her as to why she came home so early. So now she marveled at her quiet manner.

After an instant, still looking at the young man as he roared out his last question rudely, she answered steadily:

"Yes, I went home, if that is what you mean."

"Well, why? *Why* did you go? Just to make me furious? Just because you wanted to spoil the greatest event of my life for me? Was that it? Was that why you disappeared when everything was just at its height?"

"No," said Lisle quietly, as if it were a matter of very little moment. "I went home because everybody was drunk, and I was ashamed of the way you acted."

Victor gazed at the girl in utmost astonishment, that she would actually dare to speak to him that way. Then his handsome lips curled slowly into a sneer of contempt, and he drawled out hatefully:

"Says you! You poor little white-livered Victorian! You product of an antique forgotten age that was all hedged in with fanaticism and ignorance! What kind of a social leader do you think you could be with a background like that? Answer me? How do you think you could hold your own in the world today? That's what I meant when I found fault with your education. If you could have been free from your childhood's traditions, and gone into a real college away from home till you could get the college outlook today you would have got over all that funny business. Thinking you were too good to get drunk now and then as others do, and play around with other people and have a really good time. And it isn't too late yet, Lisle, if you're ready to put ideas like that out of your head and try to be like other people. I'll be with you heart and soul. We'll start and go places and see things and get that backwoods background out of the picture entirely."

A quick movement on the part of Mrs. Kingsley made Victor suddenly glance her way and catch the look of utter indignation on her nice kindly face. Quickly he added apologetically:

"Of course your parents did the best they could in bringing you up. They were sort of out of things themselves and didn't know any better. But it's time now for you to come out from under their thumbs and act for yourself. You've got to understand that everybody nowadays who is worth anything drinks, and expects you to drink. It's time for your silly old-fashioned ideas to change—"

But suddenly Mrs. Kingsley arose:

"And it's time now for you to leave our house, Victor!" She said it in the same sternly firm voice that she had once used when she sent the boy home for some misdeed years ago when he was only a child. And somehow the fire in her fine eyes and the lift of her proud head filled him with the same humiliation that he had felt then. There was something about her refined dignity, and authoritative attitude that made him feel at a disadvantage in spite of all his arrogant ideas. He straightened up and tried to gain the upper hand in the argument again.

"I'm sorry I had to offend you again, Mother Kingsley, but you know all I have said is true, and the sooner you recognize it the better for all concerned."

Mrs. Kingsley did not sit down. She kept her dignity and poise and looked the insolent lad in the eye.

"That will be about all from you, Victor," she said. "Now, will you leave the house? I'm sure no one will welcome you here as long as you hold such views.

Please go!" and she herded the reluctant boy toward the door.

"Now, Mrs. Kingsley. Don't go and get sore and spoil all our friendship of the years!" pleaded Victor, donning his engaging smile and looking down upon her as he had done many times during the years. "You know you like me better than any other friend of Lisle's. Don't spoil our friendship!"

"It is you who are spoiling the friendship, Victor. You know our standards of right and wrong. You know that you have been most insulting, and that you have gone contrary to all the standards that Lisle has come to think of you as believing."

"But the world has changed, Emily!" wheedled the boy. "I've done my best to make you see that, and you can't expect everything to stand still and go your way. Besides, haven't you any care for your daughter? You know Lisle loves me. You know she wouldn't be happy without me. And I certainly couldn't think of marrying her if she continues to hold such nonsensical ideas. You wouldn't stand in the way of Lisle's best interests would you?"

Then Lisle arose haughtily, and indignantly disclaimed what he had said.

"I certainly do not love you, Victor, and would never consent to marry you! There could be no happiness for me in having my life linked to yours, and I wish you would put that idea entirely out of your head. Never, *never* will I marry you!"

"Now, look here, Lisle, don't be silly! You don't know what you are talking about. The truth is I came in this evening to tell you that my father has made me promises tonight that practically put me in the class of a wealthy man. I shall have an enormous income, both from the business, and also from my inheritance from my grandfather, into which I shall soon come in full right. I'm going to be a rich man, Lisle, and you can't afford to quarrel with me this way. I thought you would enjoy hearing of my good fortune. You've always taken great interest in everything that had to do with my success and I supposed of course you would rejoice with me at the way things are coming out. And more especially because it will mean a wonderful future for you."

Lisle paused haughtily and looked at him coldly.

"Why yes, of course, I'm glad for you to have success," she said frostily, "if that is the kind of success you want, but it really has nothing to do with me, Victor. Not all the money in the world would tempt me to join my life with yours. You and I have definitely nothing in common any more. Now, go your way, and don't worry about me. You and I are done, Victor. We aren't even friends any more. We were old friends of childhood, yes, but childhood is past, and we have come to the end of our association. If I hadn't been thoroughly convinced of that before, I should have been the night of that awful party! So, please excuse me from any more of your attention. I'll bid you good night and good by," and she swept him a cool little bow and went out of the room.

He stood stunned by her words, her manner, watched her until she mounted the stairs lightly, not angrily. Then he turned toward her mother, who was now sitting down knitting again, ignoring his presence.

He waited until he heard her door upstairs open and close quietly, finally, and then he turned furiously toward her mother:

"There! I hope you see what you have done!" he said bitterly.

"Oh, no!" said Mrs. Kingsley. "I think *you* are seeing what *you* have done. Good night, Victor, I'm very sorry for you, because if you go on in this way you certainly are not going to be happy, or successful. The world can't offer you anything to make up for the good principles you seemed to have when you were a child."

"Yes? That's your idea, I suppose. Well, I guess I'm well rid of you and your old-time notions!" And in sullen anger Victor went out from the house that had been almost a second home to him since childhood. And the woman who had made many happy times for him and her own child sighed. For Victor certainly was changed. There was no denying that.

But upstairs in her own room Lisle looking into the future was surprised at herself that she was not regretting the break that had come so definitely tonight, and seemed quite permanently final. It was like a long heavy burden rolling off to know that so far as she was concerned she didn't care whether she ever saw Victor Vandingham again. She wasn't even so annoyed at him that she had any desire to run away to another place where she would not have to meet him again. She was utterly indifferent.

A few minutes later Mrs. Kingsley came slowly up the stairs to find her daughter, half fearful lest there might have been a reaction, and she would find her dear girl in tears.

But Lisle was sitting happily by her desk with her university books beside her, and her interest deep in her lessons for the morrow. As her mother reached the top of the stairs and came fearfully toward Lisle's door, her heart grew suddenly hopeful as she heard that sweet little happy tune. She paused and listened to the softly clear words that came from the open door:

> Oh, what wonderful, wonderful rest!
> Trusting completely in Jesus I'm blest;
> Sweetly He comforts and shields from alarms,
> Holding me safe in His mighty arms.

What was she singing? It wasn't any song that her mother knew, nothing she had heard at church, though it sounded some like a hymn tune. It wasn't a love song either, not even a modern love song, though that part about being held in somebody's arms sounded almost like it. But there! Hark! Now she was singing it again, slowly remembering the words one by one. No, it wasn't a love song, only a hymn. Where had Lisle heard it? On the radio? But Lisle never had much time nowadays to listen to the radio. She was so busy with her studies and her war work.

The tune sank into a low hum, and Lisle was deep into her Latin study. An instant later her mother stepped into her door and smiled at her.

"What a sweet song, dear. Where did you get it?" she asked with a pleasant note in her voice.

"Oh, I heard it at the meeting where I stopped for the blackout," said Lisle happily. "Isn't it pretty? Mother, I think you'd like to go to that meeting sometime. The whole thing was just like that little song, so peaceful and sure, and restful. Will you go with me sometime?"

"Why, yes, dear, perhaps. If we can find a free night, and the car can be used. I'm not much on knocking around in buses you know. We'll see, perhaps. But dearie, I'm so glad to hear your voice singing instead of weeping. I was afraid I'd find you in tears after the experience we've just had. I'm so glad you're taking it cheerfully."

"Oh, *that?*" said Lisle giving a gay little laugh. "I settled that in my heart some time ago, and I'm just glad to have it finally off my mind. That's that, and that's all there is about it. Let's not fret about it any longer. I know you feel badly on account of Mrs. Vandingham being your friend, but there'll be a way to work that out somehow I am sure, and as for Victor, he's gone sour and that's all there is to it. No, I'll never be in tears over him, so don't you fret about that. You see, mother, I lost all respect for Victor when I found he was going to stay at home from war and hide behind a sham job in his father's office, beginning with that fool party! A party like that when his country is at war! It seems almost blasphemous! When others his age are *dying* to save our country for freedom and righteousness, he has a party and gets *drunk!* Aren't you glad I'm not going to marry Victor, mother?"

There was something almost pleading in the tone with which the girl ended her sentence and her mother responded quickly, eagerly. "Yes, dear, I'm heartily glad! For weeks I've been worried about this because I was afraid it was going to mean so much to you, and you had seemed so much attached to Victor when he was a boy, but since I've seen more of him, and especially after tonight, I feel as if you had been saved from a terrible fate. Set free for a beautiful life somewhere, somehow, I hope."

"Yes, mother!" said Lisle with her eyes shining. "I don't believe I could ever have been happy spending my life with Victor. And now, mother, do you mind if we don't talk any more about him? I'm just sick of the thought of him. I'm sorry he has turned out this way, and I'm afraid he is going to have to pay a terrible price for his changed standards, but he's going his way, and I'll go mine, and I'm quite satisfied to have it that way. So that's that!"

"Yes, that's that!" echoed her mother smiling, "and now I'm going to bed. Don't study too late, dearest. Good night!" She stooped and kissed Lisle tenderly, then went out with Lisle's responsive kiss warm upon her lips, and tears of real relief in her eyes. Oh, it was good to have her fears end this way. But was this really the end? Or would the question return and have to be all worked out again? Victor wasn't one to give up easily. She half wished she could take her girl and fly to the ends of the earth, away from that selfish pestiferous young man who felt he owned Lisle, who thought he could go where he pleased and do what he wished, and still come back to her when he got ready. She went to sleep that night with something like a prayer of thanksgiving in her heart.

But Victor wended his way to a haunt of his where he felt fairly sure he would find his new secretary, Erda Brannon. He would take her places, some of the high spots of the city, and show her a good time. They would dance all night if they liked, and to heck with the plant! If they wanted to take the next day off and sleep it through they had a right to, didn't they? It was his office, wasn't it? What did the government have to say about it? It was his father's plant, wasn't it? And besides it was easy enough to explain that some supplies, or steel, or something, hadn't been delivered on time and had held up the work. He could work that out when the time came. Of course if the old man found it out he would raise the heck of a fuss, but he'd been in other fusses with his father before, and he knew pretty well how to get around him, and get his co-operation too.

But though he went the rounds of the night spots where he expected to find Erda she was not there anywhere. But at last, questioning vaguely some light-minded crony, he was told that Erda had said she was on night duty at the plant tonight. Oh, no, that couldn't be so, but in his befuddled brain he figured that he ought to go and see. And so it was at the plant that he found Erda finally, sometime in the middle of the night.

Erda had told him that she was busy that evening. She had a date with an old friend who was passing through the city and had telephoned her to meet him for dinner and the evening she said.

But the old friend who was meeting her was named

Lacey, and the dinner they shared together was in a little Chinese restaurant in the downtown part of the city which the Vandingham's friends did not frequent. And when their brief talk and dinner was over, and Erda's latest instructions explained to her, and notes passed into her hands of certain definite facts she was to obtain at once, Erda went by a devious way back to the plant, and with her own key entered the private office where she worked during the day.

When the night watchman challenged her she showed her pass, told him she was Mr. Vandingham Junior's secretary come for some papers that had been forgotten, and some letters she had promised to mail before midnight, and he let her pass. Later when the night watchman of the midnight shift passed through the hall, saw the light through the transom over the office door and came to see about it, she smiled at him, her best ash-blonde smile and said: "It's all right. I'm Victor Vandingham's secretary. I came here on some business for him. I'm just hunting now for my compact I left here and then I'm going." He went on after a steady look into her eyes, but later he met the night foreman and told him about it, his conscience being tender and his instructions having been definite that no one was to be there that he did not know, and was sure should be. The foreman frowned and volunteered to go and look at her, said he had seen Vandingham with his secretary once. So the foreman went up and Erda exercised her charms on him. He was a lanky homely fellow, and was unconsciously flattered with her smiles. They talked a moment or two as Erda got out her lipstick and did a few repairs on her sensuous lips. Then she looked up confidingly as if it was giving her great pleasure to have this bit of conversation with him.

"You're the foreman on the night shift, aren't you? Your name's Hatteras. Arthur Hatteras. Isn't that right?

I know because I've seen it on the pay roll. That comes through our office you know. Aren't you just thrilled to death to have such a wonderful job? Such a responsible position for so young a man? I should think you would be. Why, you're as important as any general in the army, for without the work that's being done in this plant the whole war might drag on for years and years! And to think it all rests on you sometimes, whether we win or not."

"Oh, no," said the young man grinning and embarrassed. "You know I'm not the only one. There are a lot of us."

"Yes, but only one foreman—when you're on duty of course I mean—and while you're on duty it all depends on you whether the job goes right. And it's such an important job! You know it must be wonderful to stand in that big building and watch those engines going, those strong men working with all their might, those machines pounding away like human beings, all for one thing, that we may win this war and make the world free for—well, for freedom. It's a great work! My, how you must be thrilled to have all that power in your hands even for a single night! It thrills me to even be connected just this much here in the office with working out figures and correspondence that help to make this work go on. And those wonderful machines down there! They tell me there are no other machines in the world quite like those. And they're making such marvelous mysterious things that are almost human, why—almost *divine*, aren't they? Of course no one says just what it is they are going to be able to do when they get the things made and assembled and all, but one can imagine they must be super to be so important. Of course I know no one is supposed to go in and see what is going on, and I wouldn't for the world desire to break any rules which I understand are very necessary for this country's safety, but I have so wished that there was some little window, or doorway up above it all where I could have a tiny glimpse of the general whole, just to carry in my mind as something great with which I was connected. There isn't, is there? Just a little gallery or something where I could get a glimpse of the great dark factory with its brilliant bursts of light and its hurrying working figures down below? Think! Isn't there such a spot somewhere?"

The man grinned at this romantic idea of making a sort of a poetic scene of what he considered mere hard labor, but so winning was this beautiful girl, with her eyes alight and eager, that he actually began to consider. Yes, of course there was the door at the head of the outside stairs that went from one building to the next, and opened on a gallery. One could look down from there. They couldn't see anything much. It wouldn't be against any rules he had been given. It wasn't letting anybody into the buildings without passes signed by the boss, but if she just wanted to get a view of the lights and the men working in the distance why that wouldn't hurt anything. And besides, she was the young boss's secretary. She likely knew everything about the whole show anyway.

And so little by little her smiles and her dreamy eagerness wore down his conscience, and he told her there was a place, but she couldn't see anything much, only light and shadow. And before long he found himself piloting her across the dark yard, up those narrow spiral stairs, and opening the door to the tiny gallery that she might peer in and get her glimpse.

But trust Erda. Her glimpse was plenty. She knew how to edge her way into the place of privilege she craved. She crept unobtrusively over to the slender rail that was put there to guard a workman when for mechanical reasons he had to observe the workings of the important machinery of which he was in charge, and she looked straight down at the bright spinning wheels, the busy gadgets, the sharp cutting teeth that gashed through bright steel with the ease of the wild beast champing up its prey.

"Oh, isn't it wonderful!" she breathed into the ear of the astonished and half worried young man as he watched her raptured face in the flickering light of the furnaces down below.

And even while this was going on Erda was wearing on the lapel of her coat a little button set modestly like the center of a flower among gay petals of metal and sham jewels, glittering brightly and entirely concealing one of the most ingenious cameras that was ever invented. The entirely trustworthy young foreman did not see the white fingers as they touched a spot in the flower and manipulated the turning of another film. Neither did he see the tiny trinket that weighted the end of the soft scarf that she wore around her neck so gracefully, and that responded so silently to the touch of those soft fingers on the fine pliable wire that regulated its operations, and took in mighty secrets in the breast of another tricky camera. No, he didn't see those things nor dream of their importance in the great job he was so proud of doing. He only looked in amusement at the pretty girl who stood there and cooed and asked silly questions and some almost wise ones.

"Oh, isn't it thrilling to be looking down at these wonderful things? Now what is that queer, funny, almost human machine down there supposed to be doing? Cutting up tin biscuits, it looks like. Are all those funny little gadgets it is making really useful? What are they supposed to do? I'm not very wise in machinery, but of course they mean something, don't they, and they all work into this great scheme to win the war, Mr. Hatteras, and as such they are almost sacred, don't you think? And what do they do, Mr. Hatteras? Do they fit into some other gadgets that are important, and do really important things for munitions? Of course I know you're not supposed to talk about these things, but then I'm a part of it all and am in on all these secrets, so you needn't mind explaining a little of it to me, you know. I'm not a mechanic myself, but I should like to understand a little of what this wonderful machine below me can do. Is this machine the one they call—now what is that name? I can't think of it, but the one that is really the heart and center of the whole mechanism?"

The young man looked at her sharply. Was she actually as innocent as she seemed? Did she really know these secrets, or was he wrong in having let her have even so brief a glimpse?

Then he became aware that she was waiting for an answer and started in hurriedly.

"Yes, something after that idea," was all he said, and then wondered just what he had been assenting to, and tapping her lightly on the shoulder added firmly: "Come, we'll have to go now. I'm needed down below."

"Yes," she said dreamily, "just one little minute more, please. This is too divine, this whole scene. I can't tear myself away from it yet. Couldn't you just leave me here a minute or two more? I can find my way down alone, I'm sure I can, and I would love so to watch the working of those machines down there and the movements of all those workers. It is like a moving picture. How I would love to ask a lot of questions about it all. Suppose I just stay here a few minutes while you go down and give what orders you have to, and then you come back here and talk to me five minutes. By that time I'll have such a lot of questions to ask. What for instance is that other machine doing over on the far side? Is it—"

But the foreman's strong fingers had grasped her shoulder peremptorily, and turned her about.

"We're going down now, lady, and this door will be fastened. I couldn't leave you here. It would be as much as my job was worth. And I can't answer any questions either. The government orders that. If you know so much about things you ought to know that."

"What, not even to *me*? Why I write the letters for the firm. I wouldn't be counted an outsider."

"Not even to you, no matter how much confidential stuff you know. It isn't my business to talk about these things to anybody. Now we better get you across this piece of the yard before the night boss comes around. He doesn't like visitors, and above all he doesn't like women around the plant. I heard him say so. Now, down these stairs and here we turn to go around the other side of the yard. That will take you nearer the office door. Shall I call a taxi for you? It's pretty late you know for a lady to be going around this neighborhood alone."

"Oh, I'll be all right. I'll go back to the office and get my compact."

"Better let that go till morning, lady, that part of the building'll be all locked up now, and under the care of the night watch. You better stay here by the door. I'll call a taxi."

And then there came Victor's voice from the taxi that had brought him down that way.

"That's all right, you c'n wait. I gotta lady friend around here somewhere!" His syllables were thick for he had had a good many too many drinks, and his steps were uncertain, but he was coming on down the hall as they entered the back door. Then they saw him halt in the dim light and scan the length of the empty corridor.

"Shay!" he called. "Ish that you, Erda? I been looking everywhere for you. Wantta go danshing?"

Erda's steps quickened as he spoke, and the frightened foreman melted into the night, stepping out the back door into the shadows of the yard and disappeared. Had the boss seen him or not? But the boss was drunk. Would he stop to think what all this might mean? And would that girl tell him what he had allowed her to do? And would he lose his job? Well, no one had seen them, he was sure of that, and he hurried into the edge of the shadows over to the other building and was presently hard at work in the thick of industry. But once he looked up from where he stood by the side of glowing furnaces into the shadows above a certain noble machine, to a frail little gallery up in the dimness, and wondered if any of the workmen could possibly have seen that girl as she hung over the railing to look down, and could have known who let her in. Then he turned his eyes to the great busy machine, with a casual wonder what the girl could have made of the glimpse she had caught. Of course the whole operation was in its earlier stages, and an outsider could not possibly understand anything important yet, but a thing like this must never happen again, not while he was foreman, not if she was fifty times the young boss's secretary—or anyone else! Then he put the whole matter out of his mind and devoted his energies to the work before him. But even so, the memory recurred occasionally, uneasily, and made him uncomfortable, as if he were greatly to blame. He had always considered himself entirely trustworthy, and didn't like to suspect himself of having weaknesses even for a lovely flattering lady.

SEVERAL times Lisle went to the Bible class during the fall and winter. She always went in the car and had the chauffeur call for her at the close, but John Sargent was not there. Another man was acting as janitor. She decided that John Sargent must still be working on the night shift. She wondered how his grandmother was, and thought perhaps she would venture to send her more flowers. But then she hesitated lest he would think her presuming, and putting him under obligation.

But one evening at the close of the lesson the teacher made an announcement.

"Word has just come to me that our brother John Sargent's beloved grandmother went to be with the Lord last week. The funeral services were held yesterday, conducted by her old family pastor from Thurston, under whom she united with the church as a young girl. We should bear our brother Sargent in prayer, that he may be comforted in his bereavement. I understand his grandmother was his only remaining near relative, and that she has been ill for some months. Her death was for her a happy release, but it leaves our friend practically alone in the world. Let us remember him in prayer."

Lisle was startled. So, the dear old lady was gone! And with her death would likely come the end of all possible touch she might have had with the grandson. If she only had sent flowers again before it was too late! And she had not seen a death notice, and therefore had not even sent flowers to the funeral!

She went out from the mission with a grieved feeling that somehow she had lost a dear one too. Strange, when she had never seen the woman. Just heard about her from one who loved her. She had a mental picture in her mind of a sweet-faced, white-haired woman. A gentle lovely lady, she was sure, both from her grandson's description, and also from what John himself was. Even though she had seen him but twice her brief contact with him had taught her that he must have a refined background.

Lisle as she made her way to the door felt greatly saddened that she had not known to send flowers at least. She bowed and smiled to those members who greeted her shyly. She wished she knew them well enough to speak about John Sargent and ask if he had been at the mission lately, though of course she did not.

But when she reached the door there stood one of the men who had seemed to follow her several times lately. He came up to her as she made to pass into the street.

"I have a message for you from your chauffeur," said the man in a low tone. "Something has gone wrong with your car and he sent me to escort you home. If you will step this way I have a car here."

Lisle gave him a startled look, recognized the shifty eyes, the crafty cringing attitude. He was the same man whom she had seen before. She was sure he was. Her instinct warned her to beware.

"Oh," she said backing into the hall again, "thank

you! That won't be necessary! I have friends here. I would rather go with them," and then she turned and went back to stand among the group around the teacher.

Mr. Evans was standing with open Bible explaining some point in the lesson he had just been giving that had not been quite understood by some of his listeners. Lisle stood with the rest and listened, her frightened heart quieting as she heard the trustful words the leader was speaking. Eagerly her mind reached out to grasp the help this man could give her spirit.

Then suddenly as he was talking the teacher looked up right at her, as if they two were the only ones in the room, as if he was talking just for her benefit, and there was a pleasant smile on his lips as though the words he was saying meant a great deal to himself. "You know," he said: "'The beloved of the Lord shall dwell in safety by Him; and the Lord shall cover him all the day long.' That makes a refuge surer, safer, than any earth can give, doesn't it?" And he smiled again as if the message was all her own.

Lisle smiled shyly back, with new wonder in her eyes.

"Do you mean," she said, "that one can so live that he can be *sure* he is beloved of the Lord, so that no matter what perils loom he need not be afraid?"

A light came into the teacher's eyes that reminded her of the light she had seen in John Sargent's eyes once.

"It is not a matter of one's *living*," he said. "We do not merit His love by the way we live. It is a matter of so trusting that you *know* beyond the shadow of a doubt that whatever happens will be what He allows, and that all will be well for you, whatever it is, because you are His beloved. His beloved because He died for you. Because He bought you with His blood, and nothing can come except He allows it. If some things come that we would not choose if we were trying to run our own lives, we can know that He sees that it is going to bring us more quickly to the place where we shall be like His Son. That is what He wants for us you know, that we may be 'conformed' from ourselves 'into the image of His Son, Jesus Christ.' And no matter what it is if it does that for us it is worth it, isn't it? For that is the ultimate that we should desire, to be what He wants us to be."

"Oh!" breathed Lisle softly, a new wonder, and a new enlightenment growing in her eyes. "Then we don't need to be afraid for anything?"

"Not if you are consciously walking with Him, *He* will do the taking care. Our care is that we are being guided utterly by Him. Living so the soul is alive constantly to His guidance. And He will not lead us into the wrong way."

"I see," said Lisle thoughtfully, and smiled suddenly into the face of a tired looking woman beside her who looked as if she wished it were true but wasn't quite certain. Lisle had almost forgotten the immediate trouble for which she had come forward, perhaps to ask help, she wasn't sure. For now she had begun to feel that there was help all about her, over her continually.

"The beloved of the Lord," she said softly to herself. "To think I may claim that!"

Presently the little company began to break up and to walk slowly toward the door, and Lisle walked with them, all at once remembering the man outside who had frightened her. Should she ask someone to go with her to the bus? Did any of them go that way? She wasn't sure, and she wouldn't like to make them go out of their way. And in her heart she prayed, "Dear Father, show me now what to do. Give me safe-keeping home, please!"

She looked up and saw the teacher hurrying. He was

going to meet a train she heard him say. She could not ask him to look out for her and make him miss the train he wanted to meet.

Then her eyes lifted toward the door. Perhaps her would-be escort was gone by this time, and she could walk out and go home by herself. Not by herself, but with her Heavenly Father. Would He help her?

And suddenly she saw, just entering the door, her good old chauffeur. Oh, joy, the Lord had sent Joseph to take her home!

Lisle walked radiantly to meet him, for she saw behind his faithful homely face the glory of the Lord who had sent him.

"Oh, Joseph! You *have come!*"

"Yes, Miss Lisle. I have come right away just as quick as I can. I telephoned a garage and had them look after the car, and I called Mark to bring the little service car, and it's outside here now waiting. You won't mind riding home in the service car once, will you? It was the best I could do under the circumstances. I've left the big car for repairs."

The little old car that was used for house errands, and for the servants, stood just outside the mission close to the curb, and she could see Mark's stubby form sitting behind the wheel. Nowhere could she see the man who had so frightened her.

Thankfully she climbed into the back seat of the service car, and it was not until they were started on their way home that she thought to ask Joseph about that man.

"Who was it that you sent after me, Joseph?" she asked breathlessly. "Was he someone you know?"

"Sent after you, Miss Lisle? I don't understand," said the puzzled Joseph, turning to look back at her from his seat beside Mark. "I didn't send anybody after you."

"Why the man who came to tell me the car had broken down. He said you had sent him to take me home."

"No, Miss Lisle. I send no one. I wouldn't do a thing like that. Your mamma would not stand for my doing that, and in these times I would not dare, either. Send a stranger after my young lady? No, *never!*"

"Well, then, who was he? And how did he know that our car was disabled? What happened to the car, anyway? Did someone run into you?"

"No, no one run into me. Just the car run over something, some broken glass maybe. Anyway *something* sharp, and the tires pick it up. First one tire explode, and then another, and another. Three tires now are out of working. Flat! Useless! And the fourth has some of the small spikes still sticking in the tire. The garage people are investigating. They are bringing it to the attention of the authorities. It was intentional. I don't know if it was meant for us. I thought maybe a accident. But now since you say a man came after you I think maybe intention. There are a great many things going on in the world today since this war started. Definitely, Miss Lisle, we must arrange that you do not go places alone. I think somebody plan to do you harm. For money perhaps. Might be. I must report to your papa. So I come quick. I am glad you do not go with that man. I know nothing about him. I did not see any man at all. It was a lonely place in the street where the car stop. The shops all shut for night. I am sure it must have been intention. But don't you worry. I take care of you, Miss Lisle. Mark and I watch over you."

"Thank you, Joseph! I'm not worrying! I am quite sure the Lord sent you for me tonight. I didn't know what to do. I was afraid of that man. I had seen him watching me before, or at least he seemed like the same one, and I was silly-frightened. But when I saw you come in the door you looked just like an angel from Heaven, Joseph!"

"Well, Miss, I sure am obliged to you for compliment."

"But you see, Joseph, that was a prayer meeting and Bible class I had been attending, and I had been praying that God would show me what to do, and take care of me on the way home. And then He sent you."

"Well, Miss Lisle, I sure am much 'bliged to God for letting me be the one to come." Joseph's tone was awed and reverent. He had never heard his little lady talk of religious matters before and it filled him with a great wonder. He felt that it was really so since his little lady thought it was, and he felt that he must walk softly the rest of the way, at least while this war lasted, for somehow the next world seemed to be terribly near to this one in these days. And if there was glory and angels about there must be then devils and deviltry about also. He hadn't been able to enlist in the great war, because of his age, and his devotion to his dear "family," the Kingsleys, but he began to suspect that perhaps there were ways of serving in this war under a greater General even than he might have had if he had gone out to fight as a private somewhere. A firmer look came about his homely mouth and chin, and a gentleness about his eyes. Joseph wanted to be a true soldier somewhere, and serve to the best of his humble ability.

Elsewhere that evening John Sargent, returning from his midnight shift at the shipyard, looked up to see Kurt Entry falling into step beside him.

It had been several weeks since he had seen or even thought of this man, and John wondered what was coming now. He had sometimes been sorry that he had not pursued the subject a little more subtly and therefore been able to discover more to report to the authorities, for the more he heard of sabotage the more he felt that he had almost uncovered something that might have proved pretty important to the country. Therefore he looked up alertly.

"Well, so it's you again!" he said calmly. "What's doing now? Another fake job?"

"No fake about it," swaggered Kurt. "It's real all right. I've come to give you another chance. It's something really good, so you better do something about it this time, for this is the last chance you'll get."

"Oh, is that so?" drawled John mockingly. "It seems to me I've heard something like that before."

"None of your lip," said Kurt, "or I'm quitting. I know another man would jump at this chance you're getting and no mistake, and I'd have folded him into it quick enough only the boss is hit hard by you, and wants you to take the job. He feels you'll do a better job than anybody else, so I had to give you a last try. But the time has come, and you better say yes at once or the other man gets the chance, and he's all eager for it. Besides, there's a little matter of a lady involved, and a good deed you can do, so that might make a difference to you."

"A lady?" said John with a laugh. "Not me! I don't have anything to do with ladies. I haven't time."

"Oh, *yeah?*" returned Kurt with a sneer. "How about that little lady you took home from the blackout that night? Know her, don't you? A dame named Kingsley? Well, she's the gal I mean. She's in real trouble now, and as far as I've been informed you are the only man who can help her out. Now, does that make any difference? She's been kidnaped and her folks don't know where she's at. It'll probably all come out in the papers in a day or two. Her parents are sort of laying low now to give the kidnapers a chance to get the ransom, perhaps. I don't know much about that part of it. But they tell me if the right man would come forward and take this job I was offering you, and carry this thing through, you could get her released tonight, that is, providing you tied yourself up to the job so you couldn't wiggle out of it afterwards. How about it now?"

John had given the man a quick look when he began this new phase of the plot, and then dropped his eyes and feigned indifference. But suddenly into the silence that followed Kurt's last statement there came an ear-piercing whistle that rent the air about them and seemed to proceed from the opposite corner, and to echo far and wide. Kurt started and looked sharply at his companion to see how it had affected him, but John was looking around casually as if to see where the sound came from.

"What's that?" asked Kurt huskily, and there seemed to be almost a note of fear in his voice. "We better beat it. You take the right road and I'll hide over there in that lumber yard. We can meet after they've gone, over there by the closed gate to the yard. Do you think that was the police?"

For answer there was another piercing whistle, sounding close at hand.

Now John Sargent had an accomplishment which dated back to his early boyhood. He could imitate perfectly a police whistle, and make it sound from any direction he chose. Moreover his officer-friend was aware of this gift he had, and more than once when John was a young boy in school, he had grinned at the lad when a whistle of his had stopped some rash driver from going through a light. John had talked over this matter of the offered job with his policeman-friend, and they had agreed that if he should hear that whistle again the police would answer it by coming at all speed, and if there was a man with him they would understand that he was one to keep an eye upon.

So now, in the not-far distance, they could hear the snappy roar of a police car heading their way, and John Sargent grinned affably.

"No need for you to get excited, is there?" he asked Kurt lazily. "If you haven't done anything out of the way they can't hurt you. What's this you say? Somebody kidnaped? You sure? Where is she now? Oh, you aren't ready to tell yet. I see. And they think *I* know her? You say her name is Kingsley? Seems as though I might have heard of her, maybe met her once, but nobody would ever associate her name with mine. I'm not in her class at all. Why should they pick me out to come to her rescue?"

"Why you see they *want* you, and if you'll agree to carry out this job in the right way, and put yourself under contract to do it, they'll put you on to how to set her free. Give you an advantage with her all righty, too, can't you see that? You set her free and bring her back to her family, and papa'll be so everlasting grateful he won't even think of that class-business you was talking about. You'll be right in the swim, and everybody happy, see?"

12

WHILE Kurt had talked a police car had turned the corner and suddenly gone silent, rolling so quietly to their side that Kurt had a feeling it had gone around another street. Then suddenly there was a voice.

"Is this your man, kid?" and looking up with a start Kurt saw the police car and several dark silent figures on the pavement close beside him, their rubber-shod feet quite unheard by the man who had thought he was just putting over a big deal, and making good on it.

"It's *one* of them," said John Sargent. "He's just been giving me a new line of talk about a kidnaping he wants me to stop. It's Big Kingsley's daughter. Better take notice."

Kurt Entry started to slink into his accustomed invisibility, but a heavy hand was laid on his shoulder, and another on his arm, and a pair of steel bracelets were snapped about his wrists. That one man was caught. A man, too, who had been most successful in many an unlawful operation, both in this country and in Europe. Perhaps he had grown too confident in his own powers, and was so sure that he was going to get away with this job, also.

But Kurt Entry was not figuring on Lacey's having failed in his mission of the kidnaping. Lacey did not as a rule fail, and the agreement had been that if anything should go wrong a small boy who was known to them both would somehow communicate with him. Lacey hadn't stopped him. There had been no small boy on hand to beg for five cents to pay his bus fare home. Kurt hadn't been able to sight that small boy anywhere. Could it be possible that some harm had come to him? He wasn't a boy who had things happen to him. He was smooth and sharp and slick as a whistle about getting out of jams. If he only was about there were ways he could send a message, signs agreed upon by gestures, or when it was dark there were sounds, coughing, clearing the throat. Ordinary little sounds that would never be noticed by an outsider. Hark! What was that? A cat squalling! That was the boy, showing that he was aware of what had happened. He would report to Lacey of course. Kurt had only to lie low and keep his mouth shut and eventually Lacey would find a way to set him free. Yes, even if they locked him up for the night he would be released later. He cheered up and cleared his throat strenuously. He blew his nose, and he put forth a pitiful plea that he knew nothing about this whole affair. That would let the boy see what was going on. He would be rescued.

But what Kurt did not know was that Lacey's part of the plan had failed. That he had not been able to kidnap the girl. She had not fallen for his plan to take her home. And that being the case, Lacey himself was in no position to do any rescuing. As for Weaver, he had departed hastily for parts unknown, not wishing to be mixed up in any trouble with the "big Kingsleys." Of course he had planned such an escape as a possibility from the first. But a quick message to Lacey instructed him to get hold of that Sargent kid at all costs, or failing in that, take the girl, and see what could be done with her in getting facts. "Definite information is imperative at once, at all costs."

There followed a number of sessions between Erda and Lacey, and Erda was more and more entrusted with delicate situations to be dealt with, involving heavy risks both to herself and to those for whom she worked.

That first trip of Erda's to the inner buildings of the plant was not her last one by any means. More and more she found means to an access that would better reveal the inner workings of the plant, and the new inventions. So, quietly, unsuspected, the knowledge of vital facts, even to the delicate measurements made by accurate instruments especially designed for this particular operation, were not only measured by expert hands, but also photographed from every possible angle, until an exact duplication of every item with which the Vandingham Plant had to do, went traveling out to the enemy.

And day by day the men who were making these marvelous death-dealing instruments, sworn to keep their secrets inviolable, labored on with the one thought in mind that they were giving their strength and the labor of their hands to make the winning of the war possible for their country, and for freedom. And they never suspected that there was one stealing in and out among them like a ray of lovely sunshine—"the young boss's girl" they called her now—giving her smiles and her laughing words here and there, cheering them on their way, who was undermining all that they did. She was giving away all their precious secrets to the enemy who was on the other side of the ocean. She was working away with a fiendish intensity to beat them to their goal and steal their ammunition before they had even completed it.

And so the days went on, and only Kurt Entry went to jail as yet, because they could not find the other men who were in absolute hiding. Only Lacey remained at large, for he had ways of disguising himself, and getting places, and he was important to the whole outfit. In fact he and Erda were quite a team in themselves. His main object now was to get hold of John Sargent, for Weaver was still determined to have him in their service. Some incident of his past that had been brought to Weaver's knowledge had impressed him as being one who would be invaluable to them, and if he made good in this Vandingham affair it would be a sort of a test case, and also bind him to their cause.

But John Sargent, after he had whistled Kurt Entry into custody, could not get away from the memory of his last words. Was it true that Lisle Kingsley was in trouble? That anyone had dared to lay hands upon her and imprison her? He ought to do something about that. Or should he, more than he had already done by telling the police? Maybe it was all a hoax, and they had merely been using her name to tempt him. But if it wasn't? If it should be true, and he was the only link between Lisle and safety he surely must do something to find out. Oh, if he had only had his head about him and made that sneaking reptile tell where she was before he gave the signal to the police. He wasn't a very wise person or he would have led this man on to further revelations before he gave him over to the police. The only thing was that he happened to know that just then the police were about to start out on their rounds, and if he gave the signal before they left he would stand some chance of having them get his man. Perhaps after all it was best so, for if it were true that Lisle was kidnaped they would have one man at least, and might be able to put him through such a grilling that he would *have* to tell what he knew.

But John was not happy about leaving it at that. He had to do something himself. He simply *had* to find out right away whether Lisle was safe or not. He hesitated to call her on the telephone, for that seemed a presumption, and if she was at home, and safe, how could he explain? He wouldn't want to say he called to see if she had been kidnaped. If she was safe then he ought not to let her know that such a thing had been considered. Or ought he? Perhaps she ought to be aware of danger and be on the alert. Yet was it fair to fill her with fears? Perhaps he should hunt up her father and tell him. But no, that didn't seem the right thing either. Why cause alarm to her father and mother when there might be nothing to it at all? Take it all in all John Sargent had never been in quite such a perplexity. But after considering a moment he walked straight into a drugstore and looked up the Kingsley number. Even after he had it he stood for a moment in the booth considering before he finally called the number. He found himself trembling as he waited. Would she be at home? Oh, if he could be sure it would be her own voice that would answer! If she wasn't there he must surely do something. He couldn't take any chances. He would perhaps have to go to the police and ask advice next if he didn't find her. What a fool he had been not to have asked a few more questions of that man! He could have acted as if he was considering taking the job, and the creature might have told him more.

Then he heard a man's voice. That would be their butler. It sounded like a servant.

"I would like to speak to Miss Lisle Kingsley, please," he said, trying to make his voice as steady as possible. "Is she in?"

"I'll see, sir," said the servant. "Who shall I say wants to speak with her?"

"Mr. Sargent," said John. "John Sargent."

The servant went away with a deferential murmur and was gone several minutes. John stood there anxiously waiting, growing momently more troubled. This was a terrible situation if he really was responsible for this girl's safety. Then the servant returned to the telephone.

"I'm sorry, Mr. Sargent, Miss Kingsley has not come in yet. Can you leave a message?"

"Oh!" said John Sargent, a great lump of fear springing up in his throat. "Do you—? That is, has she gone somewhere that I could reach her by phone? It is quite important."

"No, I'm afraid not," said the butler. "I understand they do not have a telephone at the place where she is. It is some sort of a chapel, I think, where they have classes. Perhaps it might be some of her war work."

"Oh!" said John almost incoherently, "is it a place where she is in the habit of going? I might try to find her. Did she go alone?"

"Oh, no! She did not go alone. Madam her mother does not permit her to go alone in the evening in these days. She went in the car with the chauffeur. The chauffeur has not returned yet."

John was getting his senses back, just as it used to be when he was in athletics and had made some strategic play, and didn't know yet whether it was going to reach its destination or not. Then there would come an instant of clear thinking, and his mind would be on the alert for the next play. So now he was thinking on. He had to bear this anxiety yet again. She was not back! How long dared he wait before he did something more definite?

"How soon could you reasonably expect her?" he

asked, trying to give his voice a natural business-like sound.

"Well, she ought to be in any minute now. They don't often stay as late as this. But I should say in a half-hour at least."

John considered, his heart heavy within him.

"All right, then, I'll call again," he said.

"Very well, sir."

A moment later Joseph called up to have Mark sent with the service car, and so put the butler's mind at rest. The young lady was all right. The chauffeur was looking after her. But John Sargent carried a heavy heart as he dialed the number of the police station and held a worried conversation with his friend. No, they hadn't been able to get any information out of the man they had arrested. "He said he never heard of Miss Kingsley, and didn't know what we were talking about. He's a shifty baby all right," finished the policeman.

"Yes, I was afraid that would be what he would say," said John anxiously. "I should have made him tell me more, only I was afraid you would be gone, and we would get nowhere."

"It's all right, kid. We'll call up her house and ask to speak to her. We just tried but the wire was busy."

"Yes," said John, "I was trying to get her myself, but she hasn't come in yet."

"That so? Well, we'll keep watching. Don'tcha worry, kid. You ain't ta blame. We'll get the other birds and find out all about it."

It was a little more than half an hour before John ventured to call the Kingsley house again, and then he held his breath till the answer came.

"Is Miss Kingsley at home yet?"

"Yes, Mr. Sargent. They have just come in. There was an accident to the car, that is, they ran over some glass or nails or something, and they had to telephone for the service car to be sent for them. But they are just entering now. I'll call Miss Lisle."

John stood there in the booth with the cold sweat standing on his forehead, and he found an inward trembling from head to foot. The horror and fear were over, for the time. Thank the Lord! Then he heard her voice, and it thrilled him as a voice had never done before. Afterward he called himself to account for that, but just now he was too weak with gladness to take account of it.

"Oh, I am glad to hear your voice," he said, his own trembling with relief. "I was afraid—I was afraid something might have happened to you."

"No! Oh no. They told you about the car and how Joseph telephoned for the other one to come, didn't they? But I wasn't in it, you see, and didn't know that anything had happened to it till Joseph came for me."

"Well, I didn't know about the car," owned John, "but I just had a feeling you might have gone down to the mission, and I was worried, because in a way I was responsible for your going there in the first place. And I've been hearing—" he paused, realizing that he must somehow explain this without being too explicit, without frightening her. "You see I've been hearing that there are some rather tough characters around that neighborhood. I had reason to think there were, and I felt you ought not to be down there alone. I wish you would promise me you won't go down there alone any more."

"Oh, but I don't. Joseph always comes for me, and if I go late he usually takes me, too."

"Well, please be careful, won't you? Don't trust anybody you aren't sure of. There are lots of unpleasant things happening these days. You are too—too—*precious*—to be running any risks!"

"Why, Mr. Sargent! How queer for you to talk that

way! And tonight when I really had almost a scare. A man whose looks I didn't like came to me at the close of meeting, he was right outside by the door, and he told me my car had had an accident and my chauffeur had sent him to take me home."

"Oh!" groaned John. "You didn't go with him?"

"Why, no, of course not. You see he was a man I had seen before who seemed to be staring at me. I've seen him a couple of times in different places, and it sort of made me uneasy, so I thanked him and told him he needn't wait, that I had friends in the hall and would rather go with them, and I went back to the teacher."

"Thank the Lord!" said John Sargent fervently. "I think that is the man the police are looking for, and that was why I was worried when I called up and found you were not at home, and so late! So I called again for I was uneasy."

"Well, that was awfully kind of you. I have been wondering what had become of you. And then tonight they announced that your grandmother had died. I felt so sorry for you. And yet I know it must have been good to know that she was really at rest and in Heaven."

"Yes," said the young man. "That was the main reason for my daring to intrude upon you. I wanted to tell you of her going. You had been so kind in sending her those flowers. I shall never forget that."

"Oh, but I'm sorry that I did not send her more. I thought of it several times, but I was afraid perhaps you would think I was presuming."

"Never!" said John Sargent. "How could I feel that way about a beautiful kindness?"

"Well, I would have loved to send more flowers and also to send some to the service if I had known about it. I never read the death notices, and of course I didn't know. But I did want to let you know how I sympathize with you."

"Thank you," said John. "That means a lot to me. And some day in Heaven I'm sure my little grandmother will be thanking you too."

"Oh, what a lovely thought! I shall look forward to that!"

"And now I mustn't keep you any longer. I know you must be tired. But I do want you to promise me that you will never go down to that neighborhood again alone, please? I would love to take you down sometimes if I were free, but since I can't, please get someone to go with you. Or else don't go. Will you do that? It's important, or I wouldn't ask it."

"Why, thank you for your interest. Yes, of course I'll promise. In fact my mother is rather worked up about it, and would be more so if she knew what happened tonight. She insists that I go in the car, so you needn't worry. But I'm sorry you had to miss the meeting tonight. It was wonderful!"

They talked for several minutes about the message, and then before he hung up he asked Lisle to describe the man who tried to take her home. What did he look like? And Lisle did her best.

"He's medium height, sort of slender, and drab-looking, hat drawn down over his eyes, a little round-shouldered, with his hands in his pockets and his coat collar turned up. Of course it was rather dark out by the street door, and the light from the street lamp shone right into my eyes, but that is the impression he gave me."

"Well, I guess it's the same man I saw one day. Wanted me to take a crooked job. Has kind of a whine when he speaks, doesn't he?"

"Oh yes, definitely."

"Well, thank you. Now, take care of yourself."

"Oh, but I don't have to take care of myself," said Lisle with a little lilt of a laugh in her voice. "The teacher quoted a verse tonight, and I'm taking it to live by. 'The beloved of the Lord shall dwell in safety by Him, and the Lord shall cover Him all the day long.' He helped me to see that I would not be presuming to take that for mine, and that I might count myself 'beloved' of the Lord."

"Oh yes, of course. I'm glad you feel that way. I'll be praying too that He will guide you. Well, good night!"

"Good night," said Lisle softly, and then: "But oh, where are you now? You said you had moved. May I have the address?"

But John Sargent had hung up.

"Oh," mourned Lisle. "Why didn't I find that out sooner?"

13

BUT John Sargent seemed to have disappeared from off the face of Lisle's earth again. He did not call up the next day as she had hoped. He did not write. And when she tried to call him on a telephone at the place where he had told her he worked, they said there was no such person there at that time. He might have worked there some time ago, the janitor wasn't sure, but he wasn't there now. And, no, they didn't have his present address. He hadn't left a forwarding address.

She did not know that there had not passed a day since the night he talked with her, that he had not walked by her home, sometimes several times. She did not know that there had not been a day when he had not communicated quietly over the kitchen telephone with Joseph, or with the butler, and found out in a business-like way of the safety of the young lady of the house, for he had made a compact with the butler and the chauffeur to keep a watch on her, and had told them how to let him know if anything was wrong, or she should be missing. Not that he revealed his identity, only as a friend. "One of the boys she had helped"—he called himself, to the servants—who had found out that certain gangsters were trying to pull something with her as the victim, and he was doing his best to stop it. Neither did Lisle know that he had gone that first night, as soon as he hung up the receiver, straight to her father and had told Mr. Kingsley all he needed to know to protect his daughter, without troubling her too much with nervous fears. She did not know that even her mother had been made aware that great protection should be about her. And of course she did not know that the police were a guard about her continually wherever she went.

Oh, it is true that John Sargent's policeman-friend did call at the house one early evening just after dinner and ask to see her for a brief interview. And her father, after speaking with him first, came back to Lisle with a smile on his kindly face.

"I suggest that you go in and see him, daughter," he said to her, as if it were a matter of small moment. "It is only right that we should do our best to help the police, who are our natural protectors, to do their work well. You needn't be startled, child. He merely wants to get your impression of the man who offered to take you home that night that Joseph had the accident with the car, and I think you should try your best to remember everything you can about it."

So Lisle went into the reception room, met the police officer, and did her best to describe Lacey, even mentioning the other times when she had thought she saw him watching her.

The officer thanked her, and said he thought he had a line on the man, and that her description tallied with their suspicions. He told her that it was important because it was linked up with something some spies were trying to pull off for the enemy. Although she personally just happened to be the intended victim that night through whom they hoped to work their plans. But she needn't worry lest it would happen again. They thought they had the kingpin of the gang safe in jail, and were now sure of this other man, perhaps another who was the head instigator. Then he smiled and went his way, and Lisle heard nothing more about it, and did not even know certainly that there had been a plot to kidnap her. Her main concern was that she could not get into touch with John Sargent again, and tell him of some wonderful comfort she had heard at the class that she thought might help him.

So the busy days went on, and Lisle was deeper and deeper in war work, going to classes whenever her duties at the university did not interfere, going to her Bible class at the mission whenever she could persuade someone to go with her. Sometimes it would be Joseph, or Mark, or even the butler, but often it was her mother. Once her father went and sat studying the plain simple people with the radiance of trust and peace in their faces, wondering how these people seemed to have gotten hold of such deep wisdom, half deciding that he too some day would take time to find out just what it was all about, and if there was anything in it that they with all their wealth and culture and righteousness were in the way of missing.

Every time that Lisle went to the mission, or even went abroad on the street, she was always looking for the young man with the very blue eyes, and the true smile. But he was never there. And because she had kept silent about him so long she was shy about mentioning him, so her mother and her father, who in a way were very close to her innermost feelings, knew nothing about her contacts with John Sargent.

And then, the very next time she saw him he was in uniform.

Lisle had been taking a visiting girl friend to her New

York train. As she waved farewell and turned to walk back to her car where Joseph was waiting, she saw a group of soldiers standing on the other end of the platform, and foremost among them, standing just a little apart and looking back toward the street as if he were searching for someone, stood John! In uniform!

Lisle's heart gave a sudden quick leap of mingled dread and triumph. He was in *uniform!* He had said he wanted to go, and now he was going. But oh, he was *going!* That was something else she hadn't considered yet. How she was going to feel about having him go away? Of course she hadn't been seeing him much. What right had she to have that desperate sinking feeling? He was nothing to her but a casual acquaintance. That she had allowed him to become something more in her thoughts was a matter she had not reckoned on. That would have to be dealt with later when she was by herself with her thoughts. But now, he was here, and she was seeing him! She could have this to remember! How fine he looked in his uniform!

All this was just a bit of coloring in her mind as she went with swift steps to meet him.

As if he had been drawn by her very approach to turn, he looked behind him and saw her coming. Then quickly he dropped the suitcase he was carrying and hurried to meet her, his smile lighting up his face like a flash of sunshine. He came with both hands out, a quiet eagerness upon him that she had not seen in him before. Her own hands went out to meet his, and so they met clasping each other's hands, and looking into one another's eyes.

"Oh," she said, speaking first, almost breathlessly. "You are *going!* I did not know you were in the army! I'm so glad I happened to meet you!"

"Yes, it is great luck for me! I almost got up the courage to call you and say good by, but I really had very little time. My orders just came through, and it was all I could do to rush what I had to finish and get off at the time ordered. But I wanted to see you. I wanted so much to know if you are all right. Of course I've had a report from the detective people who are looking after you in a way you know—" he smiled—"You knew they were going to do that, didn't you?"

"Why, yes, you told me something like that, but I supposed that was only for a day or two. I thought that was over long ago."

"No," said John, looking down at her with an almost loving look in his eyes. "It is still going on. They have orders to keep you in mind as long as any of that gang is at large, although I don't believe that you'll have any more trouble now that I'll be gone. You see they had tried to rope me into one of their spy gangs, and as they happened to see us together that night of the blackout, they figured that you and I were friends, and that if they got you in trouble they could bribe me into telling them what they wanted to know, by promising to let you out if I came across. Only you see they missed fire when they tried to get you into that man's car, and their man got arrested. So I really think you'll have no further trouble with any of that gang. If I thought you would I don't believe I would have had the heart to go away. I couldn't see anything happening to you."

All this time they were gripping each other's hands, and looking into each other's eyes, breathlessly aware that it was a train they were waiting for, and that when it came it would snatch them inexorably apart. They were irrationally unaware of any who might be observing them. And because it was something so new and so glad to them both to have found one another at this the last moment as it were, they had thoughts for nothing else but the moment.

She smiled gently.

"You know, it's rather wonderful to have someone— someone outside my home I mean, take that much thought for me."

"It has been great to feel I had the right," he said meaningfully. "Just because I happened to know some danger that those who were closer to you did not know. I am so glad you did not resent my interference in your affairs."

"Resent!" said Lisle with a wonderful, understanding look. "Does one resent God's care? And yours was very much like His I think, so quiet, so thoughtful, that I didn't know it was there. I can never thank you enough."

"I don't want thanks," said John with a close pressure of the hands he held. "It is enough if you will count me in a measure as one of your friends."

"Of course. In full measure," said Lisle warmly, nestling her hands softly in his. "I am glad you are my friend. Only, I wish you did not keep out of sight so much. I wish—I *wish*—you didn't have to go away. Though of course I know it is right that you should. But you were doing defense work in the shipyard, weren't you? Wasn't that just as important as going?"

John shook his head.

"Yes, it was defense work, and important, but an older man who couldn't be accepted for actual fighting could do what I was doing, and I have known for sometime that as soon as I was free, I must go. It was as if I heard a trumpet sounding in my soul, calling me. I felt I must!"

"Oh, that is a beautiful way to put it!" said Lisle. What a wonderful exceptional young man he was! The thought fairly blazed in her eyes, shone in her face, and her fingers answered the pressure of his clasp on her own.

Then steadily his clasp tightened, as he looked down

into her eyes and saw she was sincere. And something unspoken thrilled between them, some intangible sweetness that was almost like a physical touch, and a great joy came into Lisle's heart. It was so keen that it reminded her of that first time she had seen him in the street and they had smiled. That time that she had known they were friends, and would be always, even if they did not meet for a long long time. That memory flashed through her mind and became a part of her brief knowledge of him, even while she drank in the look in his eyes, the admiration in his face.

Around them the world was going placidly on, with all eyes for the group of soldiers in their fresh new uniforms. The by-standers were filled with pride in their country, and their army, and the victory they were expecting to celebrate very soon, because these fine-looking young men were going over somewhere, anywhere, to deal with the enemy.

But there was something more than just admiration and patriotic pride in the look that Lisle had for John. It was much deeper, with a hope far beyond the few months or years that men allowed for any war. It was a tender regard that looked forward into the eternities. This John was going away, yes, but wherever he was he was looking forward to a day when there would surely be a Heaven to come to, and where they two would surely meet. Yes, even if the vicissitudes of war should separate them so that he would not be coming back *here*.

Of course there was no time to think out all this. It was merely a quiet atmosphere that gave the grave lovely setting to their little meeting.

Of the people who saw them there were a few taking special notice. There were John's fellow-comrades. They were interested in "that guy Sargent." He wasn't well known to them yet, as they hadn't been together long, just a few days, and were only linked by the order that was sending them to a certain training camp together, with a common destination. But they were interested because he was one of themselves, and there was a pretty girl talking to him. An exceedingly pretty girl.

"Know who she is, don't you?" swaggered one soldier whose home was not far away. "That's that Kingsley dame. Her dad's one of the richest and most influential citizens in this city. What he says goes. That's what he is. And she's some lady! Say, that guy Sargent must be the tops or he wouldn't know *her.*"

"You're right there, comrade. I've heard about her. Gosh! He's going in company like that and he's going to be in our gang! Well he needn't think he can lord it over me. I'm really tough, you know."

"Yes, here too," said the other fellow. "But I wouldn't judge Sargent was stuck on himself. He seems more common-like and real accommodating. Anyhow, just knowing her doesn't say he's in her class."

"No," said the other, "not positively, but he sort of acts as if he might fit in anywhere."

So they stood and watched the two, noting the eager glances, the held hands, the low murmur of conversation.

"Yes, sure they know each other real well," said one of the soldiers. "They've been places together, and like the same things. You can see that with half an eye. Just watch 'em. Aw—they won't know you see 'em. They're too absorbed in each other."

Two girls across the street were gazing over at the uniforms.

"Isn't that Lisle Kingsley over there with that soldier? Say isn't he stunning-looking! Has she fallen for someone at last?"

"Oh, it's probably a cousin or in-law of some sort,"

sneered the other girl. "She's good friends with all the soldiers at the canteen of course, and every fellow likes her. But I never saw her hold hands with any of them, and right before the world this way! He must be a relative. She's just awfully prissy, you know, old-fashioned as a white violet and twice as shy."

"Well," sighed the other girl, "when that kind fall for a fellow they really fall!"

And out in the car Joseph, the chauffeur, was watching furtively. He had already identified John as the young man who had called up on the telephone that night of the blackout, after they got home with the car, to know if Miss Lisle was at home yet. And he seldom forgot the sound of a voice. He had called several times since, and there was something dependable about that young man's voice, and about the way he walked and stood. He had been watching him before, once or twice seeing him in the company of that police-detective who was handling the matter of the men who were supposed to be kidnappers. Joseph was canny. He could put two and two together, and knew the look of the blue-eyed soldier with the golden hair and the wide smile. Although he had never seen John in uniform before, he felt sure of his identity, and he watched his young lady with satisfaction as he saw her welcome this man with a light in her face. He hadn't known before this that any of the Kingsleys knew this young man more than just casually. He had not known that Lisle really counted him as a friend. So now he kept them in his vision while he sat, apparently just waiting.

Far in the distance there was a faint echo of an oncoming train, and the two young people, talking eagerly, hurried their words, an almost frantic look of haste in their eyes.

"Is that your train?" asked the girl breathlessly.

"Yes, I'm afraid it is," said the young man with a

quick glance at his wrist watch, and another up the tracks.

"Oh! I wish we had a little more time!" she said wistfully. "I,—you—!" she stopped and her voice and lip trembled just the least bit. "It seems as if I had known you a long time, and it is hard to give you up. But of course I know about that trumpet. Of course you must go! I'm *glad* you want to! But—I wish we had had a little time to talk. If we could only have had an evening!"

"I thought of that last night. I almost called you up to see if you were at home and whether I might come."

"Oh, why didn't you?" she said sorrowfully. "I *was* at home. I would have been so glad to see you."

He looked earnestly down into her lovely eyes. His fingers clasped hers closer.

"I—felt I would be presuming," he said gravely.

"Presuming?" she asked with a troubled look. "Why should that be presuming?"

"Because—Well, because you are a Kingsley. Your father is a great man. Wealthy, influential, prominent,— You belong to the aristocracy, and I am a nobody!"

"Oh! *John!*" she reproached with tenderness in her tone. "Oh, you are a child of the Heavenly King! How could you be higher? *We* are not above anybody. We are just *people*. My father and mother are not supercilious, they are not what you would call 'snooty.'"

"No, I did not think that! I was more considering the fitness of things. Comparing your background and mine. I couldn't see that your people would be pleased with a friendship such as ours would have to be, at least for a long time. Oh, it wasn't that I didn't want to come. Believe me, I did. Won't you believe that?"

His hands clasped about hers were saying deeper sweeter things even than he was daring to utter with his lips, and she was searching his eyes gravely, knowing that he spoke the truth.

"I do believe—" she said softly.

The train was almost upon them now and drowned their words, giving them a moment's sweet privacy, with the vivid consciousness that it was to be exceedingly brief.

The train came to a halt and the group of soldiers piled noisily aboard, the civilians who had been waiting farther along the platform moved up and choked the steps, filing in, anxiously stretching their necks to make sure there were still some vacant seats. The platform was all at once empty.

"All aboard!" shouted the conductor, and the engine began preparations for an immediate start, the wheels giving a preliminary slow turn.

"I must go!" said John. "This is the last train that can make it in time."

He gave her one last look deep into her sweet eyes, that all at once were filled with sudden tears. Then he bent and held her close.

"Do you mind?" he murmured as his lips sought hers in reverent tenderness.

Lisle lifted her face, and her lips clung to his for that brief instant.

"Dear!" he murmured as he turned away, caught up his luggage and swung himself on the platform of the last car just sweeping by.

"Oh, be careful!" she cried ineffectually as the train rumbled triumphantly past her, carrying away her soldier whom she had but just found.

They stood, he on the lower step of the car, she on the platform, their lips thrilling with that farewell kiss, a great wonder in their eyes, and smiled with something like glory in their faces. That smile of theirs was sending messages across the rapidly increasing distance between them.

Presently John Sargent roused to lift his cap and hold

it aloft in salute, and Lisle with tears raining down her face fluttered a small white handkerchief, watching until the train swept around the curve and passed out of sight. Then she stood still looking at the place where it had disappeared, wondering what had happened to her; her lips still thrilling with his kiss, her whole self trembling with the wonder and the joy of it.

But the train was gone. The place where it had disappeared began to look hazy and dim in the late afternoon wintry quiet, and all at once Lisle realized that this wonderful interlude in her busy life was over, and she must go home. The car was waiting for her.

She snapped into alert and looked toward the car. Yes, there it was, not very far away, although that little time with John there on the platform had seemed so very far away from everything and everyone.

She walked briskly toward the car and Joseph got out and swung the door open for her, with his kindly deferential smile.

"Getting colder, Miss Lisle," he said cheerily. He didn't appear to notice the traces of tears on her lashes. Of course not. He was well-trained, but his heart went out to her. He had been in the Kingsley family a good many years.

Lisle roused and looked up with a pleasant smile.

"Why, yes, it is colder, isn't it? I hadn't realized." She gave a little tremor of a shiver.

"Will you be going back to the Red Cross room, Miss Lisle?"

"Back?" she repeated dreamily. "Why, no, Joseph, I think I'll go right home. It does seem chilly out. That platform is a cold place."

"Yes, it is cold. There's a full sweep of wind across it. And then you stood there quite some time, you know."

"Oh, yes, I did, Joseph. I hope you weren't cold waiting. You see I happened to meet an old friend, and found he was going off to war. I had to stop and say good by."

"Of course, Miss Lisle, I noticed. No, I wasn't cold. The heater was on in the car, you know. But that's a fine young fellow you were talking with, Miss Lisle. That Mr. Sargent. He's one of the finest young men I know."

"Oh, do you know him, Joseph?"

"Well, yes, Miss Lisle, in a way I know him. He's the young man called up the house to see if you was home that night the car had the accident. And he called up often afterwards to know if you was home yet. He's been very anxious about you being took care of."

"Oh, is that right, Joseph? Well he is a fine man. I'm glad you know him. He's really worth while."

"Yes, Miss Lisle. And if he's going off to war the town will be that much worse off without him, I'll say."

"Yes, it will," said Lisle thoughtfully. "He has been very kind."

"He has that!" said the man, inwardly resolving to keep even better guard over the young girl than he had been doing, since this vigilant friend was gone.

It brought a warm glow to Lisle's heart to have Joseph speak in such glowing terms of John Sargent. And thinking back she knew that Joseph must have been a witness to her farewell to him. Her cheeks glowed in the quiet of the back seat as she recalled what that farewell must have looked like. Yes, he had put his arms about her and drawn her close. Yes, he had kissed her. They had both kissed. It must have looked very intimate to Joseph. But it was most brief. After all, girls were all kissing their friends good by. It was different from ordinary times. She need not feel embarrassed. She need not try to explain.

Well, how could she explain? What was there to explain anyway? A kiss? Some people counted that nothing. But Joseph would know that she was not the kind of girl who went around kissing every young man who said good by to her, not even in war times. How did it come that she had done it this time? Yet it had seemed so altogether right and good. It had seemed such a perfect, wonderful happening, a thing to be rejoiced over and cherished in her heart. Something God had sent.

And of course it was. She hadn't gotten any further than that yet. It was something she must think over first before she talked about it, even with her mother. Perhaps it was not anything to be told. Not yet, at least.

She closed her happy lips over the smile, and let Joseph think what he would. She was sure in her heart that he would think no evil of her. And he would never tell what he had seen. Joseph was her good friend since childhood.

So she drove to her home and went quietly to her room in a daze of happiness. It was as if she carried in her heart something fragile and very precious, like a little bird that was singing to her, and yet might break, or fly away if she even thought about it carelessly. She found herself walking into the house, and very slowly, very softly, up the stairs, glad that not even her mother was about, lest the wonderful thing that had happened might slip away into the prose of life, and she be unable to recapture it. She wanted to be alone, to sit down and close her eyes, and go through it all again, to fix it in her memory, so that she could never lose it.

And after she had sat so a little while, living over the sweetness of that embrace, the touch of his lips, thrilled with the look in his eyes, his hand on hers, she arose and knelt beside her bed and prayed: "Oh dear God, keep him safely. I thank Thee."

14

THAT very night Erda was in consultation with Weaver and Lacey, in a little town fifty miles away from the city where she worked.

The two men had sent for her urgently, written a letter bidding her go to a certain telephone in a department store, not too far from her office, there ordered her to be at a certain lonely corner on the outskirts of the city at dark, take the car that would be waiting for her and drive to meet them in an isolated farm house in the country. There would be certain signs by the way, unobtrusive lights, white rags tied on trees occasionally, so that she would know her way, and at a certain village they named she would find a boy with his cap drawn over his forehead, ear laps fastened, a scarf around his neck and a lighted lantern in his hand. This boy would wave his lantern and she must stop and take him in. He would guide her to the farm house and take over the car.

Erda went. It was her business to go. Her ample salary paid her from abroad ensured that she would.

She told Victor that she had received a telegram from a very dear friend in New York who had met with an accident, and was dying. She wanted to see her on a very important matter before she died. She left the office in the middle of the afternoon as if to catch a train to New York, but instead she went in the opposite direction, en route to the isolated farm house, going first to the place where she was to find the car, by devious back streetcar lines and buses, keeping sharp watch for any followers, making sure she was in no way watched. Erda was well versed in such devious ways of escaping espionage.

There was a fire in an old-fashioned kitchen stove in the farm house, and they sat around a kitchen table, by a kerosene lamp, in a room whose windows were covered with black paper. There was no danger of any policemen seeing their meeting or listening for their plans. Erda had been used to such furtive gatherings across the ocean. She had been trained in a severe school.

It developed on this occasion that there were certain important articles wanted which Erda alone could have any hope of procuring. For one thing a set of blue prints of certain parts of the great invention that made the Vandingham plant so secret, and so important to the government. In some way the enemy had got wind of what these vital things were, and were demanding them at once.

It was known by the enemy that the initial gadget which was desired was about to be completed, and tried out, and that others were immediately to be manufactured in quantity. The enemy wanted this first one, also the papers, blue prints, specifications, etc., relating to it at once, so that further manufacture of it would be impossible, at least for a time. Erda was commissioned to get these things without delay, and put them in the hands of the agent within a few hours. Could she do it?

But it wasn't the first time Erda had been up against

such a requirement. That was why she could draw such an enormous salary.

They found a glass in the deserted cupboard, and gave her a drink from a bottle they carried, by way of refreshment. Then the girl went to the empty parlor and put on a set of workmen's overalls from a bundle the men had brought, making up her face so that she was hardly recognizable to anyone who knew the pretty flashy girl. She put on coarse workmen's shoes, and covered her hands with worn soiled woolen gloves. She did up her own garments in a compact newspaper bundle, and came slouching into the room as the two men finished the bottle and looked up.

They watched her a moment with grins of approval, as she stalked across the room with her bundle under her arm. Oh, she was a good actress, even when the part was not quite in her class.

"Okay, Erda," said Lacey. "All set?"

"All set!" she responded cheerfully.

"Another drink?" offered Weaver.

"No!" said Erda. "After all I've got to keep cool, and I don't trust that stuff you've brought."

"Okay!" said Weaver with a grin, and put the second bottle back in his capacious overcoat pocket. "You're some girl, you are! I guess you knew what you were doing when you insisted on getting her on this job, Lacey."

"Didn't I tell you?" said Lacey.

Then they went out into the darkness, locking the door behind them. This wasn't the first time they had used this house as a hideout and a rendezvous. Erda looked back at it as she left. She knew that somewhere about the premises there would be likely to be a short wave radio. Probably in some of the outbuildings. Her quick eye studied the group as they went toward the old barn. It might be up in the haymow. But that old brick smokehouse was perhaps the most likely harbor. In the darkness she could not detect any sign that would make her sure. It might be there was an underground line somewhere that would not show on the surface.

They walked a few paces from the house and Lacey went ahead, to the old barn, presently backing out a battered car from its depths, and they climbed in and sat in silence while Lacey drove cautiously, without lights, until he reached a dirt road at some distance from the house. Then he skirted a piece of woods; and came finally to the road, a back road, which he followed for some distance, till he came to a little way station where a freight train was maneuvering on a side track.

"There she is," said Lacey, who had been watching rather anxiously ahead. "You get into that caboose, Erda. You'll likely find some other workmen there. They're used to carrying men to work early in the morning. They wait here for the express to come along and then they start. You'll get to the city in about an hour, and you better get your work done as quick as you can. Afterwards when you get a chance call me up and let me know how you're doing. Of course if you succeed in getting this accomplished tonight, go to Weaver's place. Here are directions. Probably you better stay away from your office a couple of days yet, and telephone your boss your friend in New York is dead or dying, and you have to stay to the funeral, or something like that. You can fix that up, you know, and when you get back don't look too happy about it. A few tears will throw off any suspicions easier than anything else, if I know anything about your young boss."

"Oh, sure," said Erda. "I'll fix that up all right."

"Be sure to keep in touch with me!" said Lacey, as Erda climbed down from the car and made a clumsy way across the tracks to the caboose which was standing not far away.

"Nice little number," said Weaver appreciatively, as he watched her go. "Where d'you pick her up? Shouldn't wonder if she'll pull the trick off in good shape."

"She will," said Lacey. "She's slick at her job. Been trained over in Europe under men that know their business."

"Well, I guess she's our answer, all right. Probably that man Sargent might have been too conscientious for our purpose. But anyhow, you might keep a weather eye out for him. We might be able to tempt him yet."

"Oh, he's gone to war!" said Lacey in disgust. "That's him all over. Didn't *have* to, but he's gone. He had a good job in a defense plant too, and might have salved his conscience with the idea that it was necessary. But he had to throw it all up and go and enlist. Can you explain that? I can't see any young man, good-looker, good job, chance for bigger things if he would, throwing it all away and going out to get killed. Can you? What's patriotism at such a price? What's the matter with a guy like that?"

"Too much conscience," said Weaver meditatively. "I guess that's what killed him for us. Well, we're doing very well. I think your girl is okay. And we'll see what comes. If she can get possession of that gadget and give it to us we'll be on easy street and our sponsors will be satisfied."

They drove on to a village and left their rented car at a little country garage where they had hired it early in the day, then went their way by bus and trolley to the places where they were at present hiding.

But Erda was lounging lazily in the back seat of the caboose, her hat drawn down over her eyes, which were shut except occasionally when a trainman came through, or when three workmen swung aboard and slouched down in as many seats, setting their dinner pails on the floor at their feet with a clatter, and eyeing the rough looking slender boy in their midst. They had passed her with a couple of curious glances. She looked white and dirty and tired. The world was full of such workers just now. You couldn't figure them all out, but what did it matter? Then they too lolled back in their seats and went to sleep. Noisily. In different keys.

It was still very dark when the freight train rambled into a side track down behind the Vandingham plant buildings, and rattled to a temporary pause in its goings. Erda lurched to her feet and pretended to be suddenly roused, though in reality she had been alert for the last half-hour, watching the window furtively for any familiar lights in the sky, any buildings that would show her where she was. The whole plan of her going was thoroughly in her mind. She was not easily distracted. She was perfectly calm. All was going well.

She stole a furtive look through the window and could glimpse a couple of workmen from the plant coming out the side gate that gave to the tracks. That was where she planned to go in if possible. Would any of the keys she had brought with her fit that lock?

She swung awkwardly down to the track and pretended to stumble gawkily along, acting her part to perfection, even there in the semi-darkness. Then she melted well into the shadows under the wall of the plant, and hunched herself down out of sight. If any of her fellow travelers should rouse and look out of the window they would not be able to see her here.

She walked along to a little jog in the wall where she would be well hidden, and by sense of feeling examined her bunch of company keys, selecting one she thought might open that little gate in the wall. If she could only get in there her way would be plain. This was the time when the workman on that special machine she had been sent to examine was gone to his early breakfast, and the man who took his place would not arrive until perhaps an hour later. She had been noting all such habits.

She stole back to the door in the wall, and flattening herself against the bricks, her face turned from the light, she tried to fit the key into the lock. Oh, would she never find the keyhole?

She turned her tiny pencillike flash light across the lock and off instantly, then worked again. This was the key, she was sure. She had been collecting keys for some time in view of just such an expedition as she was undertaking now. She could hear a train coming in the distance. Was that the express? It would have bright lights, a tremendous headlight, and she would be able to see what she was doing, but on the other hand, someone might see her, trying to get into the back door of the plant at that hour of the night. Oh, she must get this door open and vanish inside before it arrived!

There! The key had slipped into the keyhole at last and with a mighty effort she turned it. Could it be the right one, so stiff to turn? There! Yes, the door was unlocked! She took out the key, and with a quick look up the track where the long sharp headlight was piercing the darkness, she opened the door and slipped inside, flattening herself against the wall till she could be sure whether anyone had seen her enter.

No, the yard was quiet and empty. No sound save the steady monotony of the clashing machinery. No men walking about. The night shift was on, and they were all working of course, except a few in the room where the manager had left to go to his home. The room where she must go.

Swiftly, keeping to the shadows close to the wall, she made her way to the farther door of that special building, hoping thus to avoid meeting any of the men. She knew just about where each one would be working at this hour. She had not spent time in the Vandingham Company without discovering all these important details. It was all a part of the business in which she had had foreign training.

The key for that door? Yes, here it was. She had had that made from a borrowed key when the owner had gone to lunch and left his coat hanging on the wall.

Quickly she unlocked that door, stepped inside the building, and immediately the thrash of the machinery told her that all was going as usual, and none of the workers would be likely to notice her now. There were only two men down here who knew her, and she was sure they wouldn't recognize her in this disguise. Besides they were working at the very extreme other end of the building.

So Erda arrived at the machine she was to search, still unnoticed.

The blue prints from which they worked came first. They were most important. Then, even if she failed to get the gadget itself at once, without the blue prints they would find it next to impossible to produce more without exact measurements. And she knew pretty well where the blue prints would be. In the drawer of the metal case near the big machine. Perhaps it might even be unlocked, but even if it were locked she had the key.

Hiding in the shadows behind the machine, for the workman had snapped out the brighter lights when he left, Erda unlocked the drawers of the metal case, and gathered the rolls of blue prints, sliding them into the paper wrapped around her garments. Then she turned and cast a quick glance about. Where would they have put that gadget? She already knew pretty well its size and shape from the description. And there it lay on the top of the cabinet, just above the drawers, as inconsequential as if it were most unimportant. Just a piece of metal in the queer shape, shining there in the shadow and looking like nothing at all.

Erda's eyes gleamed with satisfaction and her heart missed a beat, but she put out a quiet hand and enfolded the gadget. It wasn't large nor heavy. Just important. The old dejected sweater she was wearing over her rough workmen's garments would easily cover it. She slid it inside her blouse, fastened a casual button of her sweater, closed and locked the empty drawers, picked up her paper bundle and held it across her breast, noting that the gadget made no noticeable protuberance. Then she slid into the shadows along the wall again, and so toward the door by which she had come in. Now, if she could only get outside and disappear before the man that had charge of that end of the room returned, all would be well. It hadn't taken as long as she had feared.

But suddenly she stopped short in her tracks and froze into a silent shadow, turning her eyes quickly to the door across the room. That was the man! He had returned sooner than usual, and he had someone else with him. They were coming across to his machine! If he should discover the gadget was gone before she could get out, all was lost!

Slowly she moved almost as invisibly as a spider might have spun his silken web. If she could just manage to get behind that next machine, she could make it out the side door, and through into the next building. Suppose someone did see her? They would just think it was a new workman, a mere boy. There were so many hundred men in the plant that one low-browed dark slender youth would not be noticed. She knew she looked very like a young foreigner She could pass for that easily in the dim shadows of the part of the building where she would walk

Clasping her bundle closely to her breast, and bending her head with a weary gesture as if she were tired from a whole night of work, she crept on. She was not looking directly at the approaching men. The back of her cap would conceal her face from them. And there! Now she was behind the next machine! One step more and she could get across the intervening space and be in the dim stone corridor between the buildings, and then she would be practically safe.

Just then she heard the voice of the operator for the next machine. He was coming down the wall beyond her, and calling to the man on the other side, "Hey, Jim. Got the finished one over there? I want to check up on something before I set that machine for the next."

Erda stopped petrified. They were coming over here. They were after it, and she was carrying it away! They would see her! They would discover it was gone, and they would raise an outcry. She would never get by if that happened. She would be caught red-handed and her reputation as a spy would be gone. And just when she thought that all her peril was past!

"Okay, Butch. Yes, it's here. Be with you in a minute!" answered the foreman.

The two men across the room paused and looked up. The one they called Jim was explaining something about the building, or the machinery. And it was just by that fraction of a minute that Erda's day was saved. The man they called Butch paused as he came, and turned toward the other two for that second or two, so that the young workman with his newspaper bundle could slip by into the corridor, and be gone when Butch came on with Jim and the other man. She was gone into the dimness of the corridor that led to the yard.

Outside she could hear the steady tramp of the night watchman on his beat, and she knew she must wait inside the corridor till he was gone by, or be challenged and have to explain her presence.

Alertly she watched beside that door, studying the

lock in the dim light. Trying the door to see if it was fastened. It was. In the darkness she felt for her keys, to choose the right one. She had practised this exercise so many times. Yes, here it was. She fitted it in and attempted to turn it but it ground noisily. Alarmed she applied a drop of oil from a little vial she had brought along. Oil quieted so many things that might make trouble.

And now there were footsteps along the corridor, coming from the upper end, the end toward the offices. She had hoped to escape through that exit if this first door failed her. Coolly she turned the key, at last, swung the door open and slipped out, just in time. Some men were coming from the other building carrying some frames between them. Those would be frames for the next set of castings. If she had met them they certainly would have challenged her and put her under arrest until she could explain her presence there.

Out into the yard she came like a shadow. The stars were dim and far away. The sky was still dark. Dawn was yet in abeyance.

Clutching her bundle firmly she made her way to an outer gate where she knew she could get through if the night watchman was not about. She could listen in the dark to make sure of that. If she only knew what time it was!

Just then the city hall clock struck, one, two, three! Ah, there was still time. She could get to Mr. Weaver's rendezvous before it was light enough for many to be abroad. If she could do that she could take the train and get to New York, where for a time at least she would be safe. It would not do for her to be found in this city. Not yet. She must have a perfect alibi.

She hurried along the dark street, her clumsy shoes stumbling at a rough stone. How glad she would be to get rid of these garments, and be clothed again in her own things. Well, if she pulled this off in good shape perhaps she would have money enough to get out of this kind of thing, live like a human being, and not like a spy. But would she be content without excitement? After all she had been raised to it. But if she did give it up would she want to marry Victor? Of course he was wealthy enough, and a fairly good sport in some things, but he was such an awful sap! There were other men in the world, and now that she had money enough to dress as she should, it would be easy to find them. But after all, why bother? She had Victor right where she wanted him, and could get anything from him she desired. Well, she would see, once she got away with this affair. And after all she could carry on her life work as successfully if she were a married woman.

And all this while she was going stealthily through narrow dark streets where no life seemed to be, vanishing into blackness. Till at last she came to a little door in a wall. She pressed a button, and the door swung inward softly, waited for her to enter and then closed. At once a soft light blurred down a passage, and she followed the way as she had been directed.

The room she entered was plain and bare, as any rooming house might have been, and presently Weaver approached from a partly open doorway where he had been able to watch her coming.

"Well, what success?" he asked, looking at her sharply. He was not yet fully sold on this girl as their main spy for this important case.

For answer Erda handed out the roll of blue prints. The grim man unrolled and studied them for a moment, then, his expression relaxing, he lifted keen eyes toward her.

"Is this all?" he asked in his severe tone.

"If that had been all I should not have returned so

soon," she answered haughtily. After all this man must be made to understand that she was slick. She always got what she went for. She took chances with her life sometimes, but she brought back the booty. She reached inside her blouse and pulled forth the coveted bright steel object. "This is what you wanted," she said coldly, and laid it in his hand.

"Ah!" he breathed with a look of gloating in his eyes. "You have brought it. And are you sure this is the one, the *right* one?"

"There are the blue prints, Mr. Weaver," she said loftily. "You can study them at your leisure. As for me I must catch my train to New York."

Weaver looked up with quick comprehension.

"Of course," he said quickly, and brought out a roll of bills, handing them to her. "Have you a place to keep this safely?"

"Certainly," she said crisply.

"Then you will go out the same passage by which you entered and you will find a car parked just outside the door. To the left. The key is in it, and it is being guarded by one of our men, but you will not see him, unless there is some warning to give you. You will drive by the back way to the Forty-third Street station. Get out of the car and someone will immediately take possession of it. You go into the station and find your train. Here are your tickets. You will find a reservation in the Pullman, but you must enter it carefully. They would probably not permit you in the Pullman in that garb if you were seen. You have your other clothing?"

"Yes," said the girl. "I'll change on board of course."

"Very well. Now you better hurry. You haven't too much time to spare, and the next train would be awkward because it will be getting daylight. Here are directions, what to do about returning, and my telephone number. Now, go quickly. You have done well so far. Be careful not to spoil it all."

"Of course not," she said with a little cocksure smile, and hurried away.

15

WHEN Lisle lay down to sleep that night it was with a
wonderful sweet peace upon her. Even the thought that
John Sargent was gone away and that she would not be
likely to see him again for a very long time, because no
one could know how soon or how far the soldiers
would be sent, could not cloud her joy. It was as if some
great gift had been given her. Something that no distance or parting or contingency of life could ever cloud
for her. She felt that now she knew him, his hands had
held hers, his lips had touched hers, his arms had been
about her and drawn her close. That made them happy
in one another in a very special way.

She didn't stop to reason about it, nor think if it was
a wise friendship, or any worldly thing like that. She
just gloried in the sweetness of it without trying to
reason it out at all. The fact that he had gone far away
somehow set the whole matter as a thing apart from ordinary happenings, took away all objections that others
might raise, all plans for the future. There just seemed
to be the now, the today with its precious knowledge
that he cared for her. How did she know that, she

questioned herself? Why, his eyes had said it plainly, as they looked into her own, his lips as they clung to hers had told her. And he had called her "dear" as he left her. Not the silly "Oh, *Do*lling!" that people were flinging about today, but gravely, sweetly "Dear!" That seemed to have more meaning than the common endearments that were not really endearments at all, only imitation ones with no meaning behind them. And he belonged to her Christ whom she was beginning to love and serve. That gave her great joy and peace. That meant there could be no question about him. Even her mother, when she came to know everything about it and understand, could not but approve. But that was something that could wait now. He was gone away, and she could keep it for herself, unless there should come a time when her mother could know him for herself.

She found herself suddenly contrasting him with Victor in a new way. She thrilled with pride over him that he had gone as a soldier. It was hard to have him gone, and there was fear and peril in the thought, yet rejoicing because it showed what kind of a brave loyal man he was. No hiding behind a safe pleasant job at home for him, even though it had been easy. He wanted to feel that he was doing the right thing. He wanted to fight for his country. He had had a safe defense job, and could have stayed, but he had heard the "sound of a trumpet" in his soul and he had answered it. Oh, he was one to be proud of, her John, her Christian soldier boy!

And once again as she drifted off to sleep she felt the thrill of his kiss on her lips, the holding of his arms about her, and his voice saying "Dear!" Oh, there was no room now for Victor in her heart, for Victor had heard no sound of a trumpet in his life, or if he had, he had not answered it. He had listened to the blare of trumpets that called him to please himself. Victor, the little playmate who had always had everything he wanted, and never wanted things for other people, not even for his country, but only for himself.

And with the thought of her young lover's kiss thrilling on her lips she fell asleep, and dreamed of clouds of glory, and a cause of righteousness that was serving their Lord. The glory of the Lord, and the sound of the trumpet!

But when Lisle awoke in the morning, and recalled the joy and the thrill of the meeting with her new friend it seemed to her all like a wonderful dream, and she wondered if it could have been only a figment of her imagination, or just a wishful vision.

Till suddenly the memory of that precious kiss thrilled across her consciousness, and she knew it had been real. And then a joy she had not dreamed existed swept in and enveloped her whole being.

She went down to breakfast with a light in her face, a joy in her eyes, that her mother noticed at once. She had not seen that look in her girl's face since she was a happy carefree little girl playing around all day long. It was something real and her mother studied over it while they ate and talked of trifling matters. She decided that the cause must in some way be connected with Victor. For Victor had been her childhood companion, and they had seemed so happy together. Somehow Victor must have done something to make her happy about him again. At last she said:

"Have you been seeing Victor these days while you were away from the house?"

"Victor?" said Lisle with a dreamy, faraway look in her eyes. "No, I haven't seen Victor anywhere. He doesn't frequent the places I've been inhabiting lately. You wouldn't catch him even so near an army as the canteen amusing the soldier boys. Victor is enjoying himself somewhere. He is a slacker!"

"Oh, my dear! I don't think you ought to say that,"

said her mother. "His mother tells me he is very much interested in his work, and you know it is most important, what the Vandingham plant is doing. His mother says he is extremely busy. Sometimes he cannot spare time to come home for his meals. He feels he is needed at the plant, and he sends out for a sandwich and a cup of coffee."

Lisle gave her mother an unbelieving look.

"I'm afraid Victor's mother doesn't know all about her son," she said, after a moment's thought. "I'm afraid she believes everything he tells her."

"My dear! You don't think Victor would *lie*, do you? Not lie to his mother!"

"Yes, I'm afraid he would," said the girl gravely. "He used to do it when he was a kid of course. Tell her he felt sick when he simply wanted to stay at home from school. Tell her yes, he had worn his rubbers, when I knew he hadn't thought of it. When I knew he had flung them back in the closet after she had gone back to the dining room from telling him to wear them. He used to say he had done errands for her when I knew he hadn't even gone near the place. And I don't believe Victor has changed much since those days. Not for the better anyway."

"Oh, my *dear!* You seem so bitter against your old friend. Don't you think perhaps you have a duty toward him, to help him to better things? How would it be if you were to ask him over to dinner tonight and spend a happy evening with games and music the way you used to enjoy yourselves? I believe you could make him happy again, and make him want to stay around among the right kind of people. His mother is quite worried about that girl he has for a secretary. She wants him back associating with you. She feels he is terribly hurt at you, and the reaction has turned him toward that awful girl. His mother feels that girl is terrible, though the only time I ever saw her she seemed a rather pretty child. A bit too sophisticated, perhaps, for Victor and his family traditions, of course, but not *bad*. Not really bad. I told Mrs. Vandingham I thought she was a little too hard on the girl, and I was sure Victor's upbringing would tell in the end. He wouldn't be led by any but the right type of girl. I'm sure that girl isn't so bad."

"If you had seen her at the party, mother, I'm afraid you would have thought so. She was rather unspeakable."

"Oh, well, at the party. I suppose the poor child has never been out much to the right kind of party, and wouldn't quite know how to act."

"No, mother! It wasn't that! Oh, you don't understand! You wouldn't have liked her actions, her dress, anything about her."

"Well, try to feel as kindly as you can toward her, dear. She probably won't trouble your life at all if Victor comes around all right. And I do think it is your Christian duty, dear, to try to be nice to Victor. Try to lead him back to his old self. To better things. Don't you think you might, dear?"

"No!" said Lisle quickly. "I don't think there is *any-thing* I can do for Victor. I'm done with him, mother, utterly done. He disgusts me. Lying around in a pretty office with a pretty secretary, taking her out to lunch and to dance, and to night clubs half the night, while other men of his age are either in training, or at the battle front."

"But my dear, you don't know many other young men, do you? You have been so exclusively with Victor during the years that you really are quite to yourself now. I blame myself for that. You haven't enough friends. I should have seen to that!"

Lisle laughed joyously,

"Oh, you dear little mother. Don't go and worry

about a thing like that. I have friends galore. Fine friends. You ought to see some of the splendid fellows we have coming to the canteen nights when they are in town. They are *real* young men."

"But you don't know them, my dear. You never went around with them. They may be much more slackers in their hearts than you think Victor is."

"No, mother, you're mistaken. Some of these fellows are true Christian young men, with real purposes in life. You'd be surprised. Some day I want you to come down with me and meet some of them. Perhaps I'll bring them home here for an evening if you don't mind."

"Why of course, child. I suppose that would be a patriotic and a benevolent thing to do, to show them a good time when they are away from home, and I'll be glad to help entertain them. But that isn't like old friends. You surely wouldn't rate absolute strangers ahead of an old friend."

"Why mother, they are not absolute strangers. I've met them again and again. I know what some of them are. You and father couldn't help approving them. Some of them have left fine prospects to go to war because they think it is right. Some are fliers, some are artillery men, some are officers."

"Oh, *older* men, I suppose."

"No, young men, as young as Victor. And they are solemnly glad to go and do their duty fighting. One of them told me that he felt as if he had heard a trumpet sounding in his soul calling him to go."

"Why, how poetic! That sounds like quite a young boy! Such a boy as Victor used to be when he came over here so often."

"No," said Lisle, "he is not so young. He's finished college, and been working for a year or more. And he's not a bit like Victor. Mother, you seem quite sold on

Victor again. I thought you had seen enough of his outrageous actions to disgust you. I'm afraid I see his mother's fine artistic hand in this. She has been talking to you, hasn't she?"

"Well, yes, I had a little talk with her yesterday. She came over to talk with me about you. She wanted me to coax you to ask Victor to come back here. She is very worried about him. She thinks you have cast him off, and she feels it is a great mistake. She says you are driving him into a life that isn't his natural element."

"Well, mother, the next time you see Mrs. Vandingham, please tell her that I am not going to coax Victor over here. I'm entirely satisfied to have him stay away. I don't want to see him any more. And we did quarrel. I guess you would call it that. He wanted me to marry him right away and I wouldn't. I won't *ever* marry him. And I don't want to go with him any more either. I'm sorry for his mother, that she has such a son, but *I* don't want him. I don't love him, and I never could. He says love is all hooey, but I know better, and I don't want any such marriage ever. You wouldn't want that for me, would you, mother?"

"Why, of course not, dear. Love is the foundation of all true marriages. Without it married life would be intolerable. But I thought you used to be very fond of Victor."

"Why, yes, *fond* of him as a playmate. But when I began to grow up I saw how very weak and full of faults and selfishness he is. And I never really *loved* him, even as a child, only in the sense that one is kind and pleasant to playmates. But he can't be even a playmate to me any more. I don't enjoy his kind of play. He's drunk half the time, mother. That's no foundation for even true friendship."

"He is? Oh, my dear! I didn't know that! Why, of course you couldn't go around with one who did that.

But I want you to be sure that there isn't anything you could do to help him, that might bring him back to reason. For his mother's sake, dear, if not for his own. Do forgive him."

"Why, yes, of course I'll forgive him. I just don't want anything more to do with him. I can't help rather despising him, either, a fellow who is downright *afraid* to go and enlist. I'm sure that is what is at the bottom of this ridiculous need for him to take over his father's business. Do you know, I met Mr. Vandingham yesterday, and he looks as well as he ever did, and he said he was feeling fine. I think Victor and his mother cooked up all this keeping him at home, just because *she* was afraid to have him go to war too, for fear he would get wounded."

"Oh, my dear! Do you think anyone would do that in these terrible days when our country needs to keep the world free and safe and happy? Of course I feel sorry for Mrs. Vandingham, but I don't think she ought to do that, even if she did feel afraid. But, dearest, if you are going to feel so hard and bitter I'm afraid you will do yourself out of having any friends at all. I wouldn't like to have you grow up and feel alone, because just your father and mother aren't enough for you. You'll want friends."

"I have friends, mother. Wonderful friends. Though I'm sure just my father and mother are better for me than getting tied up to a young man I would have to despise."

"Oh, my dear, I don't want to get you tied up, of course, not *yet*. Not to Victor unless he changes of course. But I don't want you to be supercilious. Answer me honestly, Lisle. Do you know *any*one that you admire as much as you used to admire Victor?"

Lisle's cheeks grew rosy and she looked steadily at

her mother and answered quietly with a lilt in her voice:

"Yes, mother dear. I *do!* But that's very slight praise, for I never really admired Victor, except that I always knew he was good-looking. But mother, Victor will *never* change unless he should some day yield himself to the Lord Jesus Christ, and then he wouldn't be Victor any more. He'd be God's man."

"Why, my dear! What a startling thing to say! I'm sure Victor always went to Sunday School as a child. I'm sure he has a good moral character, doesn't he?"

"I'm not so sure of that even, mother. And going to Sunday School doesn't always ensure getting to know the Lord Jesus. I went, but I never knew Christ as I do now, and it's wonderful! Of course if Victor could get to know Christ it surely would make a difference in him. But mother, I'm afraid he's so full of self he never would be willing to yield and take Christ instead."

The mother looked embarrassed.

"Well, dear, I never heard you talk this way before. Of course religion does make a difference in some people's lives, but I can't understand why you don't want to work on Victor and try to get him to understand this way of living you profess to have found."

"Oh, I do. I don't feel really well enough grounded yet to go out and teach people, but you know yourself, mother, that Victor never would accept teaching from anybody. Living is all that would count with him. Certainly I want my life to be such that he can see Christ in me. But I'm afraid that would not include making Victor a constant companion any more. Mother, I wish you'd come with me again down to that Bible class. I'm sure you would get to love it."

"Well, perhaps," said her mother doubtfully. "But child, why don't you ask Victor to go down there sometime?"

"Mother!" said Lisle breathlessly. "You know perfectly well he *never* would go, and if he did he would just sit and make fun of it all the time."

"He would go with *you,* Lisle, if you asked him in the right way."

"No, mother, I don't think he would. And besides, I can't make advances to Victor to get him to go to a Bible class. You don't want me to do that, mother. And that is the *only* way I could get him to do *any*thing. You know I can't do that!"

"No, of course not, dear," sighed her mother. "Well, I'm sorry I've troubled you, and I do hope sometime you'll find someone who cares for you who is as good and true and perfect as your father has always been."

"Yes," said Lisle cheerfully, "that is what I want, too. And if I don't get that kind of a man I don't want any. I couldn't really love and trust any other kind."

"Of course not, dear. I only thought there might be a way to help Victor for his poor mother's sake."

"We can *pray,*" said Lisle softly.

"Yes, dear, of course," said the mother again embarrassedly. She was not used to talking freely about religious matters. It almost shocked her to hear Lisle speak frankly about them. She had reserved traditions and upbringing, but she was thoroughly glad her daughter had such sound principles.

"And then, you know," said her mother, "I don't want you to go sorrowing all your days because you can't find a man just like your father."

There was a quiet wistfulness in the smile she gave her daughter, and Lisle bent and kissed her mother sweetly, her heart singing to herself, "But I've found one, mother dear, and some day I'll tell you about it." But she did not speak yet, only gave her mother a second precious kiss. And then said thoughtfully a moment later:

"I'll be praying for Victor, of course, mother. *We'll* be praying. I should have thought of that before."

Then she went to her room to pray. First for Victor, that he might some day come to know the Lord and know how much he needed Him. And then with thanksgiving for the knowledge of another man who was right and true like her father. She might not even see him any more, but she thanked God for him, and let a song ring in her heart about it, giving a radiance of joy to her face that her mother could not quite understand, and yet rejoiced over.

16

THERE was great consternation at the plant five minutes after Erda had stealthily departed with her booty. The sturdy manager had been proud indeed that the wonderful gadget had been completed at last, had passed its tests, and was ready to be reproduced. He felt as if his heaviest burden had rolled away and all things now were to be smooth and easy. And then he walked up to the place where he had left it five minutes before, with the foreman of the other half of the machine, and lo, it was *gone!* He couldn't believe his senses.

"What's the matter, Montie, where is it? What's happened?"

"It isn't here," said the big foreman, his swarthy face white with apprehension. "It couldn't have gone far in that time! What—where—*Who* has been here? Sam!" he called across the room. "Has anybody been in here? B. F? Or Smalley? Or any of the crowd that had a right?"

"No, I didn't see anybody," called Sam.

"Have *you* been here all the time?"

"Sure I have. I wouldn't go away till my stint was done. What's eating you? What's the matter? You didn't think I'd hid your precious old contraption, did you?" and Sam grinned deridingly.

"Why, no, of course not, but where has it gone?"

"Where did you put it?" asked Peters, coming over to join the crowd. "You're *dreaming,* Jim. You've been up too many nights, and got it on the brain. You're going nuts. Take it easy, man, and stop and think. Just *where* did you leave it when you went to your morning lunch?"

"I *didn't* go to lunch. That's *it!* I brought my lunch here in my lunch box, and then didn't take time to eat it. I just went across the corridor to bring Belden here. He wanted to see what it looked like before he got ready to set it up."

"Well, where did you leave it? Now think! Did you hide it somewhere? It isn't very large, you know."

"No I didn't hide it anywhere," said the foreman. "I left it sitting right on top of the metal cabinet there, just where I put it when it was finished. And it isn't there! Say, if you fellows are trying to make a practical joke out of this, it isn't funny! Hear that? It means too much to me and the plant and the government. If any of you fellows have hid that, bring it out *quick* or I'll report you all to Mr. Vandingham, and hold you responsible, every one of you. And you all know the oath of secrecy you're under."

The men looked soberly at one another, weird suspicions creeping unaware into their eyes, but they all shook their heads. No, they hadn't touched it. And one of the older men spoke for them.

"Give you my word, Montie, these fellows were all at their machines working like men. Not one of them stepped over there. I know that for I was waiting for a hot bearing to cool off, and looking around the room. *Nobody* went over by your location."

"And no outsider came into the room?" asked the foreman.

"Not a one," said they all, and looked at one another with troubled glances.

"Who would come?" asked the old man, Hardy by name.

"That young scapegrace of a Victor didn't come? You're *sure?* He's liable to do anything, you know, but I'd be responsible."

"You bet you would," said Sam under his breath. Victor was not popular among the men. They knew his comings and goings all too well.

"Not he!" said Butch derisively. "He's off at a night club getting drunk as a lord with that little smarty secretary of his. If you ask me, I think *she's* a snake in the grass, and if I was running this plant I'd get rid of her first off."

"Try and do it!" said Sam.

"Shut up all of you! This is a serious thing. We've got to give the alarm at once," shouted the foreman. "We'll have to call our guards and see if there have been any questionable characters about. Call the inspector, Butch. Tell him what's happened. But first, lock the doors and search this room. Don't miss a corner. Look *every*where."

"Is anything else gone, Jim?" asked the old man.

A look of fear passed over the face of the foreman. He dashed to the cabinet and pulled open the drawers.

"Yes," he gasped, "the blue prints are gone!" He said it in a terrible tone. "They were here ten minutes ago. I was just looking at them." He gave another desperate look about the room and then dashed to the telephone. This was something the master must know. It was awful to have to waken old Vandingham, but he had the right to know at once, and he was the only one who had a level head anyway.

From then on the plant became frantic.

The streets were deserted, stillness and darkness

everywhere, broken only by search lights, turning steadily back and forth over the neighborhood, but there in the quiet night the plant went on the alert, searching for that small important gadget that meant so much to the war and the country, and the trusted plant. And so very much to the enemy! What would happen if this went on and the government had to find out about it? What would happen to the foreman who had been so proud of the trust put upon him? What would happen to the dependable old plant with its enviable reputation that had weathered already two wars and been trusted through them both? Some of the great machines that had been working night and day to produce as fast as the government needed their work. What would happen were many of them stopped now, while the men who ran them went searching everywhere, leaving no cranny unscanned? But from the first discovery that the blue prints were gone, those in charge lost hope. The enemy had done this, that was certain! Who else would want blue prints? This was no practical joke. It had assumed the proportions of a disaster.

More soldiers arrived, were marched into the plant before day had scarcely dawned, so that the general public was not yet aware of the calamity. Policemen and plain clothes men, and detectives were called upon, and a system of tense guard planned, locking the barn after the horse was stolen. The personnel of the plant was put through a severe grilling to discover if anyone knew anything that might help in the investigation, but the heart of the head of the house of Vandingham was heavy.

Moreover, Victor was missing. Also his secretary. They thought they had gone away together. Victor had often been missing in the early morning, and had turned up later with a heavy hangover from drinking all night. But the secretary had always been on hand. Now, upon enquiry, it developed that she had gone to New York to see a friend who was dying. She had been careful to leave this word with the people at her apartment. Everything seemed to be all right in her direction, although the Vandingham family were sorely worried lest Victor had gone with her. But a telegram addressed to him from Erda presently arrived, stating that her friend was dying and she would probably have to remain away until after the funeral. The detective tried to trace that telegram to its source, somewhere in the outskirts of New York, but it was hard to trace. Erda had been most careful in all her small details. That was one of her strong points, never to call anything unimportant. But nothing was heard from Victor until late in the afternoon, when he turned up heavy-eyed and said he was sick.

They were so relieved that he had come at all that his father refrained for a time from the severe tongue-lashing he ought to have had.

Victor verified the fact that Erda had been called away by a telegram to the bedside of a dying friend. But he hadn't seen the telegram. He had no clue to her whereabouts, and Victor began to learn that the business he was supposed to have "taken over" was really something quite serious. He was questioned by the police, and an official from Washington arrived and took him in hand, looking him keenly through and through, asking him as to his whereabouts last night when the robbery took place. It further developed that he had been with a young girl named Cherry, a waitress at a big department store restaurant during most of the evening, and thus Cherry was brought into the picture and questioned, and wept, and declared her innocence, and finally was able to bring witnesses to prove that she had not been about the plant, not *ever*. Although she knew when she was dismissed that the police intended to keep an eye on her, and she wouldn't be very safe anywhere until this affair was over. She was just a silly pretty girl who quietly carried on a good many escapades with rich patrons of the restaurant, unknown to her quiet respectable little mother at home who was working hard to keep her daughter respectable. But she had it to learn that rich young men who made up to waitresses entirely out of their social class, were not usually to be depended on when real trouble came, and a girl was safer to stay in her own realm and not get her silly head turned by attentions that flattered.

Victor, sullen and unhappy, thought back to the days when he and Lisle Kingsley used to be companions, and wished he could turn the calendar back to that time and have things go peaceably, happily on in the pattern his parents had set for his life. After all, these wild nights he was practising nowadays always left a bad taste in his mouth, and nobody was quite as pretty and well-bred as Lisle. Why had he ever quarreled with her? He could have been more discreet about that. He could have kept his criticisms to himself, until he had her in his power. He could have let her go to any old college she wanted, and trusted to making her over to his plan after they were married. So he sat in his luxurious office and meditated. Cursed his luck. Decided that it was all Lisle Kingsley's fault. If she had just taken his advice and not acted so bull-headed. If she had changed her college and learned a few things she wouldn't have declined to marry him. She wouldn't have acted like a stiff little icicle at the party, and spoiled all his prospects. They would have been married by this time and everything going fine. All her fault!

Then his father came in and began to berate him. His father had usually been rather easy on him, leaving his upbringing mostly to his mother, perhaps because that was the easy way, for Mrs. Vandingham was a very determined woman. But now Victor was a man, and in a supposedly important position in the business. More important because the government was behind it, and had power to revoke contracts and make a great deal of trouble for them. Mr. Vandingham senior was greatly worried by what had happened, a "calamity" he called it, and he came and gave Victor a piece of his mind, straight out from the shoulder. He told Victor he couldn't be a mere playboy any longer. He had to rouse up and take responsibility or he would find himself behind prison bars pretty soon, and he wasn't joking, either.

Victor at last looked up with a sneer. This kind of talk irked him.

"Oh, now, dad, let up on that line, can't you? You make as much fuss about the loss of a little thing as if it was an irreparable loss. They made it in one day, didn't they? They've got the machine all set the way it made it, haven't they? Why can't they make another and nobody the wiser? The government needn't ever know anything about it. Just go ahead and work this out the way you planned. Where you made your mistake was in letting the workmen all know anything had happened. They didn't need to know. But you can tell them you'll skin them alive if they mention it, can't you? And suppose the blue prints *are* gone? The enemy will be sometime getting machines ready to duplicate the gadgets, and by that time you can get some other new invention going. I think it's time this nonsense stopped and the men got to work again. It isn't necessary to carry on when something like this happens. It's bound to happen sooner or later with all these foreigners around the country, and of *course* some of them might be spies. I think it's ridiculous to make such a fuss, and act as if the heavens were falling! I wish you'd let up."

"Be *still!*" said his father. "Not another word like that

out of your mouth! You're an ignorant little upstart! That kind of talk is dangerous. Besides it isn't true! The government already knows all about this affair, and has taken steps accordingly. What do you suppose all those extra soldiers are coming into the plant for, guarding every building?"

"What?" said Victor, starting to his feet and looking wildly around. "You don't mean you told the government? Or did the foreman get rattled and go blabbing it before you knew?"

"Certainly I told the government. Didn't you know that I am under oath to carry on this business openly with the government and report every possibility of trouble as soon as it comes? And didn't you know that *you* are under the same oath?"

"Oh, rats!" said the youth arrogantly. "Shut up! I don't want to hear any more about this. I've got a headache and you're a pain in the neck. What's an oath? Nobody pays any attention to that. It's just a form. You can get by any oath that was ever taken. If you're going to talk like this you can get right out of my office. I've got work to do, and I can't be bothered with you any longer."

"Victor? What do you mean by speaking that way to me?"

"I mean just what I say," said the angry young man. "This is *my* office, isn't it? Didn't you make me first Vice President of the plant? Well, I say get out! You can't interfere with me even if you are my father."

For answer the father arose and seized his son by the coat collar, jerked him across the room to the door, and opening it, flung him out forcibly. Then he locked the door and put the key in his own pocket. His father was a large man and strong, and it was all done so suddenly, so unexpectedly, that the boy, flabby from over indulgence and heavy drinking, had no chance to defend himself. He crumpled like a piece of pie crust and huddled in the corner where his father had flung him, blinking up at the astonishing spectacle of his father in a righteous rage.

He lay still for a minute or two, completely abashed by this sudden onslaught from a father who had always been so kind and loving. And the father walked back and forth in the handsome room, his hands clasped behind him. After a turn or two he came out and stood before his prostrate son.

"Now," he said, with an air of finality. "You can lie there and decide what you're going to do. I'll give you five minutes to make up your mind whether you're going to get up and act like a man, and a patriotic citizen of the United States. If you do, very well. We'll try to go on from there in good form and weather this thing together. Otherwise I'll hand you over to the government to put a uniform on you and make a buck private of you, unless they first decide that you belong behind bars!"

"*Dad!*" said Victor aghast, his face white and frightened. "You wouldn't do that!"

"Yes, I would, if you ever talk like that again. I won't have a son who is an utter disgrace to the family and the community."

"Dad! What do you think mother would say to you if she heard you talking this way?"

"That gag doesn't work any more, son! Your mother has protected you all your life from real discipline, and the time has come for you to step out from behind that sort of camouflage and see what's in you. And I'll tell you another thing. You've seen the last of this fancy office, and that little dressed-up doll you call your secretary. I'm done with all that nonsense, and so are you, if you expect to stay here. You've got to get down to real work and show what's in you, or *out* you go!"

There was silence in his father's plain little office for a few seconds while Victor tried to work this out. Gradually he rose, first to his elbow, then upright on his feet, and stood uncertainly, wavering, and blinking at his father.

"Do you understand?" thundered his father, in a tone reminiscent of the day when he was a little boy caught stealing apples by the police and brought to his father for accounting, with his mother far away at a summer resort for a week.

Victor's eyes were downcast under his father's steady gaze.

"Yes sir!" he managed tremblingly.

"Well, sit down then. I want to ask you a few questions. Just where is that fool girl of a secretary of yours?"

"I told you, dad, she went to the bedside of a dying friend who sent for her."

"But where?"

"She said she was going to New York."

"*Where* in New York?"

"I don't know. She was in a great hurry. She went right away."

"Do you mean to tell me that you let her go without getting her address?"

"Why, dad, I didn't think that was important. She promised to be back as soon as possible. Said she might even come this afternoon. She was in a hurry to catch her train."

"Yes? I guess she was. Well, you certainly proved your inability to run any kind of a business, even just an office. But that settles it. We'll put the police and detectives after her post haste!"

"Dad! You wouldn't do that! She was away. She wouldn't know anything about what went on here."

"Wouldn't she? It's an extraordinary coincidence that

the most important thing that we were making should be stolen the night she went away. I always suspected that little dolly. She has sly eyes. She was out to get something, and I guess she got it. I ought not to have given in and let you take her. Even your mother questioned the wisdom of having her here."

"Now dad, she's a good secretary! Hurried as she was to catch her train she waited to finish a letter I had just dictated."

"Yes?" said the father dryly. "What was the letter about? Some night club bill you hadn't paid?"

Victor's eyes went down and his face flushed angrily. He opened his lips to speak and then closed them fearfully as he saw the glint of anger in his father's eyes, and the sneer on his lips. Perhaps, just possibly, his father knew more about his private personal affairs than he had thought.

"She's a good secretary all right," said Victor. "The letter was some business about that steel that hasn't shown up yet. I think that was it."

"Oh no," said his father. "I came into your office and got that memoranda and answered it myself two days ago, and the steel has already arrived. You'll have to get a better alibi than that. Remember you haven't been here for two days, and you don't know what has been going on. Now, if that is settled, and you actually don't know where this excellent Miss Brannon is hiding herself in New York, suppose you go into the little side office over there and have an interview with the government man who is waiting for you. And be sure you speak the truth, remember, for I have a dictaphone over there and I'll go over the interview afterwards. So be careful. Your future rests largely on this interview."

Thoroughly scared, with white face and trembling hands, Victor went out, wishing there were some other exit through which he might vanish until this man from

Washington was gone. What was coming now? And wouldn't his father come to the rescue if they began charging him with any connection with this robbery?

Of course he didn't know anything about it, and of course his father must know he didn't. It was likely some of his own pet workmen, old fellows too old to really work, who wanted to feather their nests. Or more likely still, foreigners who were somehow connected with the enemy. He had told his father he ought to get rid of all foreigners, just in case.

With this reflection he stepped into the little waiting room designated, and met the eagle eye of the government detective, and so his grilling began.

Victor put on his most arrogant air and endeavored to awe the government detective with a good dose of the Vandingham lofty manner, but the keen eyes did not flinch, the hard line of the man's mouth did not soften. He was definitely unfriendly and unbelieving. And Victor, mindful of his father's warning about a dictaphone, and extremely conscious of the unbelieving attitude of his tormentor, had a hard time. He emerged from that interview minus most of his dignity, and certainly not any farther from the doubts of his examiner. It was perhaps the first time that Victor had ever been up against any person who utterly frightened him. At school when the professors had been ugly he always had recourse to complaining to his family, and having himself removed from the school. This had been extremely successful during his childhood days when his mother was the arbiter of his fate. Later, in college, there had been other ways to manage. His father would promise a big donation for a new building or something of that sort if they didn't anger him by complaints of his son. Of course not every college was open to such bribery, but most of them could be managed along such lines and made to forget their worst grievances at himself.

But this was the government, and this would be law, and he must go cautiously. So he stumbled along from question to question, until he got himself pretty well tangled up, and if his father had been present, even *he* would have felt sorry for the boy who had always been so hard to manage.

He found himself, too, having to defend Erda. Not because he wanted to, but because if he did not he would have the worse blame for letting her go so inconsequentially. In fact he found they were suggesting that he had been in collusion with his secretary in pulling off this miserable robbery, and more and more its importance in the whole scheme of American life just now became apparent to him, until he was appalled.

His mother had never seen such a look of soberness in his eyes when he finally came home to get a little rest, and some food. She plied him with questions which he would not answer, and with food which he would not eat, and then she wept at him till he cursed her and locked his door.

It was about that time that word came to the plant that a dead man had been found down under the outer wall, in the dark of the railroad bridge. And when at last he was identified he turned out to be one of the workers at the plant. Then they sent for Victor again for more questions, as he was supposed to be in charge of the men who would work on that location. They wanted to know when this man was last seen, whether he had permission to leave the plant, who would be responsible for him, and Victor had nothing to say except that he was away that day and didn't know. He named the man whom he had put in charge, but it turned out that the man had been discharged by his father the week before and had not been around the place since. It was said he had joined the army and been sent to camp. That proved that Victor had been doing some pretty crooked lying.

He tried to excuse himself by saying that his secretary looked after such matters for him, but that too seemed an obvious lie, as Erda had been in New York that day, if his former statements were correct, and the evidence loomed against him. He was not arrested, but he was told to keep within certain limits and be ready to answer a call at any time.

Victor would have been still more frantic if he could have known that the dead man was one who had been rounding a corner of the wall, next the railroad, as Erda had come forth from the gate with her booty, and that it had been but the work of an instant to flash forth the small neat weapon she had carried concealed in her sleeve and do in the man whom she feared might have seen her at this last minute when she thought she was safe. It had passed with Erda as one incident of many, and she hurried on as he fell knowing only that he had not followed her, as she fled to Weaver's rendezvous. Erda had had much practice in shooting, and never did her work half way. And the dead man told no tales.

But the men who were watching everything had seen that startled look in Victor's eyes, that catching of his breath when he heard about the dead man, and put one more link in the chain of evidence against him, and so, as murder entered the picture, the chain began to tighten about Victor himself. Oh, if only Erda would come back! If only he could find her!

So he put a private detective on her track. But the days went by and there was no sign from her.

Then suddenly she called up and said the funeral was over and she would be returning the next day. Victor, breathless, tried to warn her what had happened, and then bethought him just in time that perhaps she wouldn't come back if she knew her danger. So he hesitated, and then went on, only imploring her to come quickly, that there were some important letters to write and he needed her. He added a question. "Where are you, Erda? How can I get in touch with you tonight in case I need to ask you a question?"

But Erda had hung up.

17

BECAUSE the government was in charge there had been no publicity so far concerning the robbery at the plant, and the Vandinghams were not as yet in the public eye. Even Mrs. Vandingham did not know to a great extent all that had happened. Her husband had learned long ago that anything told at his home could no longer remain a secret. And Victor, though he was not as close-mouthed as his father, at least not for the same reason, realized that if he wished to keep his mother on his side he must not let her know what was going on. Their only great difference of opinion was about Erda. She did object to Erda, and Victor no longer desired to hear the subject of his chosen secretary discussed. If his mother knew what was being said about her by his father and the detectives and others at the plant she would be quick to remind him that she had "told him so." So he did not tell her of the trouble at the plant, and she went serenely on, trying to plan great things for Victor's future, in which no war possibilities figured, and hoping some day to be able to bring Victor and Lisle Kingsley to-gether again. That was her great desire. She liked Lisle and thought her the most fitting person to be her son's wife. And in that thought her plans fitted nicely with those of her son. Of course as she knew nothing yet of what had passed between Victor and Lisle so far, she was not utterly hopeless. Lisle would come around pretty soon, and smile as sweetly as ever at her old playmate, when she saw what a great man Victor had become. And when, somehow, they could get rid of that little viper of an Erda, whom she blamed for every indiscretion and mistake her son had made.

And so the excitement went on quietly with not even the public press getting hold of a hint of it.

It was just at that stage of affairs that Erda in a becoming and very smart black costume arrived at her job one morning, becomingly tearful and pensive at the death of her dearest friend, and ready to enter upon her duties with a vim.

She had not been very intimate with the other women in the office or else they would have approached her about the recent happenings while she had been absent. They just bowed distantly and eyed her with scared looks, for there had been many wonderings among them, just what was going to happen to Erda, and they were somewhat reassured that she had returned so apparently normal and in good form. There had been whisperings that she might have been connected with the disappearance of the precious gadget. But now she was back, apparently unafraid, it seemed hardly likely that she was the thief.

She essayed to march into Victor's office and take her former place, but she found the door locked, and her key did not seem to unlock it. Upon questioning she was told that there had been changes made during her absence, and that Victor's former room was closed for the time. She would have to take one of the empty desks in the main room until Mr. Vandingham senior arrived.

Erda had not reckoned on anything as drastic as this happening, and began to wonder if it wouldn't have been better to disappear from the picture entirely, rather than to return and hope to bluff it off. But she was here now. It was too late. And of course it was better to allay any suspicion that might arise either now or later, so she settled down cheerily, took off her wraps, put them in the cloak room, took out a paper she had bought on the way from the station, and prepared to wait.

Soon, however, an office boy came to bring a message for her. Mr. Vandingham senior would like her to come to his office at once.

In some trepidation Erda went. She had been through many alarming experiences in her daring young life, and she wasn't sure what she feared just now, certainly not detection. For whatever happened she had done the thing that she had come there to do. It might cost her the loss of her job, but there were other jobs, and of course she was not working mainly for the Vandinghams. But where was Victor, and what attitude would he have toward her? If she could only speak to Victor first she was confident that she could put up a good story. She could make him understand how sad she had been at losing her friend, and what a frightful time she had been through. She could excuse herself for her so-long absence. But the older Vandingham was an unknown quantity, one that she did not particularly admire. He was grave and stern. He had not warmed to her beauty nor her coquetry. Could she in any way get into his good graces? Then she tapped at the door of his office, and in response to his crisp "Come" she entered.

He was not alone. The detective from Washington was there too, had in fact been waiting for her, since ever his men had, by the process of elimination, found out her abiding place in New York. They had trailed her down on the train and kept the office in constant touch with the situation. Erda had not dreamed that such careful detection could be found anywhere on this side of the ocean, therefore she felt no alarm as she entered coolly, smiled a good morning in a grave sweet way to Mr. Vandingham, and said cheerfully: "You've been making some changes in the office, Mr. Vandingham?"

The head of the plant bowed gravely.

"Yes, Miss Brannon. And now, will you sit down? This is Lieutenant Armes of the war department in Washington, and he wishes to ask you a few questions."

Then began a grilling of two hours which was worse than anything Erda had dreamed could possibly come to her, in this country, certainly. Not after all her experience and training.

"Where were you on the afternoon of Thursday, five days ago, Miss Brannon? What train did you take to New York? Where did you buy your ticket? Had you reservations on that train? At what hour did you receive the telegram which you say was the cause of your journey?"

Every step of the way, moment by moment, through the hours of each day and night since she had started on this fateful escapade.

She was quick-brained and for the most part she answered coolly enough, through the routine of the first questions. She was even able to keep a quiet mien, and control any tendency to trembling when the lieutenant sprang sudden surprises on her, and watched her sharply. Though she was the more conscious of the elderly Vandingham who kept his solemn eyes upon her every instant.

"Are you accustomed to using firearms?" The question was irrelevant in the extreme.

"Firearms?" said Erda sweetly with a girlish shiver. "Oh, dear no! I'm just terribly afraid of a gun. It almost throws me into hysterics to see one shot off!"

"H'm!" said the lieutenant. "I would not have judged that you would have that sort of reaction."

"No," said the older man. "No, I certainly would not."

Erda gave him a quick glance and was not quite sure whether he had more in his voice than appeared on the surface or not.

There were some more questions asked, commonplace enough in themselves, and then the lieutenant aimed another.

"Were you well acquainted with the workman who was shot that night?"

"Shot?" said Erda, lifting a face suddenly white with startled astonishment. "Was there a man shot? One of the workmen, you say? I wouldn't know. I have been in New York, you know. What was his name?"

On and on the questions went, sometimes seeming to get near to the thread of a story, and then veering off to the commonplace of times and places and dates. What were her habits of entertainment? Where did she spend her evenings? What clubs and night life was she fond of attending? Then back again to the line of the story. Not a word about the lost gadget! Hadn't it been missed yet? Surely it wouldn't have been so long before they found it was gone. Sometimes she almost began to hope that this questioning had nothing to do with the loss of the gadget and blue prints. Then would come another question.

"Has Mr. Victor Vandingham ever taken you into the buildings of the plant?"

"Oh no," she answered promptly. "You know the office force are not supposed to know anything about what goes on inside those sacred precincts. They are the government's secrets of course. We never even talk about them. My work has been mainly matters of finance, records of workers, orders for material, that sort of thing."

"Then you have never been inside building number A in the plant? You would not know where the different machines were placed?"

"Oh no, of course not," said Erda sweetly, although she grew restless under the sharp eyes that were watching her.

"And you knew the man who was shot quite well, did you not?" went on the relentless voice.

Erda paled visibly.

"I? Why no, I didn't know any of the workmen, of course, although they were always polite and pleasant to me, and I usually smiled and nodded good morning to them if we happened to pass. But no, I do not know who was shot. What was his name?"

"It is immaterial. I thought I understood you to say that you knew him. How often have you been at the plant in the night? Has Mr. Vandingham junior been in the habit of bringing you to the office at night?"

"Oh no," said Erda, coolly again. "Just twice when there were important letters to go out by the midnight mail, something about ordering steel that would be needed the next morning early."

Oh, Erda was clever. She skirted around those questions as one who knew her way about anywhere. And then, just when she thought he had reached the end of his long list of questions, and was turning over another page of paper, he lifted his eyes and asked, "How long have you been in the habit of carrying concealed weapons?"

Erda almost started then, but she managed a pretty well-feigned stare and answered:

"Concealed weapons? *Me* carry concealed weapons? I thought I just told you how frightened I am of them."

Then suddenly she turned to Mr. Vandingham with a weary appeal in her eyes:

"What is the meaning of all this questioning, Mr.

Vandingham, please? And why have they selected me to grill this way? I am really very tired. I've traveled all night, and have been through a most trying experience seeing my dearest friend die and attending her funeral. I do wish you would excuse me from further questioning. I can't understand what it is all about. I didn't know a man was dead, and I didn't know the man. What should all this have to do with me?"

The detective looked her straight in the eye.

"Miss Brannon, in case you don't know the situation, some important documents have been stolen from this plant, and Washington is interested to question all the employees. That will be all this time. You will please stay within call." And he bowed her out.

Erda went back to the desk where she had been parked earlier that morning and tried to think what she should do next. If it was at all possible she would like to get in touch with Weaver. Perhaps he would want her to vanish. But of course there was no opportunity at present to go to the telephone without attracting attention, and she had sense enough to know that her strongest action would be to sit quietly and wait, as if nothing disturbed her. At least she would have plenty of opportunity to observe what went on about her and that would be something to report. If only Victor would come she might be able to find out something. But Victor did not appear, and the morning went on quietly. The old trusted girls who usually worked in that outer room were going on about their business, typing and filing and addressing envelopes. The office of the young Vice President was not open. No one seemed to be going that way. She wondered if Victor might be in there. If only his father and that detective would go away she would get up and try the door. Perhaps when most of the girls went out to lunch she could venture to do it. But the day wore on very slowly, and then at last she was sent for once more to go to Mr. Vandingham's office, and again under the same keen observation she went through much the same grilling as before, only this time the questions were a little more abruptly phrased, a trifle more astonishing, to catch her off her guard.

But through it all nothing was said about the gadget which she had supposed was the most important item of the whole setting. Could it be that somehow she had not got the right article? She had been so sure. She had heard so much about the thing from Victor, and workmen who occasionally came into Victor's office. Or hadn't they discovered the loss of the thing? Didn't it mean much to them? Perhaps there was a flaw in it, or perhaps it had just been left there as a decoy. Over and over again she reviewed the circumstances of the night while she was stealing through the dim building behind the machines. What the men had called to one another. Hadn't she got the right thing? Wouldn't Weaver be satisfied? Oh, if she could only get into contact with him right away. Perhaps she ought to say she was sick and wanted to go to her room. Would they let her go? Why hadn't they said something about it? Documents they said. That would be the blue prints of course. But here they were just harping on the dead man. Just a dead workman. What was that to make such a fuss about? In the land where she was trained she had been taught that when you died you died and it was in a way the end and aim of life, to have done the best to further a cause and die doing it. But here they were acting as if this mere workman was important. If she had shot him they would never find it out. She hadn't thought her aim had taken effect, just scratched him, or made him faint perhaps. She hadn't bothered to look behind to see what happened to the man. She had been too afraid he might cry out and maybe someone would come who would recognize her. And now she was glad he was gone. He, at least, could not rise up and testify against her. She had shot people before, in another land, and even been commended for it, so she was not particularly worried. But they had no evidence to prove that she had fired that shot.

So the questioning went on, and the day wore to its close. She was weary and faint, but they did not send her out to lunch. Instead they brought a tray with coffee and sandwiches, and twice more she was called in to be questioned again. There were other girls called, questioned, also, but not as many times as herself, and they were not kept in the office so long.

And all this time where was Victor?

She had counted on Victor to help her through this return. Perhaps she had been wrong to come back at all. Perhaps she should have stayed in New York. Only police were wise, and quick to search out lost people, and returning had seemed to her the best way to disarm suspicion. If only Victor were here he would take her part of course and defend her from all this silly questioning. She could wind Victor around her smooth little finger, she was sure. That was one reason why she half thought she would marry him, because she could always do with him what she wished. But she needed him now. Why didn't he come?

And now they were asking her more about her relation with her employer. Didn't he talk the business of the plant over with her often? Hadn't he told her of the secret things that were being made for war purposes? Hadn't he described articles that were being made? Hadn't he taken her into the work rooms at odd hours when the shifts were changing and no one would observe them? Wasn't she interested in machinery? Hadn't she once asked him to take her to see it?

Oh, the endless questions! Would they never cease? If

only Victor would come and put an end to it all! Was he under espionage and questioning too? Oh, surely not. Perhaps he had been drinking badly and was having a hangover. He was doing too much of that. She must get him out of that if she really took him over.

But as the day wore on Erda was almost of the opinion that she was going to escape from this setting and get away to pastures new. She would contact Weaver and Lacey and get sent elsewhere. They didn't need her here any longer. She had accomplished their purpose for them, and they could afford to pay her a little more and send her to parts unknown. Now especially if they were getting this murder slant on things. They were stressing it so much that it almost seemed to overtop the robbery. Though of course if they could prove who did the murder it would help to solve the mystery about the robbery.

She was surprised that she did not hear any whispering about what had happened from the other girls, but they were absolutely mum. No talk whatever, unless it were to ask for paper, or letters that they were working on. Well, this too was a part of their scheme to put her on the spot, she supposed, and being Erda, and proud of her shady record, she held up her head, determined to see it through and show them that they were barking up the wrong tree. She would come out of this innocent as a lamb. It wouldn't be so hard to fool the government. She had done it before with other governments, and she would do it again. So she sat smiling through the hours, and waiting for what came next.

18

LISLE went about her daily program like one walking on the clouds. Rosy clouds, too. War might be in the world, and sorrow and disappointment. Separation might loom, and undoubtedly would on her horizon, but just for the present her soul was filled with ecstasy. Just to know the touch of John Sargent's lips, the feel of his arms about her in that quick parting clasp, just to hear over and over that quick whisper "Dear, good by!" That was enough to give her such joy as she had never known before.

Oh, there would come a time when she would want something more to satisfy the questions that would come. But she knew he was honorable. All the rest would come in due time. It simply hadn't come to her consciousness as yet.

And then one day later there came a letter. A dear letter. It brought back the thrill of his presence.

It began very simply:

Dear:
I didn't ask you if I might write. We had no time for questions. No time for me even to say, 'I love

you,' though I am sure you know that. I am sure our lips told all that was necessary, though we could not say it formally.

And there was so much that could have been said that perhaps were better left unsaid, since I am going away, and since we both know that I may never be able to return. That is hard to speak of, but because it is true, perhaps I have no right at present to say more than I love you. Just this much I'll tell you. I think I have loved you ever since I first saw you, that day the lady made such a fuss about the mud spattered on her "imported frock." Our eyes met, and I loved you. I knew I had no right, no future to bring to such as you. But I loved you. And I love you still: I had your dear smile to cherish in my heart then. Now I have the touch of your precious lips. I shall always love you.

If I were stationed near home, I would feel that I must wait until you knew me better before I told you that I love you, until your parents knew me, wait until I had something besides my love to offer you. But since, in this strange war-world in which we are living today, it may be that this is all we can ever have on this earth, I must tell you of my love.

And I am taking it for granted that you love me too, for I seemed to read that in your eyes and your lips on mine as we parted. But I want you to feel that this is a sacred thing between us, so if anything should happen to me, and you should find someone else to love, that our love was so pure that you could speak of it without hurting another love.

I do not like to write these words, but I know they should be written. I want you to be free as air, if anything happens to me.

I shall not speak of this again, for we must not be sorrowful. If God is willing I shall come back, and then we can plan for the future. But now I am at least glad I have the privilege of telling you that I love you. Later when I can I will give you an address that will reach me. I shall be longing to hear from you. Till then God keep you tenderly,

Yours,
John Sargent

Lisle read the letter over and over until she knew it by heart. She rejoiced in it almost as if it were a sacred thing. It seemed to her that it was the most beautiful love letter that anyone ever wrote. Later it occurred to her with a happy little relief that this was a letter she could show to her mother and father when the time came. A letter to be proud of. A letter of such dignity and sweetness that even the showing of it to her parents could not take away from its intimacy and beauty.

And the next day Victor came to see her!

The butler brought the word of his arrival to Mrs. Kingsley who was in her room making out the menus for the day. The butler understood that Victor was not in good standing with the family, and especially not with Lisle. So instead of going at once to Lisle, for whom Victor had asked, he went to the mother.

Mrs. Kingsley looked up with a frown and a worry in her eyes.

"Victor? *Oh!* Did he ask for me?"

"No madam, he asked for Miss Lisle, was she in?"

The mother considered.

"All right, I'll tell her," she said, and putting down her pencil and pad arose and went to Lisle's room.

"Dear," she said gently, "Victor is here. He has asked for you. I think perhaps you had better go down and see him, and try to be as kind and pleasant to him as you can. That is the way to help answer those prayers you said you were going to be remembering for him."

Lisle looked up with a glance that seemed to come back hastily from somewhere abroad with the armed forces, and a capable, weary cloud went over her face, though she tried to brush it away and put on a cheeriness she did not feel about this particular caller.

"Why, yes, mother, I'll try," she said with a little sigh of annoyance. "But mother, suppose you come down too and then you will see how quite impossible it is for me to do anything for Victor."

"Oh, no, dear," said her mother. "That wouldn't do at all. It would only make him angry. A young man doesn't want a mother hanging around when he comes to call on a girl."

"But mother, that's just it. I don't want it to seem like a young man come to call on a girl. Victor knows how I feel about him and all his propositions, and I want him to be reminded of it. Please come down, mother."

"No, dear," said Mrs. Kingsley emphatically, "I really couldn't. I have committee work to finish before this afternoon. A list to make out and all those ladies to call up. I really haven't a minute. Run along, dear. You'll be all right. And remember this is your opportunity. Perhaps he has come to answer your prayers."

Lisle made a little wry face.

"More like he has come to answer his own prayers, mother," she said with a mocking laugh. "But I'll do my best. Only don't expect me to stand any more of his insolence."

"Now dear, remember his poor mother, and do try to have a little patience."

"Yes, I'll be remembering his poor mother, and how she has spoiled him all these years. It's her fault largely that Victor is so unbearable. All right, run along to your committees, mother, and I'll take this thing over and settle it once for all."

"Now don't be so hard, Lisle dear! Don't, I beg of you."

"Mother I'm not hard, but I've got to be true, you know."

"Yes, you've got to be true of course," sighed her mother, "but be sure you are not blinded as to what is truth. You don't want to say or do anything that you will regret all your life. Remember there are not so many old true friends."

"Well, *he* certainly isn't one," said Lisle annoyedly, and resolved as she hurried down the stairs that she would show John's letter to her mother the first opportunity that offered. It really was time that her mother understood that there was somebody else she loved, somebody who was real. She had hoped to wait a little until her mother got Victor off her mind, but if Victor had started in on another siege of friendliness it was time he was settled once for all, and time her parents understood that her heart was occupied and happy. Only she did so want them to know John, to *see* him, before she had to tell them. They would be a bit horrified perhaps that she had actually fallen in love with someone they didn't know, hadn't even seen. And John was so winning in appearance. His blue blue eyes so trustable, the light in them could not fail to win at once. His wonderful gold hair, and his gorgeous smile! If he were only here for an hour! Mother might admire Victor's handsome face, but she surely could not fail to see the strength and beautiful trustworthiness of John's face. She must get him to send her a picture in his uniform.

He did look so wonderful in his uniform!

Then Lisle entered the living room and Victor arose from an attitude of dejection on the couch over in the orner, and lifted a hang-dog expression to her face. Woebegone! That was it. So he was going to take that attitude, was he? And blame all his troubles on her! It was an old trick of his with which she had no patience.

But Victor was really dejected. He didn't attempt to smile or crack any jokes. He just nodded to Lisle as if she were an old rag of a friend to whom he had come as a last resort, and then he dropped back to the couch with his old cap in his hand, which he continued to twirl and watch as he talked, for all the world like his little-boy self when he came to pour out his troubles to his girl friend.

But Lisle was not moved by any such manifestations. She merely said good morning briskly and dropped down on a chair halfway across the room from where he sat. This was nothing to her but a business to be got through with as soon as possible, for she had been writing a letter to John when this summons reached her, and she wanted to get back to it. Of course she knew that she could not send it yet, because she had no address, but it was as if she had been having a pleasant talk with her lover and she hated to be interrupted by something she knew would turn out to be unpleasant.

But there was something about Victor's appearance that was different from any attitude he had ever worn before. He seemed almost humble, and utterly dejected. His old arrogance was gone, as if he had been through some terrible experience that had changed his whole view of life, and the way he tossed his cap around and around restlessly was terrible to see. She watched him with a puzzled look. She hadn't of course heard about the trouble at the plant. She only knew that there was a large detachment of soldiers guarding the vicinity, but that would be natural if they were making something important for the war, some secret weapon. That was what had been given out to the general public, and as

yet no one knew the terrible catastrophe that ha[...]
pened. It would have to come out soon of cours[...]
until it did Victor naturally would have held his [...]
high and gone smiling on his way. Lisle could not m[...]
out what was the matter with him.

"Are you still my friend?" he managed to stumble ou[...]
presently, into the midst of her attempt to be pleasantly
impersonal and talk about the weather, and sports, and
ask him if he had met many of the soldiers in town.
Then he suddenly burst in with his pitiful question.

Lisle looked at him sharply.

"Friend? Why, yes, your *friend*, I suppose. Why?"

"Does that mean you would be friend enough to do
something to help me out in a jam?"

"Why—I guess so—that is—I couldn't promise of
course until I knew what it is you want, what you
need."

"Yes, you would say that!" sneered the old Victor bitterly.

"What is it, Victor, what is the matter?"

"Matter enough!" he said sourly, tossing his heavy
lock of black curls off his forehead. "I'm in a heck of a
mess, and as far as I can see you are the only one who
can help me out. I wouldn't have come to you if there
had been any other way, because you've been so hard
on me, and so sort of fanatical and sentimental. But
there isn't anybody who can help me but you, and if
you won't help I might as well go out and drown myself
in the river."

"Why, Victor! What in the world is the matter? What
has happened?"

"Plenty!" said the boy, basking under her kindly distressed tone. "But there isn't anything the matter that
you can't help me out of if you really will do it. I knew
if I came to you you would forget you're mad and be
ready to help. You always were a good little sport that

…henever I got into a scrape. Why, you see, that …old-digger I've been having for a secretary has …caught giving away our plant secrets to the enemy. …des that, she stole some of the important parts of a …ret machine we're making for the government, and …can't be found. And she stole the blue prints. Impor…tant blue prints that the enemy can use to duplicate our machines, and on top of all that they think she killed a man trying to get away with it. They've searched her room and found the gun the bullet came from, hidden in one of her shoes, and they have proof enough to electrocute her. They've found she's got in touch with a short wave radio and she's been giving away our plant secrets to the enemy right and left and they've got her hard and fast. But you see the government men are trying to tie me up to it. They think just because I've been kind to her and taken her out socially to help her have a good time here, away off from her home and friends, that she and I have been in cahoots on this, and they're trying to ring me in on it too, get me in the trial, and get me all tangled up asking questions. Of course they'd try that with dad too if he wasn't so darned respectable they know he didn't do it. And it's pretty near killing him. It isn't out in the public eye yet of course, but it soon will be, and I've got to do something about it right away or I'll have to go to jail, and mighty quick too. They took Erda yesterday along with a couple of men who planned the whole thing, and she'll ring me in on it too, plenty. She hasn't a bit of conscience about it. So I came to you. I knew you'd be willing to forget old scores, and let bygones be bygones, and help me out."

"But I don't see how I could help you out in a situation like that. I haven't any influence with courts, and policemen, or the government."

"Oh yes, you can do it all righty. You don't need influence with police or courts. If you'll just drop past ar-

guments and marry me nobody will trouble an
about it. They will know if you married me
right. They'll know you have confidence in me,
that would settle it for most people. And a daughte
old J. D. Kingsley! *He* has influence, plenty. And he
course would do all he could to get me off if I was you
husband. Oh, it's a cinch I wouldn't have any more
trouble if you'd marry me right away. You know you
and I could go out now and be married and then put it
in the evening papers, and everything would be all
okeydokey. Will you do it, Lisle? If you will I'll be a
model man from now on. I won't even drink much, just
a glass or two now and then when we're at parties. I
won't ever get tight. And we'll have all kinds of a grand
time. Come on, Lisle, say you'll do it. It'll be all right.
Your parents won't care, seeing it's to save my life, and
keep me out of jail. You're a good scout, you'll marry
me, won't you?"

Lisle looked at her former playmate aghast.

"Victor! How perfectly *terrible!* I'm awfully sorry for
you, but you know I can't marry you for a reason like
that. I can't marry someone I don't love, even if it were
to save everybody's life. It wouldn't be right! And it
wouldn't do a bit of good, either, to get married. The
government wouldn't have any more faith in you because you got married in a time like this, no matter who
you married, and they wouldn't stop arresting you and
trying you because you'd gotten married. That's a silly
idea. Getting married is too solemn a business to be
rushed into to save your neck when you're in trouble.
No, Victor, I couldn't *possibly* marry you, *ever*. I don't
love you and never will. And you know it wouldn't do
any good any way."

"Oh, yes it would. If people saw you had confidence
in me enough to marry me—"

"But I *haven't*, Victor. I don't know that I *ever* really

nfidence in you. Certainly if there was some
way in which I could help you I would, if it was
but this would be *impossible*."

You mean you'd let me hang if it came to that? Sup-
se they charged me with murdering that workman
and you knew you could save my neck by marrying me,
Lisle, wouldn't you do it? Lisle, I ask you, *won't* you
take pity on me?"

Sadly she looked at him and shook her head.

"I couldn't, Victor. It would be wrong. Marriage
isn't a thing like that."

"There you go again preaching! When I'm nearly
crazy, and all but dead, and you *preach,* what's right and
what's wrong. As if there was any such thing as right
and wrong! Is it right to refuse to save a life when you're
asked to? If you didn't want to stay married afterwards
there is always divorce, you know. I know you don't
think that is a pretty word, but it's modern, and fits the
times, and it would be a way out for you afterwards in
case you didn't like it."

Lisle sprang to her feet.

"Stop, Victor. Stop! Stop! You shan't say such things!
They are *awful* and they make me simply hate you!"

"Yes, there you go again, getting sentimental and
preaching, and all the time my life is hanging in the balance. You know after all, this is *your* fault. I wanted you
to marry me long ago. I wanted the wedding to be announced at my party. If you had done that then there
wouldn't have been any of this trouble. I wouldn't have
even known Erda, nor invited her to my party, nor had
her for my secretary, and none of this could have happened. The government wouldn't have been in trouble
either. It's all your fault. I just took up with that little
snake of a girl to spite you, because you wouldn't get
married when I wanted you to. I picked her up off the
street and got acquainted with her, just so you would

see I could get anybody I wanted to. And n̲
know what will happen to you, because you
ticular and won't marry me? You'll never fin̲
that's up to your ideas. You want somebody tha
fect and there isn't such an animal. You'll just be ṳ
maid, and then how will you feel?"

"That isn't a bad fate," said Lisle serenely. "I'd mṳ
rather be unmarried all my life than marry a man
didn't love nor respect. But I *have* found a man I can
both love and respect, so that is not the point."

Victor started to his feet and gave her such a look of
hate as she hadn't imagined he could harbor in his shal-
low soul.

"You've found another man that suits you, have you?
One you can love and respect? Show him to me. I demand to see him. I'll bet a hat I could find a lot of flaws
in his character, even judged by your narrow standards.
Where is he, I say? I demand to meet him!"

"He's in the army and far away from here. In the
army where you ought to be this minute. If you'd been
in the army you wouldn't have been in all this trouble."

But Victor's anger was by no means under control.
He was white with rage.

"In the army, is he? Some poor low-down buck private I suppose," he sneered. "I'll get him sometime, see
if I don't. Just a little old rat of a buck private."

"That would make no difference to me, even if it
were true, which it isn't," she smiled, for she suddenly
remembered the insignia she had seen on the arm of
John Sargent as he swung onto his train. "But a buck
private is more honorable than a man who doesn't want
to help fight to defend his country, just sits at home in
a luxurious office and does nothing but amuse himself
But Victor, I don't want to talk this way to you. I can
see that you are in awful trouble, and if there were any
right way to help you I would, even if I can't marry

s only one thing I know to do that will really
o to God and pray for you. If you knew the
is Christ I am sure He would help you to a
here you wouldn't get into great unhappiness
is. He would change your life and make you over
into a happy man."

Victor stared at her, and then sneered.

"New line of preaching," he said hatefully. "Sounds
a little childish, don't you think? Men in trouble don't
swallow such old-fashioned chaff. You can't put a little
religious salve on my hurts after you've refused to help
me out of purgatory."

Lisle looked at Victor with compassion.

"I'm sorry, Victor. I can't help in the way you ask,
and I honestly believe that the only one who can possibly help you is God. I know what I am talking about
for I have got to know Him myself, and He is wonderful!"

Victor stumbled to his feet and looked at her as if she
were a viper.

"Well, I'll never go to Him, do you understand? But
I didn't ever think you'd go back on me, not when I
asked you to save my life." He walked unsteadily out
of the room, across the hall, out the front door, and
slammed it dramatically behind him.

Lisle stood staring pitifully after him, with tears blur-
ring into her eyes, for the young man who had so
scorned the only help she could offer him.

Lisle went up to her room, deeply saddened by the interview. It had seemed so dreadful to refuse an old
friend something that would help him in his terrible
situation. But of course it was something she could not
do, to marry him, even if her heart were not elsewhere.
She could not marry Victor, *ever*. She could not marry
one whom she did not love.

"Well?" said her mother, suddenly appearing at the

door, an anxious red spot on each cheek. "Wr
do? Did you try to help him?"

"Yes, mother, I tried to tell him about the L
he wouldn't listen. He said he would never go t
for help. You see, mother, he is in awful trouble a.
wanted *my* help, not God's."

"Oh, my dear! And couldn't you give it to him?"

"No, mother. The only thing he wanted was for m
to marry him, so people would have confidence in
him."

"I'm afraid I don't understand. Have confidence in
him? How? And what an extraordinary reason for
marrying anyone!"

"Yes, mother. Wasn't it? You see the Vandingham
plant is in great trouble. That girl Victor had for a secretary has stolen something important that the plant was
making, as well as the blue prints of the machine, and
sent them to the enemy, and she has been sending messages out of the country, secrets of the government.
Also a man was killed the night she got the stuff out of
the plant, and they have found the revolver with which
he was shot among her things. And now because Victor
took her out to night clubs they are trying to tie him up
with the sabotage outfit and say that he and the girl had
arranged this robbery between them. Victor thinks if I
would marry him the confidence of people would be re-
stored in him, and that our name and influence might
help him."

"What an unspeakable little selfish creature he is!" said
the mother indignantly. "Willing to take a girl who used
to be his friend into a situation like that! Willing to lean
on a wife instead of standing on his own merits! Oh, my
dear! Of course you couldn't marry a creature like that!
Oh, I am ashamed that I asked you to be kind to him."

"Well, mother, I tried to be kind. I told him I was
sorry for him, but that I could never marry him. I

nat God was the one to help him, but he just
ay with a sneer. He said he didn't care to have
like that!"

dear, I think he is the most contemptible young
ever heard of. The idea that he would be willing
de behind a girl for protection! That he would wish
drag you and your respectable family into a mess like
iis! Drag us all into court and into the contempt of the
government. I am sorry for his mother of course and it
goes without saying that she can have had nothing to do
with this whole affair. She is suffering the consequences
of spoiling her son of course, and I guess we can't do
anything about it. But now I think we shall just have to
put Victor out of our thoughts. Certainly your father
will be furious that Victor should have made any such
outrageous proposition to you now."

"Well, mother, don't tell him anything about it tonight. Father looked so tired today."

"Yes, I know," sighed the mother. "I was really
troubled about him when he left this morning. I guess
he is carrying some pretty heavy financial burdens these
war days. He doesn't talk much about it. That has never
been his way. But I hear him sigh, every little while,
and when I ask him what is the matter he tries to smile
and says, "Oh, well, nothing much perhaps. Nothing I
suppose in comparison with what they are bearing across
the waters. Maybe everything will be all right by and
by, but things are most uncertain now."

Lisle went to her room and finished her letter to John,
and forgot all about Victor and his trouble, except when
some little reminder saddened her with the memory.
Poor Victor, who didn't want God to help him, even in
his trouble! But she kept on thinking about her father.
Suppose something should happen to her father! Suppose he should get very sick, and she hadn't told them
about John yet. Somehow she couldn't feel satisfied not

to have them know. But yet, perhaps it was ﹐
tell. He had spoken in his letter as if he would ﹐
to know. Or had he? She would wait a little and
anything until the way seemed to open.

19

THE days went by and the trouble at the Vandingham plant went quietly on. The government had power to keep the most of it out of the press, even if the Vandinghams didn't. There was a mere mention briefly of sabotage discovered among the workers in the plant, definitely settling around one woman who had worked in the office, and her fellow-plotters, two men from outside. Erda's name wasn't mentioned at first, but it got around who the young woman was, and Erda was seen no more in the night social life with Victor. People mentioned Victor's name with raised eyebrows, and wondered. Victor was not in evidence anywhere. If he was held in jail, or his family had had influence enough to keep him out on bail, or what, wasn't known, but there was much speculation.

Later there was more mention of Erda Brannon and a trial she was undergoing, but only most briefly. There was also the word murder in connection with the item, but there were no head lines, and the trial was private and secret. The government saw to that.

Another item weeks later announced that Miss Bran-

non had been found guilty, with a word o.
her lineage which connected her definitely
enemy and spies. With her three others had b
and sentenced. Their names were Entry, Lac
Weaver, but nobody seemed to know them and
interest failed to connect them with any known de
group.

Sometime after this Victor appeared now and the
from whatever confinement he had been under, but he
had an ugly hang-dog look and was scarcely recognizable for the handsome youth he used to be. He went no
more to the Kingsleys, and was not seen in social life.
He seemed to have dropped out of everything. A little
later it was said he was in the army. His mother wept a
great deal and continued to blame Lisle Kingsley for it
all. She would scarcely speak to Lisle's mother, who
was very indignant at her attitude.

So life was going on. Lisle's graduation had been
quiet and she immediately joined herself to more war
work. Gossips watched her and tried to pity her that she
seemed to have lost connection with their social group.
They wondered if she wasn't broken-hearted that Victor seemed out of the running. Of course she wouldn't
want to *marry* Victor, now that all this talk had been
going on about him. Now that people were hinting the
Vandinghams were not as rich as they used to be. Or
was that so? Some said they were richer than ever and
that the government was not holding Victor's father to
blame. They were still using the plant for some important work. But of course nobody knew anything much
about it, and what they made up varied so much that
one scarcely could tell what to think.

Letters had been coming from John Sargent from a
distant point, and Lisle had been able to write to him,
sending on some of the letters she had written at the
first, also, so that their heart-life should be unbroken.

...en promoted. He was doing something im-
...onnected with investigation. His title carried
...he idea of what he was doing. It was secret
...and Lisle gathered that there was often danger
...cted with it. It involved going among fighters,
...being one of them at times, but it was a position of
...st and John was proud and happy that his officers had
...ounted him worthy.

Then one glorious morning there came word that
John was being sent home on leave to take some special
word to Washington. He would probably arrive a few
hours after she received his message and would try to
call her on the telephone as soon as he had opportunity;
and he might be able to be a few days in her vicinity.

The message came in an official envelope and created
quite a sensation in the Kingsley household. Mrs. Kingsley carried it to her daughter, greatly apprehensive lest
it might in some way be connected with Victor Vandingham, who was now in the army, and much to his
chagrin as yet was only a private. He didn't call it "buck
private" any more. He tried to dignify it as a "temporary" place to wait for his fine commission that he con-
fidently expected would come his way some day again.

But Lisle's voice fairly lilted as she took John's letter.
Then, with radiant face, and voice that was full of joy,
she took her letters, the few she had selected to show to
her parents pretty soon, and went to her mother's room
to reveal the story of her soldier-lover.

"But why didn't you tell us before, dear?" reproached
her mother, when the question of John Sargent's
respectability had been settled to her entire satisfaction.
"We would have been so pleased to enjoy your romance
with you."

"Mother dear, I wanted to wait until you could at
least see him, before you knew. I was afraid you would
blame me for taking up with an almost stranger, a per-

son who was practically insignificant as far as this
goes. Just a person I got to know best at a plain
religious meeting."

The mother looked thoughtful.

"Yes, dear, perhaps I would," she admitted. "But
can see there is true worth in this young man. And o
course there is reassurance always in the fact that he has
to do with religious affairs."

Mrs. Kingsley had learned a great deal in the few
times she had attended that Bible Study class.

"Dear mother," said Lisle, tenderly kissing her forehead. "Wait till you see him. Wait till you look into his
blue blue eyes, and see his shining hair that is like spun
gold, and his smile that is like sunshine."

"Dear! I'm so happy for you," said her mother draw-
ing her daughter into her arms and holding her close.
"And your father will be delighted."

"Yes, father will like him I know. Oh, mother, I'm
so happy!"

"Well, now we'll plan to have him come here of
course as soon as he is free, for as long as he can stay."

"Mother," said Lisle eagerly, "I'd like us to be married before John goes back, and if he thinks it's at all
possible, I'd like to go with him. For I'm sure his leave
won't be so very long. Would you feel very badly to
have me do that?"

There were sudden tears in the mother's eyes, but she
managed a trembling smile

"We'll see!" she quavered. "Your father and I—we
all—will talk it over. If—your—John thinks—it's right."

They were married very quietly, no stylish wedding,
but there was great joy in all hearts, and it was a happy
going away. The mother and the father felt they could
have perfect confidence in trusting their girl to this
young man.

"Such a pity!" said Lisle's girl friends from her old

group, "not to have a *real* wedding, when there
have been so many uniforms, and uniforms do
such a dressy wedding! And Lisle has certainly
ed a swell looker! Funny how quiet she was about
ll. One would have thought she'd want to show him
f. All the girls would have been envious. He's a great
deal better looking than Victor even. Queer how Lisle
always picked good lookers! Of course she's beautiful
and all that, but she's so awfully quiet, and she doesn't
seem to care to go to night clubs or parties. Somebody
told me she is getting interested in religion. Can you
imagine it? Lisle Kingsley? Of course a little religion
doesn't hurt in an unobtrusive way, but it certainly
doesn't fit with a modern girl's gay life. But Lisle just
isn't gay any more!"

"Not gay? But she never did drink nor smoke, you
know. And she certainly *looks* awfully happy now."

"Yes, she does, but anybody would, getting married
to a good-looking man like that one. Well, I only wish
she had had a big wedding. I was just dying to get a new
dress, and I know she would have asked me to be a
bridesmaid. We always were such close friends."

"Yes," said the other girl, "here too! But this is war
times of course, and you can't have everything."

Victor, languishing under the cloud of public suspicion in a uniform of the most insignificant soldier he
could possibly be, read the notice of that quiet wedding
with a bitter feeling of humiliation in his heart. His one-
time girl had married another man! And when he read
the man's name and found that Lisle had married his old
college enemy, he felt that he had reached the depths of
utter humiliation, and it wasn't fair! All this to come to
Victor Vandingham! Victor had not yet learned to recognize his own follies and weaknesses. He thought he
was something noble that rated everything he wanted in
this life.

But back in the Kingsley home the fath⸱ were talking it over.

"Lisle looked very happy, didn't she, Fa⸱ the mother, brushing away a bright tear. sweet! It seemed to me I had never seen her look since she was a very little girl."

"Yes," said the father, "she looked so entirely s⸱ fied. And she's got a wonderful man! I *like* him! ⸱ more I see of him the better satisfied I am. And I'm ⸱ glad he went right into the army as soon as he was free to go. Of course I know he had a good defense job and all that, but I'm glad that he *wanted* to get into danger and do his part. He wasn't just trying to save his hide, like that young Vandingham! I do admire a man who has courage, a sense of right and wrong, and isn't all for himself. I *like* him!"

"Yes," said Mrs. Kingsley. "Lisle told me he said the reason he went into the army was because he heard a trumpet sounding in his soul and he had to answer it. I thought that was beautiful."

"Yes, beautifully expressed," agreed the father. "I'm proud of him. A young man who hears the sound of a trumpet in his soul and *answers* it!"

About the Author

Grace Livingston Hill is well known as one of the most prolific writers of romantic fiction. Her personal life was fraught with joys and sorrows not unlike those experienced by many of her fictional heroines.

Born in Wellsville, New York, Grace nearly died during the first hours of life. But her loving parents and friends turned to God in prayer. She survived miraculously, thus her thankful father named her Grace.

Grace was always close to her father, a Presbyterian minister, and her mother, a published writer. It was from them that she learned the art of storytelling. When Grace was twelve, a close aunt surprised her with a hardbound, illustrated copy of one of Grace's stories. This was the beginning of Grace's journey into being a published author.

In 1892 Grace married Fred Hill, a young minister, and they soon had two lovely young daughters. Then came 1901, a difficult year for Grace—the year when, within months of each other, both her father and husband died. Suddenly Grace had to find a new place to live (her home was owned by the church where her husband had been pastor). It was a struggle for Grace to raise her young daughters alone, but through everything she kept

1902 she produced *The Angel of His Presence*, *of a Whim*, and *An Unwilling Guest*. In 1903 books *According to the Pattern* and *Because of* were published.

asn't long before Grace was a well-known author, she wanted to go beyond just entertaining her read-. She soon included the message of God's salvation rough Jesus Christ in each of her books. For Grace, he most important thing she did was not write books but share the message of salvation, a message she felt God wanted her to share through the abilities he had given her.

In all, Grace Livingston Hill wrote more than one hundred books, all of which have sold thousands of copies and have touched the lives of readers around the world with their message of "enduring love" and the true way to lasting happiness: a relationship with God through his Son, Jesus Christ.

In an interview shortly before her death, Grace's devotion to her Lord still shone clear. She commented that whatever she had accomplished had been God's doing. She was only his servant, one who had tried to follow his teaching in all her thoughts and writing.

Don't miss these Grace Livingston Hill romance novels!

If you are unable to find any of these titles at your local bookstore, you may call Tyndale's toll-free number **1-800-323-9400, X-214** for ordering information. Or you may write for pricing to **Tyndale Family Products, P.O. Box 448, Wheaton, IL 60189-0448.**